the
glass mountains

cynthia kadohata

the glass mountains	*cynthia kadohata*
cover illustration	*terese nielsen*
book design & layout	*larry s. friedman*

White Wolf Publishing
780 Park North Boulevard
Suite 100
Clarkston, GA 30021

Printed in Canada

for my husband.

part (one)

The range of climates on my planet—Artekka—is staggering, but in the sector where I was born dust rises like steam from the fields, and the dogs groan all night from the painful dryness in their throats and from the bites of legions of sand fleas. We take for granted the sounds of their groans filling the night, just as we take for granted the sound of the wind blowing across the plains and the sound of sand raining on our homes. The founders named my sector Bakshami: "dustfire."

As a young girl I'd learned to accept the land of dustfire and to feel safe there, but I never thought about whether I loved my homeland. I lived there the way all my ancestors before me had, and the way I assumed all my descendants would. That was just the way it was.

During the driest season the dryness ate at my eyes until they itched so much I couldn't stop myself from scratching, even if I'd already scratched my lids bloody. My lips cracked, and the air I breathed bore a mix of sand and dust so light and buoyant it seemed almost capable of levitation on a windless day. The only time I'd ever seen a person—a stranger—cry, the sight amazed me because I couldn't believe that water from his eyes could be wasted in such a way, over nothing.

Bakshami was not without charms. By day the long, sleek dust clouds with edges as sharp as razors circled the sky like the rings of certain planets, and at night the moons illuminated the sand dunes and lit up the dusty clouds in the air and shone on the fervent faces of the storytellers as they regaled us with tales of worlds beyond even the faintest stars in the sky. The leaves of the dry but regal tansan trees would rustle prettily as we listened to stories, and my youngest sister, head in my lap, would smile in her sleep.

One languid evening while my family relaxed at the storytelling, I looked up and saw a wave of sand in the distance rise and swallow a man. The man, a stranger, had been walking with difficulty near a dune; the wave devoured him and then settled down immediately. The man disappeared, and all was peaceful, the moons gleaming off the still sands just like always.

I jumped up: Everybody looked at me, surprised. Nobody ever interrupted the storytellers.

"I saw a stranger get buried by a sand wave!" I pointed, and all of us ran across the sand toward the point where I thought I'd seen the man.

Much later, under the light of lanterns and two full moons, we finally found him buried in the desert. Though he wore clothes similar to ours, he was not a native—his skin was pale and his face long—and even the most experienced among us could not guess his origin. He carried trinkets in his pockets, though trinkets meant nothing to my people. You couldn't eat or drink them, and they were heavy to carry. In my hot, wretched village we rarely saw any strangers at all, let alone dead ones.

I couldn't understand this man who had broken the rules of rationality and visited my sector, where

the glass mountains

the heat and sand could kill a stranger. I lived in a world where we each followed the rules of tradition. The traditions possessed their own type of rationality, a rationality proven by time. I understood that perhaps the dead man's traditions might include traveling, but if so, then why not travel to a sector like, for instance, Artroro?

As a child I'd heard often of Artroro, lush and green and filled with sweet waters and ripe fruits. I'd heard tales at the nightly storytelling, listening to the way those *R*'s rolled off the tongues of the storytellers and the way the storytellers' eyes grew greedy as they spoke of that paradisiacal sector's wet splendors. We all felt excitement imagining a place where no one among us had ever set foot. If I were ever to leave Bakshami, I supposed Artroro was where I would go.

Because it was the second largest sector, and because Artroro's army was renowned for its fierceness and courage, Artroro dominated many of the other sectors, and many sectors paid it fees for their "freedom." Bakshami, which didn't interest the Artrorans, paid no fees. Artroran was the planetary language, the language all children on Artekka learned after they'd mastered their native tongue. Many people spoke the language as well as they spoke their own tongues. In this one way, my otherwise fragmented planet was united.

The inhabitants of Bakshami had never needed an army—who would want to take over a land of such dryness and desolation, a land filled with a peaceful populace whose greatest talent was reproducing and whose greatest joy was their evening storytelling? Our people owned no valuable resources, and Bakshami had never held any particular strategic value in the constant push and pull among the largest sectors. Although I say our greatest talent was reproducing, most of our children died young, and many of our elders possessed a talent that the rest of Artekka revered and envied. The residents of Bakshami lived to around two hundred—short by the standards of Artekka—but while not long-lived, our elders were wise, even those, maybe even especially those, who seemed crazy. In reality they possessed wisdom; however, in legend they possessed powers of seeing and knowing. Inhabitants of other lands traveled for years to seek advice from our wise men and women. Of course in other sectors they'd invented fancy contraptions to fly across the skies and between the stars, but we never used mechanical transportation in Bakshami.

The elders asked no payment for their services, but they did require outsiders to follow the policies and customs of Bakshami. The policies forbade weapons, and the customs allowed for no fancy contraptions. So the outsiders journeyed by foot through the dustfire to learn from one of the elders what the future might hold. Some of the wealthiest left behind enormous riches, riches that would mean something in their own lands but meant little to the elders, except perhaps as decoration for bare walls. Any Bakshami who wished could travel to the hotlands—the hottest part of our sector—and the elders would give them whatever riches they desired. But few wished to waste their time in this way.

the glass mountains

Because life in Bakshami didn't change much, the seeing and knowing powers didn't ignite the ambitions of my people. On Bakshami so little was hidden or unpredictable that most of us saw and knew our futures from birth. We went about our simple lives. Our elders believed that our goodwill, and our neutrality in planetary wars, would protect us indefinitely.

That night after the village had fallen asleep, I sat with my dog in the sand in front of my house. My dog, Artroro, or Artie, was bigger than any dog I'd ever seen, and fiercer by far than anyone in my quiet sector. Artie's white fur grew fairly long, and for some reason it stood straight up on the top of his head, making him appear even bigger than he was. Artie was my best friend, and to sit with him in the sand usually made me at peace. But this night I felt fear.

The sun started to rise, but still I did not go in. Instead I fell asleep with Artie, dreaming of strangers raining down from the sky like rocks.

The next day, we heard rumors that strangers had been spotted in a number of other villages. We heard they wanted to barter, trading trinkets, food, or jewels for items we owned. They apparently eyed my people as if we, too, were items for barter. And no one knew why. My people held a number of meetings about the sightings, but no one knew what to do. When approached, the strangers used sleight of tongue to avoid direct answers.

We didn't speak of the distrust that set in among us; outwardly, we went on as we always had. We were a culture of habit, one of the oldest continuous cultures on the planet. We had been happy and unchanging for the whole of our history and had no intention of letting one dead man and a few strangers alter that.

At the time the sands buried the long-faced stranger, I was almost a young lady, no longer quite a child. I'd always been much like other children. On the other hand, my adored oldest brother had always been different. The seeing and knowing powers of the elders did indeed ignite his ambitions, inflaming his. He wondered obsessively what it would be like to travel to the hottest regions of Bakshami where the wisest elders lived and speak to someone who could tell him what would become of him if he left the sector. I was born adoring him, and it was as if I was born with a pain in my heart, a pain I assumed came from his ambitions to leave our family and travel. Those few who did leave rarely returned and were rumored to have become corrupted, which meant that when they got old they would certainly not develop the seeing and knowing. But instead they got to see forests and to know the taste of fresh fruits every day, instead of once a year when we celebrated the sun's farthest point from Bakshami.

My brother had the blackest and most lustrous eyes on Artekka. Thus his name, Maruk, "black-bright." My eyes were almost as black and as bright as his, and from babyhood I clung to my brother. Thus my name, Mariska: "little black-bright."

2.

I was born into the Ba Mirada clan. There were about seven hundred of us. It was a new clan, founded by my grandfather Samarr when he left his old clan to form his own, as was traditional for the most legendary elders, the wisest ones. There were thousands of clans, millions of people in Bakshami, and not one of us had ever murdered another.

Discussion at night was often of things past, while discussion at morning meal was usually of the present. Not long after the sand ate the stranger, breakfast talk revolved around this: The sector of Forma, which adjoined Bakshami, had invaded and annexed a neutral sector on another Forma border. Such invasions weren't particularly unusual in other parts of the world, but Forma had always been an ineffectual and unimportant sector not prone to expansion.

Every morning, my parents would discuss Forma with each other and then, even having asked him the same question yesterday and the day before, they would ask my grandfather what the chances were that Forma might invade Bakshami. And always Grandpa Samarr would say the same thing: The chances were what they were, and nothing he could say would change that. And so I realized that knowing and seeing had limited power.

Grandpa was a thin man who steadily grew thinner, and every morning he grew more impatient with my parents' questions. We expected him to die at any time. When I was born he lived deep in the hottest areas of Bakshami, and he'd already reached the unprecedented age of three hundred.

I was twenty-four and a half; Bakshami come of age and set out on their own at twenty-six. I'd lived a typical Bakshami childhood. My brothers, sisters, and I played with dolls as many Bakshami did even into adulthood, and most nights we sat outside to join the audience at the nightly storytelling. We were happy children, plagued by the heat but comforted by our family.

Like all children with grandparents in the hotlands, we'd looked forward to our grandfather's return. I had still been entrenched in childhood when he came to our home, a wizened old man with the darkest skin I'd ever seen, a sort of bluish brown. He'd left the hotlands because he believed he would die soon, and, following tradition, elders always left the hotlands to come home to die.

I had not yet started the great ritual, or education. My parents decided that since their children were fortunate enough to live with a legend, he would lead our education ritual. Usually, parents educated their children, and grandparents only helped. Unfortunately, my parents couldn't admit that by the time Grandfather came to live with us, much of his brain was battered by age. He insisted that he could soak up the meaning of a book by turning each page and looking at it quickly, or, when he was in a hurry, simply riffling through the book, first backward, then forward, and even, for full effect, upside down. Out of respect for him, we accepted his way of reading.

In a supposedly lucid moment, Grandfather told me that over my lifetime I would have several important guides, as well as some lesser guides, and that the most important guide would live in a place opposite from the village in which we lived. He did not say whether this guide would come to me, or whether

the glass mountains

I would go to my guide. Elders were famous for such cryptic remarks, remarks in which lay whatever truths one might find. After he spoke, my grandfather happily returned to skimming through a favorite tome upside down.

Grandpa's words about my future had startled me because he'd spoken quietly, though he usually talked as if he were making an announcement to the whole town. At that moment, standing in my grandfather's shadow in the sun, watching him turn his book upside down, I felt a sort of splendid fear, imagining that I might receive guidance from someone who was now far away, even if I did not then know what far away meant, or imagining that I might be torn from the sand and dust of my childhood in search of guidance. I did not become like my brother, however. For Maruk, the desire to visit Artroro hung constantly before his eyes, so even when he looked directly into our mother's eyes he really saw the fruits of Artroro, and even when our father lectured him about how he should study hard with our grandfather, in his mind he was drinking water as clear as the water of Bakshami but a hundred times more plentiful. He imagined bathing every night instead of worrying about picking the fleas out of his hair, and he thought about how he would reproduce with one of the robust women of Artroro, creating a new race that would unite our people and all those in between our two states. They would create the largest and most varied sector on Artekka. I dreamed similar dreams from the comfort of my bed, as I was drifting off to sleep. But in truth I was most pleased with my betrothed, Sennim—the meat-seasoner's son—and I had no intention of ever leaving Bakshami.

My grandfather seemed enormously happy to be with us. Sometimes he groused and muttered, but just as often he sat in his chair smiling or even laughing with delight over nothing in particular. I might walk into the room and find him alone, guffawing at some private joke. He was unsentimental about his time in the hotlands. He said that "the damn traditions" were the cause of the only decadent village in the sector. The village where the elders lived was infamous. As a favor to outsiders visiting the elders, this village was the only one in Bakshami that served intoxicants and contained a library. In the village, Grandpa had started to like getting intoxicated and reading, especially books that didn't weigh too much.

Grandfather didn't tell us much about the outsiders who visited him for advice except to say that they were fools to come, and he was a fool to listen to them. But my father told me that the outsiders who braved the hotlands—where, it was rumored, the sun reflecting off the nearby Glass Mountains could set fire to wood a hundred measures away—were honorable, and that Grandpa was only joking. My father believed in tradition. He was the most decent man in our land of decent men.

Sometimes at night after storytelling, my mother would let my sisters, my brothers, and me sit on the verandah with her, our father, and Grandpa. To keep out the dust and the fleas, the verandah was surrounded by a veil of fabric spun partly with strings of special glass. Seeing the moons through the veil was like seeing them through a sparkling layer of clouds. Sometimes as we sat quietly I felt a sadness set in, and I knew that though by tradition death of old age was no cause for sadness, my parents already mourned Grandpa, and so did I.

Meanwhile, talk about Forma among the people of my village began to reach a frenzy when that sector accused mine of encroaching on Forman land. We kept no advanced weapons and had made no meaningful protective alliances, so rather than talking about protecting ourselves, we all discussed what my parents called "bringing the Formans to their senses." Each day I would follow my brother Maruk as he followed the grownups and listened to their discussions. "We must make them realize that their accusations are wrong," the grownups would say. Or, "They won't attack us because there would be no logic in that, no logic at all." They were sensible discussions that, in retrospect, had no root in reality.

One day my grandfather secluded himself in his private hut in back, where he used to contemplate and sometimes sleep, and we didn't see him for days, until we thought that perhaps his tomb would need to be readied quickly, but finally he emerged and announced he planned to die any moment now but would take the time to give us some advice.

"This advice has nothing to do with the seeing power. It's just an old man's logic. You must hide from the Formans. Go to the hotlands. Now let an old man have some fun before he dies. Where's that book I was reading?" He grabbed a book and riffled urgently through it.

That was the longest day of the year. The air blew cooler, and the clouds ringing the horizon turned pink, blue, and pale green. My grandfather stayed inside, "reading," and when my siblings and I got sent in for bed, he looked up and shouted at me, "The great ritual is a crock!" Then he turned to my middle sister—Leisha—and shouted, "The ritual is a crock!" He nearly screamed at my brothers: "Long live the ritual!" He turned back to his book and didn't seem to notice us, even when we rubbed our cheeks against his and wished him good night.

"He's having a bad day," whispered my parents. "Now go to bed."

As my siblings and I combed our dogs and picked the fleas out of each other's hair before bed, we spoke of the day's events. Katinka was just out of infancy; Jobei was Leisha's twin—in time of birth only, not in looks or disposition.

"There's going to be a war," said Maruk. Leisha, Katinka, Jobei, and I leaned forward, scared but fascinated, as if we were at storytelling. Maruk had wanted for many years to become both a soldier and a storyteller one day. His eyes bugged out and he repeated, "There's going to be a war." When he could see how scared we were, he leaned back with satisfaction, and then a shrewd look came over his face. I marveled at the beautiful blackness of his hair and eyes. Since everyone in Bakshami possessed black eyes and hair, one learned to distinguish between the nuances of the various shades of black. His eyes were huge, and the blackness held no other colors, no blues or browns or reds. He made his eyes into slits as he sat thinking.

"A war?" we all said.

"I have predicted it," he said grandly.

"But I won't fight in a war," I said. "I'm getting married, and then I'm becoming a dog trainer."

"They need dog trainers in a war."

I rarely challenged him, but now I did. "How do you know what they need in a war?"

"Because I plan to be a general, and I will decide what is needed. You can train my dogs for me."

When my mother came in to braid our hair for the night, Leisha asked whether there would be a war. "There will be no war," Mother said, the same way she sometimes said to the younger ones, "There will be no more horseplay." She continued, "and if there was, I would put a stop to it." She was supremely confident. The rest of us glared at Leisha for mentioning this supposed war to our mother.

We could all braid our own hair, except little Katinka, but we liked to spend this time with our mother, sitting on our bedmats as she sang soothingly and smoothed our wild locks. Every night, for as long as I could remember, she sang us a new song, a song different from and yet the same as yesterday's song the way a day is different from and yet the same as the day before and the day after.

That night I sat up at the window, listening to the sand rain on the roof and watching the rings on the horizon slowly shift, fading and deepening in color, stretching and thickening as the dust blew toward the sky as if called by the heavens. I was struck as I had never been before with my world's peacefulness, with the way the houses in the distance blended into the landscape as if they were not artificial but had pushed out of the ground like the immense glass hills of the hotlands that I'd seen in pictures. And I thought of everyone in my house sleeping as the light from the moons shone on their faces. If there was ever a war...if there was ever a war...and then I couldn't think of anything more. There had never been a war in Bakshami.

The next day Grandfather didn't come out of his room, and in a few hours a sweet smell wafted from his room and through the house, and we knew he had died. Death is a time of sweetness in Bakshami. We believed that after the deceased's tomb and its contents eroded into sand, this sand all blew away toward the hotlands, where it became a part of the Glass Mountains, the most glorious sight in Bakshami.

In his room Grandfather had carefully laid out his possessions into six piles. In the pile he'd left me I found maps of several places, some familiar and some not: Artroro, Soom Kali, Restophlin, and Mallarr. He'd also included a note saying I might possibly go to some of these places, but not to others, depending. The sight of the maps scared me as much as it excited me, and the two warring feelings, fear and excitement, caused my stomach to feel such pain that I had to lie down for the rest of the afternoon, without even looking at the other things he had left me. I resented Grandfather because I didn't think he was seeing, but rather was causing this future, this travel to places far away. And why a map of Soom Kali— the Land of Knives? It was the largest sector on the planet, and rumored to be the most violent. It was

the glass mountains

only the strength and proximity of Artroro that kept Soom Kali at bay.

"That he should give a child such a thing!" my mother said.

"It's only a map of a place she'll never see," said my father. "And she won't be a child much longer."

"It isn't a map of a place, but a map of danger," replied my mother firmly. "I would not even have allowed him to give such a thing to Maruk." My parents had resigned themselves to the idea that Maruk might someday face the dangers for which he longed.

Even my father, who revered his father, couldn't disagree.

Mallarr was another sector; Restophlin was one of Artekka's twelve sister planets. These planets were all settled by people from the same place, what we called the Hooded Galaxy, which I'd once seen from the only telescope in Bakshami. The galaxy was a pink-hued swirling mass of stars that seemed to bend over, like a hood over somebody's head. At some point, all parents took their children on a pilgrimage to peer through the telescope to see the Hooded Galaxy, and to identify a few of the stars around which revolved the sister planets of Artekka.

The day after Grandfather's death, my parents, who operated a glass-making shop in addition to their civic responsibilities, spent hours finishing up his burial case. My sisters and brothers spent the day contemplating his notes and the things he'd left us, in my case the maps and some trinkets and treats from each of the lands of which he'd given me maps. From Artroro he'd left me one half-eaten piece of dried fruit that tasted both fruity and nutty at the same time and stuck to my teeth in an extremely satisfying way; from Soom Kali a carved knife; from Mallarr a flea comb for my dog, whom I'd named after Artroro; and from Restophlin a box of diaphanous cloths of pastel colors. The knife, encrusted with a few jewels, was not a cooking knife but one of those useless glittery things that Maruk so favored. He collected fancy knives from other sectors and said that someday he would open a museum. I shook out the cloths one by one, handling them carefully.

But for days I didn't join my siblings in studying our inheritances. I lay in bed in a fever of overwhelming fear brought on by Grandfather's predictions and the threats of the Formans. In the past, nothing had ever changed in my sector; now it seemed that change would come. My entourage of friends, my handsome betrothed, might all be lost. And what would become of me, the mayor's daughter!

Later, at the death ritual, I sat with Artie. I couldn't understand why I felt so much loneliness at an event whose only purpose was to recognize the inescapable. I could see Grandpa clearly through the smooth parts of the glass tomb, and he looked not pale as I'd been warned he might, but as full of vigor as I'd ever seen him. I waited to hear his thunderous snore, the one I could sometimes hear even from my bed, and that my whole family had sometimes suspected was proof of the life force that would make him outlast us all. He looked as if he could be playing a practical joke—he'd liked to pretend to be asleep and then pounce on us children.

Death's sweet smell filled the ritual parlor. I knew from other deaths I'd witnessed that the smell would grow stronger and stronger, lingering even after the body had disintegrated. Whenever I visited burial grounds the wondrous smell filled the air and brought a smile to the lips of all visitors. But even this smell didn't appease my loneliness as I sat with my family in the parlor, listening to the speeches of Grandfather's friends. Each speech ended with, "May Samarr's grandchildren know peace always."

At the end of the funeral we all played drums. Children in Bakshami learned the traditional rhythms as soon as they were old enough to control their hand movements. We played drums at solemn rituals, at celebrations, and sometimes just for enjoyment.

The brief rainy season was far away; still, rain fell in fast, harsh drops that night, the storm clouds obscuring the rings at the horizon. Afterward, the wind blew the rings away and cleared the clouds, so that the sky was black as our eyes. And one of the elders who lived in the village, a woman who'd been the oldest except for my grandfather, said that instead of going peacefully as one of dignity ought to, Samarr was putting up a fight; thus the storm.

The day after the ritual, tradition dictated that everyone talk about the bereaved. Yet talk of Forma dominated our lives, and the storytellers, previously the center of our nightly gathering, sat quietly and uselessly to the side.

"Let that be a lesson," my father told us at home. "What's of value one day may hold no value the next."

My youngest sister, Katinka, whose translucent skin shone with the slightest tinge of sky blue and whose baby fat still clung to her smooth cheeks, said, "What about me? Will I have value tomorrow?"

"Yes," said my father. "Tomorrow, and tomorrow after that, and after that. As long as your mother and I live, my children will be treasures of great value."

3.

The next evening before storytelling my parents sent Maruk and me to get some meat. I took some glass pots my parents had made and put a couple on my back and several in Artie's backpack. Maruk did the same, except my dog carried twice as much as Maruk's could, but Maruk carried twice as much as me. We took everything down to the meat-seasoner's house and traded it for several slabs of dried and seasoned meat.

The meat-seasoner belonged to a distinguished clan, and he and my father were good friends. My parents had made arrangements for me to mate with Sennim, the meat-seasoner's handsome son, shortly after I came of age. Maruk, too, was already betrothed, to a girl in another village. Maruk and Sennim were good friends, but despite our future together, I didn't know him very well. We might have been friends had our parents not decided to mate us. As it was he made me more curious than all the other boys put together, but I didn't know whether that was because I knew we would mate or because I liked him particularly.

the glass mountains

There was less meat to be had than usual, and the seasoner said that since his supplier was late we should be judicious about how much we ate. There was nothing unusual about that—often there was a shortage of game. We ate mostly roots, anyway. But because of the fears about Forma, the shortage left me worried. We walked out with our meat into the sunny evening. Sennim had sat down casually in front of the house, as he often did, as if he just happened to be there while I happened to be leaving.

Maruk sat next to him, and I found a place on the ground a few measures away.

"There wasn't much meat today," I said. Sennim squirmed, as he always did when I was around.

"I can get you extra," he said shyly.

"Really!" I said.

"She doesn't need extra meat if others must go short," said Maruk sternly.

Sennim caught my eye, to tell me that if I still wanted, he would get me meat. But now I felt annoyed with him, as if Maruk's rebuke were his fault.

"Look!" said Maruk to me. "Another stranger."

This time it was a man. Usually years went by between each sighting of a stranger. This one had dressed himself in the garb of Bakshami. He found it difficult to walk in the sand, moving clumsily, without even a vestige of grace.

He approached and eyed us critically—he seemed to think we were game to evaluate and capture. Instead of greeting this stranger effusively, as tradition dictated, I was surprised at how by tacit agreement we continued to sit nonchalantly. Later, we all agreed we'd disliked him immediately. He had a long face like the man the sand swallowed, and his mouth turned cruelly. At his side hung something hard and shiny that I instinctively knew to be a weapon.

Sennim yawned. "Can I help you?"

I scooted closer to the man, but Maruk pushed me back protectively. The man ignored us at first, pacing back and forth, falling and slipping and shielding his eyes. Finally he deigned to speak with us. "I'm a busy man," he said.

None of us knew what to say to that. The man, while handsome, seemed tremendously vulgar, and the fleas seemed to like him quite well. Bug bites covered his face. But we felt such curiosity about him that we waited eagerly for his next words.

Maruk, of course, would take over talking with him. I looked at Maruk in admiration. I was the most mischievous in our family, Katinka the loveliest, Jobei the most generous, and Leisha the funniest. But Maruk was the most dauntless, and the most admired.

The man studied Maruk, then settled his eyes on me. "Perhaps the girl would like some dried fruit?"

Maruk scowled at me, so I reluctantly said, "I don't like fruit."

"It's the best fruit from Artroro."

My heart beat faster, and I knew it was instinctively copying the beating of Maruk's excited heart as he heard the word Artroro. "Have you visited Artroro?" I asked. I didn't believe a flea-bitten man such as he could be native Artroran.

"Young lady, I'm wanted in Artroro and every sector on the planet, except Pussan, where everyone is an outlaw, and Bakshami, where no one is." He bent to pet Artie, but my dog bared his fangs.

The stranger eyed us with a sort of bored hopefulness. "I understand some of the elders have fortunes stashed away. A fortune isn't much use to a kid, is it?" He scratched at a bump on his skin.

"Oh, I don't know. If I stay in Bakshami, I can use a fortune as building material for a house. I'll pound it into bricks. And if I don't stay I can spend it in other sectors," Maruk said.

The man continued to scratch, then began picking the scab on another bump. He nodded and pulled something out of a pocket. "Did you ever taste dried fruit from Artroro? Let me be your friend."

Maruk hesitated. I knew his mouth watered over the fruit, as mine did. But he came along when Sennim grabbed my hand and led me away. Sennim had never touched me even by accident. The man's eyes bored into our backs as we left.

Sennim, Maruk, and I parted ways about halfway between our two houses. Sennim had held my dry, flaky hand the whole way. He didn't say goodbye to me when he left, just to Maruk. Sennim often ignored me, except to look at me slyly when he thought I wasn't watching. When we officially began the romance ritual, we would smother each other in attention. But that was for later.

As Maruk and I walked back to our home, Maruk pranced about and pretended to be pointing the man's weapon at rocks. He would soon be of age, but he acted like a child today. It was strange, I could see my brother's infatuation with his imaginary weapon, the way his face grew serious and intent and the way a feeling of power made his eyes shine. This new kind of shine had always existed in him, needing only a weapon to bring it out.

He was prancing about in this way when we heard a low hum that seemed almost to surround us. It came from above. It was a ship, flying over our village in an aimless, roundabout fashion. The ship flew very low, as low as a lazy bird out for some ordinary afternoon exercise. On one hand I was Bakshami and raised to remain levelheaded, but on the other hand I'd never seen a ship before. Just by flying lazily above, it seemed to belittle and challenge all our traditions. I gawked, and Maruk pretended to point a weapon at the ship. Just as he did that, the ship vanished, and I felt for an illogical moment that he'd destroyed it.

"They broke our laws, they deserved to die," said Maruk.

"But we have no laws."

"They're unspoken laws. The elders will agree, then they'll refuse to give an audience to whoever sent that ship."

"Maybe they don't want an audience with the elders." I could see in his face that such a concept had never occurred to him: Didn't all outsiders want to speak with the elders if they could? And in fact such a concept hadn't really registered with me either until I spoke. "We'd better get home," I said.

On our way home, we passed groups of people talking about the ship. Most hadn't seen it and looked doubtfully at those who had. "And then it just disap-

the glass mountains

peared," said one person. Another said, "It was as big as a dwelling." As I watched Maruk walk calmly and gracefully, I felt I'd never admired him so much. But I didn't know what good his calm and grace might be in a war. I didn't know anything of the powers of Forma or any of the other sectors. My life previously had been my family, my dog, my daydreams, and my occasional thoughts of Sennim.

One question we heard everyone ask over and over as they talked about Forma was: Why? Why would anyone want to take over Bakshami?

In front of our own home several people stood out front talking with my parents. One of them was Tarkahn, whom my sister Leisha called The Man Who Never Paused. His quiet, giggly daughter Tarkahna was my best friend. She followed me a lot, and we giggled together over various jokes. Actually, Tarkahn did manage to finish his protracted sentences sometimes, but he always started a new one immediately. But Leisha liked to joke that he was still speaking the first sentence he'd uttered when he first began talking at the age of seventeen—most Bakshami begin talking by four. Leisha theorized that because he'd started so late, he had to make up for lost time. Tarkahn talked and talked and always finished his meal last because he was so busy talking. But he was so good-natured that everyone loved him despite his reluctance to pause. Everyone always laughed when his wife related how Tarkahn talked in his sleep, in the shower and while having sex. Naturally he was a thin man, since he preferred talking to eating, even when he was hungry.

But now he stood quietly, lips moving, but quiet nonetheless, staring at the sky and pointing. I think the ship overhead surprised us all as much as one of our dogs speaking would have. Something we'd always known to be true was suddenly proved false. We knew that no one would invade our skies in the same way we knew that dogs could only bark, not speak, the same way we knew that Tarkahn would never pause in his speech. But now he stood there before my family and said simply, "I know what I saw." His lips moved a bit, and then he recovered himself. "Of course it has to do with the Formans, and as some of you may know they have bombs in some of their ships, not that they would have any reason to want to drop a bomb on us, especially since we've always been a peaceful neighbor and never did anyone any harm, and, speaking I hope not just for myself but for all the village, I would certainly not be interested in seeing any harm befall anyone in the world, not even whoever was driving that ship, because I was always taught that to harm another person..."

I stood tucked between my parents, their gowns brushing my hands. The sky above us shone an effulgent blue, almost moonlike in its glowing quality. I could already see our moons in the afternoon sky, but because of the early hour they didn't glow but possessed a transparent smokiness. So the sky was like the moons, the moons were like smoke, and the smoke I could see still rising from my parents' glass firing ovens was like a sign of safety to me. When my parents sent us to visit relatives in another town, on our way back we always knew we were almost home when we saw the smoke from our house rising into the sky. Now, the smoke rose thickly; my parents had stopped working just a short while ago.

Everyone had a theory, and in a moment everyone was talking without pause like Tarkahn, everybody talking and nobody listening. I caught sight of the stranger Maruk and I had seen earlier, lurking about a distant house. He was showing his weapon to someone else and speaking earnestly. But when he saw me looking he turned and walked away, obviously trying to walk gracefully and failing by a wide margin. Then, above the cacophony of voices, we heard, the way my parents could hear us children no matter how much noise—a low hum from the sky. And so Tarkahn was silenced for the second time in one day, probably only the second time since he'd first started speaking as a child. The ship glided overhead, lower and then higher, lower and higher as it passed out of sight once more.

That night no one felt like eating. Instead everyone in town sat in storytelling groups, but rather than telling stories we talked about the ship. I fell asleep in my mother's lap, something I hadn't done since I was a young child. When I awoke I could see by the placement of the stars that half the night had passed. My mother always came silently into our room to check on us at about this time. When she was a child, her sister had died of a virus at exactly half-night, so she always came in around that time and stayed until shortly after, to make sure no virus suddenly stole our lives. It never occurred to her that she was too big to wrestle with a virus.

Some of the groups had broken up, and Tarkahn was walking home, talking to himself. My mother said to my father, "Dear, tell someone what your father said. It may be important."

My father looked thoughtful. "Maybe you're right. I don't know whether my father was losing his mind as he died. But he left me a note, a long note, most of it rambling, and in it he said my wife and I should take our children someplace safe. But where that someplace safe is, he didn't say."

The other elder in town hadn't spoken for several days, and no matter how much her children and grandchildren cajoled, she refused to speak. My parents and some others decided that a delegation of several villagers should go to the surrounding villages and talk to what elders they could find and ask advice. The interclan council met only once every few years, and the members lived at every corner of our sector, so it didn't make sense to call them together. I lay in my mother's lap with my eyes open, wide awake now. I felt strange, on the one hand cozy and precious, lying in my mother's lap as I had not done in so long, and on the other hand apprehensive and fearful. I could not imagine what turn of events the ships might bring. I fell asleep, and in my sleep I walked with my grandfather again, laughing as he exclaimed, "I love the traditions but they drive me crazy!"

When I woke up next morning, everybody and everything lay in silence, except for a slight, almost familiar humming from above. In a sort of vigil, many of us had stayed out all night. We all looked up, to a

the glass mountains

smooth white ship, smaller and shaped differently from yesterday's ship.

And in the silence I heard one voice, a voice I hadn't heard in days, the voice of the only other elder in town, saying, "It's time to leave." They were the last words I was to hear her speak for a long time.

4.

In the next few days, the ships passing overhead became common. No matter how common the sight became, I knew I would never lose the sense that something extraordinary was happening. At times Maruk and I caught sight of the stranger we'd seen on the day we saw the first ship. With his flea-bitten face and clumsy ways, he became a threatening yet unexceptional sight. No one got much sleep because of worrying, and the sounds of people debating what to do could be heard at all hours. At first we all believed the ships were reconnaissance vessels of the Formans, but we later realized the ships carried strangers of uncertain character like the flea-bitten man. His own ship apparently had landed unnoticed.

More strangers than I'd ever seen at once had descended on our village—maybe forty of them. When the contingent of our villagers returned from their survey of neighboring towns, they said outsiders had descended on those towns as well. The meat supply grew shorter, and the air became so dry that at night as I lay in bed the groaning of domestic dogs all around the village became as insistent and insane as that of the wild dogs one sometimes heard after dark.

The residents of nearby towns were as confused as we were.

One morning, after a restless night of listening to groaning and of scratching my crusty eyelids, I could tell something was wrong. I saw by the sun that our parents had let us oversleep. And there was no smell of breakfast. Maruk got up at almost the same moment I did. But while I lay unmoving, wanting the world to revert to what it once was, he pulled aside the curtains and sat watching. When I got up I could see crowds of people gathered around something, craning their necks, aghast. After a while the group parted to let through a doctor, and shortly after her arrival several people helped carry a man away.

My brother ran outside, but later refused to speak. We ate breakfast in silence. Finally I burst out with, "What is it? What happened? Who was that?"

"That was a man from across the village," said my father. "A Bakshami man. He's still alive."

"What happened to him?"

"Stabbed."

"What?" I'd never heard of such a thing. I knew one of the strangers must have tried to murder the man, but I didn't know why.

"The town is filled with scavengers," said my mother. "None of you are to go out without your father or me."

My father shook his head, signalling her to say no more. All day they prayed that this Bakshami man would not be the first to die because of the troubles with Forma, would not be the signal of many more deaths to come.

My parents made us children stay in the house all day, so we didn't know what was going on outside. Every so often, my mother or father would go out briefly and return to talk softly with the other. The injured man died later that day. All that day and night we listened to the sound of drums beating for the death of the man, and also for whatever deaths might follow his.

My brothers, my sisters, and I didn't have to wait long for a decision from our parents. They sat us down the next day for a meeting and announced that we were going on a trip, and that we'd be leaving tomorrow.

"Tomorrow!" we all said. Katinka started to cry, not that she cared when we were leaving, but I think our consternation upset her.

They told us they'd heard there had already been several skirmishes at the Forma-Bakshami border, and tens of Bakshami had been slaughtered, their skin burned off their bodies by the Formans, who thought it fitting that the people in the land of dustfire should be burned to death. Many who were spared were taken to Forma as servants. Others, in despair, left voluntarily for Forma, as they could no longer find food in their villages. We didn't live close to the border; neither could one say we lived far.

"Are we moving to Artroro?" I said.

"We're going to the hotlands," said my father without emotion.

"The hotlands!" we all said.

Maruk's face fell, but his adventurous spirit rose to the occasion. "Well, we can visit the wild village there. Are we going to consult an elder?" The village in the hotlands had no name, yet it was the most famous village in the sector.

"We're going there because some elders in the neighboring villages have suggested it. Even Forman ships can't penetrate the air above the Glass Mountains. The air above them is said to be as unpredictable as the heat is predictable."

"But that's only legend, it isn't real!" said Maruk.

My father, who'd never raised a hand to any of us, slapped him hard across his left cheek. "In this house your parents will decide what is real." We all sat in terror at how the threat from outside had moved into our own home.

"What will we be safe from? Safe from war?" I said.

"Safe from the future," my mother said.

I pondered this, as did my brothers and sisters. Maruk hesitated to speak but finally said, "Doesn't the future come no matter where you are? Does time stop in the hotlands?"

My mother said that, in a way, she hoped it did.

"But how can we go tomorrow?" said Maruk. Every time he spoke he glanced to my father, out of both defiance and fear.

"How can we not?" said my mother. "It's no longer safe here."

"I don't know when we'll be back," said my father.

I couldn't remember a time when I hadn't been safe in my own hometown.

Maruk asked, "But why can't the Forman army walk to the hotlands as we are?"

"Because they're lazy, and they're cowards," said my mother passionately.

the glass mountains

"You should pack only what you can easily carry yourself," said my father. "The dogs will have to carry our necessities, either on the sand sleds or in backpacks. None of you has to worry about packing food and water. Furthermore, we'll be taking some tents and the bedding if there's room. And remember, no personal items in the dogs' packs." We kept ten dogs in my family. They were superb protectors and workers.

My father looked outside at the position of the sun. "We've decided you can stay up for half the storytelling tonight, but only on condition that you're all packed before then. So you'd better get started now. There'll be more time for questions later."

"If we're really going to the hotlands, there'll be much more time for questions," said Maruk dreamily, as if in a trance. "Days and days for questions."

"Maruk, Mariska, Jobei, and Leisha, you must all make sure that Katinka has everything she needs in the way of clothes and personal items. And you are to divide what she needs among yourselves to carry. What she needs you must carry, and what she wants, she must carry. Now hurry, it's important."

But I couldn't do what my father wanted. I lay down and groaned while Artie licked me, pawed me and generally tried to make me come to my senses. I writhed on the floor and vomited the food I'd eaten that day but had been unable to digest. My mother cleaned up around me but didn't pay much attention to my groaning and writhing; she was not an indulgent woman.

The others had hurried into their rooms. They probably wished they could talk to each other, but there was no time.

By the time I joined them they had almost finished packing. My sisters and brothers did start to talk somewhat while they packed, but I didn't—it took a lot of consideration to decide what to take and what to leave. Each of us owned a personal chest that our parents made for our first birthdays, when we'd survived the scourge of dust virus for five years. At that time it was traditional to become optimistic and give children a gift they might use for the rest of their lives.

I gathered together all the gifts my family and friends had given me over time, dolls and glass trinkets and so forth. Sometimes we spent hours playing with our dolls. My parents even joined in occasionally. They weren't dolls only in the shapes of humans, but in all shapes. There were dolls of animals, dolls of moons and planets, dolls of colorful shapes sewn together, dolls of trees and flowers. But the dolls alone were more than I could carry by myself. I picked a few of my favorites and put them in my "take" pile. There were certain robes and gowns I preferred over others, and I placed these in my pile as well. But like the dolls, the clothes alone were more than I would want to carry a long distance. I chose the coolest gown I owned, the warmest, and one in between.

Jobei, who'd been watching me choose what to take, offered to help. "I don't need much myself. Would you like me to take a few of your dolls?" Because we were all used to his generosity and had been taught not to take advantage of him, it usually didn't take much effort to say no to his big-hearted offers.

But this time I couldn't bring myself to say no at first. I knew he would carry my dolls to the hotlands and back if only I asked. The others watched me. If I said yes, they might ask Jobei to carry things of their own, and then he would have nothing.

"No, I'll just have to decide which to take."

For Artie, I put in a flea comb and a couple of rocks he especially liked to chew on. I visually judged the weight of my pile and put the larger rock aside. Looking through my personal chest, I realized that even among my meager belongings, I wanted more than I needed. For instance, the many mementos of Artroro that people had given Maruk and he had given to me. Years earlier an aunt had given him a couple of pieces of dried fruit that he'd passed on to me and that I'd never eaten. The fruit had metamorphosed into hard black blobs.

There was a storybook about the Artroran strongmen and strongwomen, and a blank cloth to hang in the wind and stare at. This cloth was supposed to enhance the watcher's imagination. A Ba Mirada clan member from a few villages away had given it to Maruk to help him picture Artroro, and he'd given it to me. These items had been among my most valued possessions, but I didn't want them badly enough to carry them across the sweltering landscape of Bakshami. Artroro had never seemed so far away as it did now, when we actually were about to walk closer to it.

In the end I took three of my own robes, two of Katinka's, one doll, one rock for Artie, and the knife from Soom Kali from my grandfather. Someone had carved a face full of fury on the knife handle, with jewels for eyes. I couldn't tell what kind of luck it would bring me, but I knew it would bring me something. I looked at my brothers and sisters, to see whether I could learn anything from their decisions. But they'd come to the same conclusions as I had, just a logical assortment of clothing, and a couple of items that were special to them. In addition, we each brought a razor, to shave hair off our legs and bodies and discourage fleas. We kept our head hair long out of tradition. Only the rare rebel shaved his or her hair, making me wish at times that I could be more of a rebel so I could get rid of all my hair. Leisha brought her list of jokes, though she'd memorized all the jokes and told them to us so many times we'd memorized them, too. Maruk took seven knives, one for carving; one for his shaving; one for slicing game; one for eating; one for a tool; one for luck; and one for killing. So far as I knew Maruk had never killed anything, even the smallest furrto, but he always slept with his killing knife under his bedding because he said that's what members of the Artroran army did.

When we'd finished we sat with our bags on our mats waiting for our mother or father to come and tell us what to do next. Leisha occasionally threw tantrums in between her joketelling, but we were all obedient by nature. Despite everything we had to say, we sat quietly: stunned, scared. I wished I had more to do, more to pack. I left our room to go to the front room, but stopped in the hallway when I saw the flea-bitten man talking to my parents.

"A war is coming," the man was saying. He waved

his wandlike weapon at them, so that I almost screamed, but he was waving for emphasis, not to threaten them. "You may need a weapon like this. Look, I'm not a killer. I could kill you and look for Samarr's fortune, but I'm a peaceful man at heart. I have no quarrel with Bakshami or anyone living here. Oh, it's the most horrible sector on the planet, but that's not your fault. So come on, be reasonable."

I ran to stand by my parents. "We saw him the other day," I said.

"He's a scavenger," said my father. "And I don't deal with scavengers."

The man looked shrewdly at my mother. "You may feel differently."

"We own no jewels," she said. "We own only our dwelling, if you want that."

"What are you saying?" said my father. "My parents built this home for us."

"I am saying that a weapon like that may be of use. You're forgetting the more practical elements of present circumstances."

"We'll be traveling with a hundred other families. We'll be safe."

"Safe from a hundred ships?"

"There are no hundred ships."

I had never seen my parents disagree before, only overheard them a few times when they spoke louder than they realized from their room. So here it was again, the troubles from outside invading our home.

My mother turned to the man. "Samarr left us no fortune. If he did, we would give it to you. Such things mean nothing to us. We're leaving almost everything we own. Is there any price you would take besides these jewels that don't exist?"

He squinted and winked at me so that it seemed he had a flea in his eye. "How about this one? Is she strong enough to work hard until I need her to bear children?"

"Leave now, or I'll kill you," my father said evenly.

"My dog will kill you," I shouted.

"Wait," said my mother.

"Mother, what are you doing? Did you hear what he said?"

"What he said is ridiculous, of course."

"We have our honor," said my father.

"And we'll have no less of it if we can come to terms. But what if I do end up with less? What good is honor if my children die on the way to the hotlands?"

"We may die of thirst, but no Bakshami has ever died for lack of a weapon."

"Lack of precedent is irrelevant in a changing world," said my mother.

"Your intelligence honors me," the man said. He bowed extravagantly to her. "All right, forget your daughter. I have a servant already in another sector. Do you have any of those fierce dogs?"

"They're not fierce," I said with disdain. "They just don't like you."

He scowled at me. "I don't like this one anyway. Have you any children who are more pleasant?" Scratching at his face, squinting his eyes, the man looked around the room. "I don't want your house. A home in a dying land is no home at all." His eyes brightened. "Do you think Samarr might have buried something around here?"

"Who can say?" said my mother.

"Here's the deal I'll make you. To prevent you from running off with any riches Samarr may have hidden, you must let me check all your bags and then you must vacate the dwelling immediately. In return, the weapon is yours."

"Woman, are you mad?" my father said.

"Perhaps so. But not so mad that I would make this deal without my husband's agreement."

My father rubbed my face with his hand. "Are you scared, Mariska?"

"Yes."

"I am, too," he said. Then, to my mother, "You're right, of course. What's the point? He will take the house anyway, once we leave tomorrow. It's best to bargain for a weapon that can save our lives. But I would have wished for more time to say my good-byes to the finest dwelling in the village."

So the deal was made, and the scavenger handed her a weapon. And just like that, we no longer possessed a house. Instead we possessed a weapon. Later we were to find out that half the village had purchased similar weapons, and that none of them worked. By some act of prestidigitation, they'd worked only in demonstration. After coming to terms, the man checked the belongings we planned to take, and we walked out into the dry, lukewarm night. As soon as we stood outside, I began to wonder whether I'd chosen to bring the right clothes, the right doll. But it was too late to change my mind.

The wind was still and the air clear. Above me our moons hung across the sky. Lomos glowed orange-yellow at the horizon. We looked at our parents: where to?

A number of people had gathered for the storytelling, so we posted nine of our dogs with our belongings and went to listen to the stories. Artie stayed with me. I looked around for the meat-seasoner and his family but didn't see them. A couple of the better storytellers had already left town, but my favorite raconteur, Cray, remained. He stood off to himself a bit, his lips moving, his eyes darting, as he warmed up for his story. Cray was an average-looking man when he walked about town, but when he told stories he got a lunatic glint to his eyes, and you suddenly noticed the weird looseness to his joints and a nimbleness that transcended even the natural grace of most Bakshami. He ran suddenly to the center of where we sat with a few dozen others. His eyes were alight with lunacy, and his limbs shook with the looseness of a skeleton. He leapt in front of me. "Mariska knows this story is true!" he exclaimed. He leapt to someone else, the old woman who had never developed much seeing and knowing powers. "And the honorable Fu-fat knows as well!"

Cray gazed up toward the sky, then eastward. "Toward the east lies one of the oldest civilizations on the planet, also the most barbaric: Soom Kali," he intoned. He faced north, then south. "To the north and south the same: Soom Kali. To the west, Forma. We're surrounded.

"The Soom Kali are rumored not to need much

sleep because they're too busy learning to be warriors. Before people began measuring time, the residents of Soom Kali were some of the meanest and craziest inhabitants of the Hooded Galaxy. They chose our planet Artekka to populate because of the size and emptiness. They wanted the emptiest world they could find, a giant kingdom to rule and perhaps to destroy.

"All the children of the original settlers in Artekka turned out to be as ferocious as their parents—except one, a boy born so good and kind his face glowed with benevolence and his smile enraged all those around him."

Cray's face began to radiate benevolence.

"The neighbors taunted him and his parents. They thought he was a weakling.

"So, the kindest man in Soom Kali traversed through his life alone, moving from state to state, hoping to find one other kind person. He would hear a rumor that another kind person lived here or there, and he would instantly drop whatever he was doing and travel to where this other kind person supposedly lived. But when he got there, he would find out the story of this person was really a mangled story about himself, and so he'd ended up traveling all that way in search of what he already lived with and saw reflected in glass or metal every day. Meanwhile he worked in sewers and gutters and dangerous caves. Nobody would hire him for a better job, and nobody would frequent a business that he might start.

"Finally, when the kindest man was two hundred years old, he made a mistake. He broke down and cried while working in a cave. He cried for only a short while, but that short inattention caused him not to notice that the air was running low. It was his job to warn the others. He thereby caused horrible deaths to several people who were lowly workers but respected nonetheless. For that's the way it was in Soom Kali—one thing that must be said is that, except for their feelings about the kind man, they respected each other.

"So the kindest man was brought to trial and condemned to death. While he was waiting to die, he decided to throw himself over a wall. This he did, and he fell down a cliff and into a hole so deep he continued to fall for forty days, until he'd almost starved to death. Soom Kali was said to have a vast network of tunnels beneath it, and when he stopped falling and found himself in a tunnel he assumed that he was in that network, which had been built during a civil war among the original inhabitants.

"For a long time, he lived in tunnels, feeding the meager amounts of food he obtained by killing rodents to the cavedogs that befriended him. As I said, this all happened lifetimes ago, when there was more magic in the air than there is today. The magic made sparks in the rocks that helped him start fires when he was cold, and the magic cleaned the air of smoke when the fires died. Every day, with tools he made and by hand, the kind man dug more tunnels until after a hundred years he'd dug so furiously and blindly and in so convoluted a pattern that he didn't know whether he was far from Soom Kali or right beneath it. Unbeknownst to him, he'd passed under seas and mountains, pastures and deserts, then circled here and there, back and forth, and now, when he emerged, he saw that he was in a vast desert land. He caught a glimpse of a beautiful blue wild beast, but as soon as he saw it, it was gone. It was a legendary flame beast, who moves with the quickness and grace of a flame across straw."

Cray pranced about, at times leaping over our heads and seeming to change direction in midair. It seemed as if he could fly one moment, and the next moment he became a flame in its fullest glory. When he calmed down he continued.

"In the meantime he was able to catch some slower animals to eat, and to feed the loyal dogs that still accompanied him. The people of Soom Kali are unusually long lived, so he was still a reasonably young man by their standards. Every day he lived in fear that someone might follow him down a tunnel, so his new project became to close off the tunnel. After a year, he managed to accomplish this to his satisfaction. No one could get through. But then he realized that a part of him had hoped that someone would follow him, so at least he wouldn't have to be alone anymore.

"He came to realize that his escape wasn't a triumph at all, but another type of death. In order for his escape to mean anything, he thought, he needed to reproduce, so he tried with some dogs, but they miscarried, and with all manner of birds, trees, and lizards with no success. Finally he remembered the blue beast he'd seen, the wildest but most graceful beast that ever lived. Completely untamable. One day when he was hot, and low on water, and wondering whether he would die soon, he saw in the distance a blue cloud, and the cloud was a herd of desert flame beasts. He jumped on his sled, and his dogs pulled him across the sand, for even after all this time he couldn't move very well in the sand. He managed to lasso one of the beasts. And that night, after a meal of fried rodents, and while the dogs howled to the moons, the kindest man and the wildest most graceful beast on the planet copulated. In four cycles, the graceful beast bore a child: the first Bakshami, descended from warriors and wild animals, with the grace to move over sand like a flame over straw, and with the kind nature to give hard-won food to another being who needs it.

"I tell this story not just for the children but for the grownups as well, so that in the days and years to come, as all of you travel to the hotlands in escape of domination, you remember your kind spirit and untamable ways."

Cray's eyes grew sad. "I won't be coming," he said. "Tomorrow I'm going into my dwelling and staying there until they take me out. I built that home myself. The spirits of five of my dead children live there."

Way in the background I saw the flea-bitten man lurking. I looked around at my neighbors, with their dogs and packages and sand sleds, and I looked around at all our shining dwellings, reflecting the large round moon and misshapen small one, and I knew that whatever remained in those dwellings would soon be robbed by the flea-bitten man and his peers. I knew I might never set foot in my house again. And with a newly born hardness in my heart, I knew that my mother was right: At least we'd gotten a weapon in the deal.

•‿

the glass mountains

part (two)

When my brothers, my sisters, and I were all very young we traveled only with our parents. But dangers were few in Bakshami, and because Maruk had begun to grow older and stronger, if a journey was less than a couple of days we traveled only with him. Maruk was impulsive, but he was responsible, and also a sort of maverick general. That is, he liked being in charge, but he also respected the good qualities of his sisters and brothers and enjoyed delegating authority and exercising his independence. By the end of our projected journey to the hotlands, he would be old enough to build a house for himself, to become an apprentice storyteller, or, if he wished to do so, to mate with his betrothed if she survived the trip. Depending on hardships encountered, the trip might take as long as a year.

Our house gone, we slept outside, covered only by sheets and flea netting. The wind grew surprisingly cool. I huddled close to my sisters and brothers, the dogs surrounding us in a protective circle. Once, I woke up and saw Maruk propped up on an elbow, staring at our house. "Maruk?" I said. "Maruk."

But he just said, "Go to sleep. We have a long walk tomorrow."

"Maruk?"

"What is it?"

"Have you seen Sennim?"

"Yes."

"Where is he? I want to know my future."

"He is no longer in your future. His family left today."

I felt a pang of sadness that Sennim and I would not mate, but my sadness did not come because of how I felt about him now but because of how I might have felt about him in the future. I knew I could never again take my future for granted. Things had changed so much that even if I did run into Sennim again, we would probably no longer be betrothed. The only constant in my life was my family, whereas before all things had been constants. I scooted closer to Maruk, so that I could hear his breathing better.

He closed his eyes and pretended to be breathing evenly but I knew he was awake. The moons had passed through the sky, and our houses no longer glowed with reflection. The houses made smooth dark shapes in the night, except for one, lit up inside, full of shadows moving and bustling, no doubt as a family hurried to get ready for their journey with us. Our house, farther away, lay in darkness. I clung to my doll. In Bakshami, a grownup might play with dolls, and a young child might walk alone to a village several hours away. But I doubted I would want my doll in a year.

I stared at the sky and saw another ship pass overhead, the hum strange and distinct in the night. No one else saw the ship. Maruk had fallen asleep for real now.

In the morning we cooked roots in meat oil, our usual breakfast, and drank a cup of water with herbs. Some of the parents sat around discussing where the maps of the trail to the hotlands showed water, and whether it was better to go out of our way and take the less dry route, or whether, to save time, we ought to take the shortest distance. There were several lakes the long way on the map, but there was no telling whether or not they'd dried up. Lakes dried up and formed in Bakshami for reasons no one understood. Most people who traveled to the hotlands went the long distance, and apparently the ground along the shorter route was riddled with skeletons of the intrepid but foolish. Their gowns, once brightly colored, had crumbled and faded from the heat and wind. But the skeletons belonged mostly to outsiders. A number of Bakshami had gotten through taking the shorter route. On the other hand, more had gotten through on the longer route, even if some had perished there, as well. My grandfather had traversed the longer route going, and the shorter one back when he moved more slowly but also needed less water like all the very old.

"But we have children," said one parent. "How will they survive the thirst if we take the short distance?"

"They're used to going without water," said another. "My daughter once went without water for seven sunrises."

"Seven, yes, but what about twenty? And can your daughter do without for thirty?"

"I say if we plan right, we can make it the short way."

"Our plans may all be useless if we're bombed from above by ships."

"Remember, this is a border dispute with the Formans. They don't want the hotlands, they want more land at the border. Why should they bomb people trying to get as far as possible from the border?"

"I agree. Even in a ship, how many Formans are eager to fly over the hotlands? The air is too wild for ships to fly. And I heard a rumor that at least one ship that tried ended up catching fire."

"Yes, even a bird might catch fire in those deserts."

"I saw it happen once."

"No! It's only legend."

"It burst into flames in midair."

"No! How is it possible?"

"I don't know. Perhaps the heat of the sun combined with the reflections of the Glass Mountains worked like a magnifier shooting out a hot ray of sun. A fluke for sure, but not an impossibility."

My mother shook her head and leaned in to us children. "They comfort themselves with legends," she said with distaste. But my father looked on with interest.

"When was this?" he said.

"Many years ago."

"Why did you visit the hotlands?"

"To find a wife. Someone in my clan had told me there was a woman there who would suit me, and I her. We've been married seventy years now."

"And now you're returning," someone else said. "You know, they say no one makes the trip to the hotlands twice."

"You're trying to spare my feelings. I've heard that saying, and that's not quite how it goes. What they

the glass mountains

say is that no one makes the trip to the hotlands twice and lives. But my wife and I plan to arrive alive."

There was a vote—each person in the village could cast as many votes as years lived. The long route won. Certainly there were hazards both ways. The animals one might encounter in the area of my former home had no interest in the taste of human flesh. But in other areas lived a type of wild dog that had never been mastered, even by the best trainers in the sector. Supposedly some of the Soom Kali who went to see the elders captured a few of the dogs and took them back to Soom Kali, where one got loose and killed fifty people before being stopped.

My parents were trying to attach a sled harness to Artie, but he began to growl at them. "Mariska, you put this on him," said my father. "When is he going to learn to stop growling at everyone but you?"

I gently tightened the harness around my dog. "I'm sorry, Artie, but you're going to have to work hard for a while." Artie had always been a hard-working dog. He was so big everyone always wanted to use him to drag something or other. When I first got him he was the runt of the litter, but he'd grown as large as any dog I'd ever seen, with the strength of three dogs.

After the cool night, the next day's weather surprised us by its ferocity. We donned the white hoods that came with every gown and set off, almost five hundred strong. Many villagers had already left; others arranged to leave in groups soon. Along the way we planned to pick up more people, members of our clan or members of the clans of our neighbors. Clan members were people you would die for, and who would die for you. The Ba Mirada was known as especially loyal. All clans were loyal to each other, there was no question of that, but some were more loyal, just as in Bakshami all afternoons were hot but some fiercely so.

Full of energy and eager to get as far as possible before the afternoon heat pierced our hoods and robes, we glided across the sand. At the next village we stopped to snack and to wait for a family readying itself to leave with us. The village looked much like my own, but with more trees and darker earth and sand in the ground. Seven aunts of mine lived here with their families, but they'd all left the day before. The girl Maruk was betrothed to had lived here, but she, also, had left. They probably were not betrothed anymore, either. Because the sun hadn't reached its highest point, we decided to leave sooner than we'd planned and rest at midday when it got too hot even for us.

Katinka, already tired, cried when we started to leave, and my mother attached her to Artie's sled. I didn't want Katinka to have to walk more, but at the same time I hated to see Artie's load increased. He already carried far and away the heaviest load, and I could see his fatigue. I would always put my family before anything, yet I can't honestly say that I didn't love my dog as much as I loved my family. Artie had walked by my side since my first dog ran away when I was barely out of infancy. Dogs rarely ran away, but that one had, frightened by unusually loud thunder during the brief storm period.

I walked near Tarkahn, who was talking to himself as always. I didn't know where he got the energy.

"Here's what I imagine," he said to everyone in earshot. "When we get to the hotlands the elders will tell us where to settle. They'll probably tell us to walk even more, to settle in some other land. We'll create a new town closer to the Soom Kali border. The Soom Kali are animals, but they're not buffoons like the Formans. They know they have no need to expand to Bakshami, a land where the population might be easily conquered but the climate can't be conquered by human, beast, or sorcerer. Of course I say that knowing full well that in our own way our people have conquered the climate. I don't mean to offend fate by saying that, I only mean that the way to conquer such a climate is to surrender to it as we have, but the Soom Kali are incapable of surrender..."

Meanwhile Maruk mumbled as he walked, and every so often he whipped his killing knife out of the folds of his orange gown. The material scarcely rustled during the maneuver. Leisha, usually high-spirited, dragged her feet more than anyone else I could see. Jobei moved along with both the determination and the resignation of one who knows his fate is inexorable. By being determined, he probably believed, he could at least exert his will. It was similar to what Tarkahn said about the climate. Jobei would conquer his fate not only by surrendering to it but by relishing it. Katinka slept. My parents walked together almost touching, silent. I, too, walked quietly, observing everyone else until my mind wandered and I dreamed of a vast waterland or, better yet, an iceland, where the people constructed houses of ice that sparkled in the sun the way our houses did, and where you could lick the sides of your ice house whenever you got thirsty.

I stared at the sand until it looked to me like the ice I'd seen in renderings. I began to love ice. I attributed religious and transformative qualities to it.

"Mariska! Mariska!" Maruk was yelling.

"What?"

"Hurry, you're falling behind." Almost everyone else now walked in front of me. Artie trudged by my side with Katinka in tow. She stared ahead, a weepy look to her face.

I climbed to the side of the sand sled. "Go, Artie!" Artie sped up until I told him to slow down so I could hop off. He'd taken me up near the beginning of the pack. A woman I'd never seen before wailed not far away. No tears fell, but she kept making noises almost like the mating call of a larabird, each wail starting out full and throaty and slowly becoming high-pitched and full of pain. I walked nearer her, watching, feeling politely yet patronizingly curious about this exhibition of pain that differed so much from my parents' stoicism, in fact from the stoicism of all the other grownups.

Tarkahna leaned in close to me. Her hood had fallen down, and her long black hair was braided and wrapped several times in a circle around the top of her head, so that it looked like a shiny black cap. "That lady you're watching is from my clan, but she's not a native Bakshami."

the glass mountains

"Where is she from?" I couldn't remember someone from another sector who'd ever actually moved here. Forma bordered us on one side and Soom Kali on the other three. And certainly no one from those cultures would ever choose to live here.

"She's from Mallarr."

"Why did she come here?"

"She mated with a Bakshami man."

"Who?"

"I saw him only from afar. He played the drums like a demon. Such a man! He'd traveled to Mallarr to set up a trading station. She loved his peaceful ways and thought he planned to spend the rest of his life in Mallarr. But he got homesick, and she agreed to come back here with him. They had four children, and then he died of dust virus. Apparently his virus defenses weakened in Mallarr, and ever since he came here he got sick all the time."

"When did he die?"

"Only one cycle ago."

"Why doesn't she take her kids back to Mallarr?"

"She likes it better here."

"I thought only the natives liked to live in Bakshami."

"My parents say she's a rare woman. I say she's rather odd."

My friend hurried to break up a fight her dog had started. I walked close to the woman and her children but didn't say anything. Actually the sound of her wailing unnerved me, and I could see it was starting to vex everyone within hearing. It almost made one feel that this whole expedition was hopeless before it had even got started. I waited for my family so that I wouldn't have to stand so near the woman.

Walking with my backpack had already grown dreary. Usually when we traveled we didn't take much, and our pets happily carried everything. But the pack on my back weighed me down. I couldn't believe how heavy a few robes could feel. I thought of abandoning a robe, but I never considered leaving Artie's chew-rock behind. At the same time I was starting to feel optimistic and excited at what we were doing. I dreamed this was Maruk's and my chance to get to Artroro. Anyplace new already had started to seem nearer than my old home had. My dreams occupied me while I walked all day. Sometimes that day Tarkahna and I fantasized together.

"And then I'll marry an Artroran man as big as a tree," I would say while she giggled.

"And he should have a pool as big as a house for you to luxuriate in," she would answer.

"We mustn't marry anyone without a big pool."

Families from my village surrounded me, their dogs dragging sleds piled high with possessions. A couple of people had piled their sleds a bit higher than ours, and a couple had piled them lower. But no one seemed to have taken too much or too little. To take too little might mean starvation or dehydration, and to take too much was to strain the dogs so that they wouldn't be able to drag anything. My parents had taken enough food and water, they hoped, for the trip to the first lake. At the first lake, we hoped, we would find more food and water. Hope! That was all there was. Of course, if we caught animals along the way, they would provide more moisture for us. And even I understood an unspoken part of the plan: Some people would die, leaving more dogs to carry supplies for those who lived. We all accepted this part of the plan.

The dogs toiled obediently. Even the small ones, barely larger than furrtos, carried or dragged something, and even the smallest children, if they could walk, hauled a package on their backs. The Bakshami are hard workers and the weather has made us stoic.

At the height of the afternoon heat we stopped near a tree. It was just one tree in the dust, but it was the first we'd seen in a while, and it felt refreshing to be able at least to see the slight shadow the green leaves threw on the ground and to imagine the roots reaching deep into the earth in search of water. We clustered around the tree in a circle, the dogs sitting as usual on the outside, too hot to play or fight except for an occasional short growl or truncated wrestling match. We ate dried meat and sipped water. Unlike people in other sectors, we perspired little and so needed less water. Our temperatures regulated themselves somewhat differently than people from cooler climates. Otherwise we wouldn't have survived.

The woman who'd been wailing sat quietly with her four children. Her hair, hanging in a braid out the front of her hood, was so light it was not really black but brown, and one of her children had distinctly brown hair. She was a tall girl about Maruk's age, the only one of the children not crying.

Everyone started to rise after we'd eaten. The dogs

began to bustle, and one person began trudging, then another, until all but a few stragglers remained. As I got up I heard a slight hum and saw a ship in the distance behind us. Everybody stopped and watched as it caught up and flew over and past us. It was very disappointing to see how easily the ship covered ground when our walking had already grown so tiresome. But I knew from experience that a long journey was first hard, then easier, then twice as hard as it had ever been, then you grew immune to its difficulties, and then you were there.

At nightfall, when the moons first began to push their way over the peaks of the small sand hills before us, we stopped and pitched tents against the winds that had already started acting up. The families hammered long stakes into the ground to secure the tents against what I already knew would be a severe wind storm. Through the tent window I could see the huge swirling dust storm that still lay ahead of us. We worked fast, burying in the sand whatever wouldn't fit in the tents and then hurrying inside with our dogs.

When the storm arrived, sand and pebbles buffeted the tent with a force we knew could slice skin. My family sat quietly, thankful that our tent was near the middle, surrounded by others, and at the same time knowing that in fairness next time we would have to take an outside spot. Maruk clutched at a map of Bakshami he'd brought. He studied that map the way Leisha studied her list of jokes, and he even slept with it. My mother lit one of the candles we sometimes used for rituals, and I watched the tent

the glass mountains

list perilously with the bursts of wind. Outside the window, I saw swirls of dust rise like apparitions. The tent tilted so much I felt certain that in a moment everything would fall apart—our tent and everybody else's—and a hundred and some-odd families would go flying into the night air like the smallest pieces of sand in the desert. I closed my eyes, but that made the sound of the sand battering the tent seem louder, louder, as powerful as the wave of sand I'd once seen engulf a man, and I opened my eyes once more. This time I stared at the ground rather than the wind against the tent.

We needed our rest, but we sat unmoving until the storm calmed down. When it finished, sand covered the window and we could no longer see outside. Then we got up and laid out our bedmats. They felt soft on the sand. I felt so relieved the storm had ended that for the first time all day, I felt safe, even cozy, there squeezed into a tent with my family, all of us listening to the funny snores of our flea-bitten dogs as they lay at peace on their blankets. Artie always remained awake until I fell asleep, and though exhausted I combed out his fleas.

"Don't spend time only with him," said my father.

"But Artie hauls more than anyone."

"Just a bit more time then. The other dogs work hard, too." He looked very sad for a moment. "A long time," he finally said softly. "A long time."

I didn't know precisely to what he referred, but I knew it wasn't good. I had never seen my father look so burdened. My mother was firm, kind, extremely practical, but my father was the philosopher, more delicate and more outwardly emotional. He thought about every step he took, thought about it when his children or wife smiled at him and thought about it when they frowned at him. He evaluated how much food and water we needed and then evaluated whether his evaluations were accurate. On the other hand, generally whenever my mother finished evaluating something, that was that. On to the next thing. If her evaluations proved right, well, why was that surprising? And if she'd erred, she would simply start over again. But to worry, what a waste of time! She might check on us each night, but she didn't worry about the viruses the rest of the time.

I got under my covers. The sand sprinkled softly on the tent, making a comforting pitter-patter that I'd heard many times before. Artie came over and lay down across my legs, which I gently pulled out from under him. The candle had died on its own, and I wondered sleepily how many candles we'd brought. Then Maruk asked: "How many candles did we bring?"

"Ten," said my father.

"Just ten, and we used one tonight?"

"That's right, it was important to have light tonight. You children are in charge of saving the wax and making new candles out of it. In fact, since you asked the question, Maruk, I put you in charge."

He nudged me and whispered, "And I delegate you."

I kicked Leisha and whispered, "Maruk says you should make the candles."

I heard her whispering to Jobei, and I knew he would accept without question. "I'll help you, Jobei," I said softly.

"Help him what?" said my father.

"Make candles."

"I said that Maruk should do it."

"Yes," I said.

"Yes," said Maruk.

I could hear wailing from a nearby tent. It was the woman from Mallarr, and I could tell she tried to control herself, wailing softly so that you almost thought the wind blew. But we knew it was her.

"Maybe you should talk to her," said my father.

"But she's not in our clan," said my mother. "I don't want to interfere."

"But what the storyteller said—try to remember your kindness."

My mother had already settled in, so she rose wearily. She tried to leave the tent, but the sand had piled itself up around the door flap. My father and I helped clear it away without letting too much pour inside. Maruk and my other siblings had fallen asleep. After we got the flap open, I stepped outside with my mother and saw large mounds of sand, some of them with the round tops of tents sticking out the middle. The tops flickered from the candlelight inside them. Every time a slight wind blew, the mounds of sand rearranged themselves. But the wind had calmed down. My mother and I smiled at each other. The end of a sandstorm like this was a time of quiet joy. When my mother left to try to talk with the wailing woman, I got into my bed, but my father sat up, waiting for my mother. In a moment I could hear the soft voices of women wafting into the tent the way a scent might waft through the air. I fell asleep to those voices.

2.

The days passed more quickly than one might think. While the trek itself was monotonous, the proximity of the families and the lack of privacy made us not bored with each other but fascinated. The smallest disagreement loomed large, and the minutest flirtation drew the interest of five hundred people.

Much remained the same. Tarkahn still talked incessantly, the wailing woman continued to wail, and Leisha still told the old jokes. My mother had befriended the wailer. Her name was Ansmeea, and sometimes at the end of the day she sat with us in our tent and discussed matters with us. It was amazing how much there was to discuss. For instance, the subject of how today's weather was different from yesterday's and would probably be different from tomorrow's; and of how the windstorm the night before was not the worst but perhaps the third from the worst we'd encountered so far; how no one had spotted a ship overhead for many days; how for all we knew a full-scale war had never started. But that last bit of gossip was proved false when a man traveling with twelve dogs and no people caught up with us on his sled. He'd left the border twenty days earlier, about the time we'd started our journey. At that time the Formans had already destroyed many towns near the border. A dog trainer, he'd owned forty dogs

but had traded most of them for meat before beginning his journey. His dogs sat at attention as he
spoke. When he motioned them down, they lay
calmly, their eyes roving from their master for the
first time. The man didn't look much older than
Maruk. He had a high forehead and delicate pro-
file. Many dog trainers were mysterious and inde-
pendent people, preferring the company of their dogs
to that of their neighbors. They were generally both
kind and firm, and nearly always loners.

One night at storytelling, he said he had something to tell us. "I have news of your village. But it
isn't good news. When I left the border, at times I
imagined I could hear screams in the distance, as if
the war were always just an hour behind me. I hurried on, trying to put more time, more distance, between me and the war I imagined raged behind me.
But when I reached your village, I found hundreds of
Bakshami, with their packages piled on their dogsleds
and their packs tied to their backs. What I mean to
say is I found them dead. So I knew that while it was
possible that the war raged behind me, I saw then
that it had also raged in front of me. Yet all I could do
was follow my map. Returning to the border meant
certain death, while heading toward the hotlands
meant only probable death."

And so we had the scant comfort of knowing we'd
done the right thing to abandon our village.

The next day the dog trainer was gone.

We all thought that was very romantic, the way
he'd come and gone alone. Maruk said when he grew
up he would own a thousand dogs, and if he were

ever killed in battle I could choose my favorite to keep, and the rest would go to his wife and children. That made me love Maruk more than ever, because I knew that one good dog might sometimes be worth a thousand other dogs. I knew I would always adore dogs. I loved the way sand stuck to Artie's black nose and the way his oversized paws made him look half-puppy. In Bakshami we respected animals for helping to make our lives livable.

Ansmeea and her daughters, except for the tall one, sometimes rode on sleds. I seethed when they rode on the sled pulled by Artie, who already carried such a heavy burden.

No one else could escape the long trek we made each day. Back home if you really didn't want to do a chore, you could plead sickness or fatigue, or you could even exert your stubbornness. But out here to refuse was to die. Those who got sick struggled to keep up with us, maybe spending time on a dog's crowded sled, but they knew that if they couldn't keep up they would die: We would not wait for them. If we didn't keep going, we thought we might all perish. So for the good of everyone, we felt sympathy for the sick and the tired, but we didn't wait for them. One day I offered to carry a sick man's pack, and by the end of the day I was so tired I'd fallen well behind. Artie and Maruk walked beside me, but I refused to let anyone else carry my load, feeling that I'd made the commitment and should keep it. But I knew I couldn't afford to help the man the next day. It didn't matter. He died that night. I was so tired I fell asleep during the burial ritual.

In the evenings after we ate, there might be brief storytelling periods, and there was always a group who played the rhythms. I joined them sometimes. Playing the rhythms, listening to them, gave our lives continuity. The rhythms were older than anyone alive and would be played after all of us traveling together had died. So by playing them, we felt ourselves to be a part of time, the way the howling of the dogs was a part of time, something dogs always had done and always would do. But we spent the bulk of our time walking quietly or sleeping. The rhythms, the howling, the storytelling, all were aberrations in the world of silence we lived in all day and most of the night.

At night my exhausted mother continued to braid our hair and sing to us, and sometimes children from other families gathered around, braiding their own hair and listening to my mother's songs. My father would ruminate on why events had occurred as they had in Bakshami. He would play the rhythms absently and speak an occasional thought about how the Forman attacks in no way undermined the long-standing Bakshami belief in nonalignment.

"We're the only sector on the planet that has never fought a war," he said proudly. "If the Formans killed every one of us, it wouldn't equal a fraction of all the people of Artekka that have been killed in wars over time." Even as others began to have their doubts, my father clung to the belief that our way of life was superior to all others. I was still forming my beliefs. I agreed with my father, and yet I agreed with the handful of warmongers, too. What was wrong with my father's theory was that if the Formans killed every one of us, our culture would disappear. But Bakshami was incapable of fighting a war. We were not just the only nonaligned sector on the planet, we were also the only sector that didn't use advanced machines. We used the power of the sun and wind for all our needs, but we didn't use electric lights at night. When it got dark, we told stories, and then we went to sleep. We did the same during our trek, except the storytelling didn't last as long, and the sleep was deeper.

Every so often, Maruk, along with Ansmeea's tall daughter—named Sian—would take short journeys ahead for reconnaissance. They made a striking couple, brave and exotic. When he got back, he replaced our storytellers. Sometimes he told us what the maps couldn't show, where changes in the sand had made it easier to take a path other than the one the maps indicated. Everyone listened. I so wanted to believe in our safety that I developed the sense that Maruk was a savior and that as long as he helped us, we would survive. Many nights he stayed not in our tent but in the tent that housed Sian and her family. There was gossip, but they didn't care. They ignored the gossips.

Always, Maruk's reconnaissance was completely accurate. He memorized every dip and rise in the sand and predicted the future direction of even the slightest breeze. Some of the older among us grumbled that they didn't see the advantage of knowing the inevitable. "Has it come to this?" they would say. "Must we know the future in the same way as the fools who visit the elders?"

But most of us waited eagerly for his informa-
tion; and every night he was gone, if the weather
permitted us to sleep without a tent, I would stare up
at the stars and moons and the Veil of White—our
galaxy—and pray to the beauty of the sky that my
brother would return safely.

Because my mother was Ansmeea's closest friend
and Maruk's mother, she was chosen to officiate at
the wedding of Maruk and Sian one torrid evening.
The ceremony was simple, since we'd brought no frills,
but we kept candles burning all night in the sand,
filling the air with the smell of wax and with the soft,
soft sound of a thousand candle flames fluttering. I
felt great pain that night, knowing for the first time
in my life that I would not always be first in my
brother's heart. And in a fit of unfamiliar bile I wished
the worst for Sian and Maruk, and then hated myself
for wishing that.

I fell asleep wedged between Artie and Leisha
on a blanket in the sand, but I woke up somewhere
around half night after dreaming that two ghosts as
magnificent as the Veil of White passed through me,
and the ghosts were my parents. My eyes shot open.
All around me candles burned. A few people had
lapsed in keeping theirs alight, and wisps of smoke
dissipated in the night. I thought that as lovely as
the stars above me were, if someone were to look
down at our camp the sight would be just as lovely as
the stars. And as this occurred to me I heard a whine
in the sky, a noise like the humming of scavenger
ships yet somehow more threatening. I was still half
asleep and watched unbelievingly. Across camp,

Maruk must have heard all that I'd heard, and more, because he jumped to his feet and shouted, "Run! Everybody run!" Trusting Maruk completely, I grabbed Katinka and didn't wait to see who followed, just ran as fast as I could. I saw my dog gliding behind me, and to my side I saw Jobei, and I knew that Maruk's voice had caused my whole family to run. I didn't have to turn around to know that they were all there. We ran into the black until we could run no more, despite our tremendous stamina. When we stopped we stood on a slight incline and could still see the faraway camp, but not clearly.

Many other families had heeded Maruk, and as we stared at the camp I could tell he felt embarrassed to see that we could make out the candles burning, since nothing at all had happened. The sound of the whine had gone. All was peaceful. The camp appeared quiet and normal, like the sands covering a dead man appear normal.

"There's the lake in the other direction," exclaimed Jobei. He was excited, but I knew he'd really spoken to take attention away from Maruk's embarrassment.

Maruk spoke breathlessly. "I don't care what my eyes tell me. Something is wrong down there."

"Perhaps it was a dream," someone said. I felt sorry for Maruk, but I admired the way he refused to give in to what his eyes told him. The whole way back Maruk walked several measures to the side of my family. He walked quietly and inefficiently, kicking sand, hardly ever looking up, digging in his bare toes—no one had had time to put on shoes. Sian walked by his side. We'd run with abandon, and after our day of walking and night of celebration for the wedding, the run had exhausted us. We spent nearly twice as long just to get halfway back.

Except for the dogs, Maruk smelled it first, the smell of death, filling the air as the smell of wax had filled it just a short time earlier. "There's danger," he said simply.

Altogether there were about a hundred of us. Tarkahna and I held hands so tightly my knucklebones cracked.

We continued barefoot into the sand, which was still warm even at this hour, and I watched the sand ahead of me alertly. My parents walked holding hands. They were as attached to each other as a planet to the sun. When they fought sometimes, it was like arguing over which of them was the planet and which the sun. I prayed to the sand that ruled the lives of the Bakshami: Make my parents safe always.

We walked back to camp without talking. It was just starting to get light, the black sky filled with whispers of blue and red. With every step the sweet smell grew stronger, until finally it grew so overwhelming it seemed it couldn't possibly have grown more. But it did.

When we got closer we saw that what we'd thought from the incline were candles burning had been the burning of many of our possessions. When we got closer still we saw that bodies had burned as well. Smoke now hung in the air like a raincloud over our camp.

"Hurry!" someone called to us. "There's a lot of work to be done, and they may return."

I felt I needed to pause a second to take it all in, the burnt shapes of my neighbors and some of their dogs and the camp. The camp, which had seemed so large when last I sat inside it, now seemed small and inconsequential in the vast desert.

We all gathered up the remains of our possessions: a few items of clothing, and, fortunately, a few slabs of meat. In certain ways the Formans had done a merciful job. There was probably not much suffering or forewarning. Under charred covers lay charred bodies, facing toward the sky. There was no screaming or groaning because no one was alive. Maruk said the Formans may have used some sort of heat-seeking bomb. He said this not as if he knew what he was talking about but as if he liked the sound of the phrase, "heat-seeking bomb." Since the day we'd first seen the flea-bitten man with the weapon, Maruk had changed. But what the change would come to I didn't know. I'd never heard of such a device as Maruk spoke of, but then I'd never even heard of any kind of bomb at all until the current troubles.

I worked quietly, breathing through my mouth and trying not to look around. I also tried not to think about who might have lived and who died. There were those I'd befriended who'd probably died, but I didn't want to think about them now. We needed to work quickly. One family had gathered all the sleds the Formans hadn't destroyed and lined them up so that we could all pile goods on them. I knew that nobody owned anything anymore, that there were no personal possessions. If one of us starved it would be because we all starved.

We went quickly through the whole camp. Sunlight bled over the horizon, through the clouds that seemed to ring only Bakshami but that for all I knew ringed the whole of Artekka, ringed Forma and Artroro and Soom Kali. Before I left camp I permitted myself a deep breath through my nose, so I would always remember what the Formans had done to my people, and I let my eyes search for anyone that I might recognize. I saw only one—Tarkahna's brother—and then I couldn't bear to see more.

"Mariska, hurry," said my mother, and I ran to follow the others.

I usually loved sleep and dreaming, and this was the first night ever I could remember that I didn't dream at all. The Bakshami see sleep as another one of their necessary rituals. I'd never slept so little. Leisha and Jobei looked pasty, but Maruk, if anything, appeared flushed. He no longer pulled out his knife repeatedly with a flourish, yet he struck me now as stronger and infinitely more lethal than he had when he used to show off his knife by whipping it out of his robe. Now he looked as if he could use that knife.

I carried a knife, too, the one my grandfather had given me from Soom Kali. It was the only one of my possessions that had survived the attack.

For the last few days, Katinka had refused to walk, and she rode now on Artie's sled with some of our charred possessions. Katinka's eyes scared me, the way they stared at nothing and the way the whites had taken on a yellow cast. My parents had already lost several children, including three after I was born. Deaths of children were solemn but expected events.

But now, having lost many of our neighbors, I didn't think I could stand it if anything happened to Katinka. When it came time for a short break, I gave her my water ration, which she drank voraciously without even noticing where it came from.

I'd never been so tired and thirsty. If this trip was like other long trips I'd taken, we were not yet living our hardest moments. But I couldn't believe that. I knew that if things got harder my eyes, too, would turn yellow, and I would have to hope weakly that others would take pity on me. There were certain types of brutality that one got used to in Bakshami: the brutality of the sun, the brutality of the sand and dust, the brutality of living two hundred years in the sun and sand and dust. But I think my people always tried to make up for the brutality with their kindness, their fortitude, and their peaceful ways. We kept no jails; we bore no murderous thoughts. So this hate I felt rising in my heart was new to me. Just as the sight of the flea-bitten man's weapon had made Maruk's eyes flame in a new way, so the smell of hundreds of dead Bakshami had created a malignity in my heart that I would not have believed possible just a short time earlier.

3.

I think we'd all believed that the day we arrived at the first lake on our journey would be a day of triumph. Instead we plowed despairingly through a weedy, dried-out forest and sat around a lake so small I almost felt I could swallow it in a single gulp. We dropped our packs and fell upon the water, taking huge gulps with a fervor and passion that at times made me forget what had happened and feel a type of gluttonous joy. The dogs yelped with pleasure, and we had to prevent them from jumping into the lake at least until we could fill our bottles. When we finally let the dogs go in, they splashed furiously to rid themselves of the fleas that tormented them.

We ourselves bathed in the warm water and then sat quietly near the lake. I swore the water level looked lower than it had when we arrived. Ansmeea's daughter, alone now but for Sian, sobbed uncontrollably, and it was as if she sobbed for all of us as we sat stoically in our new camp.

Finally someone spoke, the woman who'd been the oldest in my village after Grandfather. She hadn't uttered a word since we left our village. "I go no further," she said.

We all looked at her without speaking, since speaking wouldn't have been our place. But her daughter placed a hand on her mother's arm and said gently, "But you must."

"I go no further."

"We can't leave you here."

"How many times does an old woman have to repeat herself?"

Actually, the idea of staying appealed to me. Where there was a lake there was bound to be plenty of roots, and where there were a lake and roots a person could live. My mother and father scarcely listened, instead bending over Katinka as she coughed on a sheet still smelling of smoke and death.

The elder's daughter said, "We can't all stay. The lake will run dry."

"I don't propose that we all stay. I stated only that I go no further."

"You can see—how many people could this area support?"

"It supports what it supports. I ask no one to remain with me. I only say that this is as far as I go."

"Mother, don't make us carry you."

"The sled doesn't exist that can carry me where I refuse to go."

My parents had begun to pile up things around Katinka. So far they'd piled around her a toy that hadn't been destroyed, some bedding, a sheet, several bottles, and a piece of meat. I'd seen my parents do the same before, and other parents as well. It was a traditional ritual, an attempt to keep the child alive by surrounding it with chosen items. We all started to help, gathering up strong rocks, or leaves that still had life in them, and placing the items in a circle around my little sister. Every time she appeared to gain more light in her eyes, we redoubled our efforts, but after a while it was clear that she'd begun to slip away.

My mother turned to the elder. "What can I do?"

And the elder said, "Nothing. She's dead."

Indeed, Katinka's lovely black eyes now stared into a world none of us could see. My father looked first at my dead darling sister and then at each of us children in turn. "Has anyone considered negotiating with the Formans?" he said sadly.

"The Formans don't negotiate, they give you choices," someone replied.

"Isn't having choices better than having no choices? And if one of those choices means that no one else need die? I have a daughter dead."

"I don't mean to be unsympathetic, but many have lost children, and more than you have. How can you negotiate with murderers?"

My father said, "Like everyone here, I knew nothing about murderers before the current troubles, but now I think I do know something. I know that murder must be stopped. Someone must see what choices Forma offers us."

Maruk stood up boldly to my father. "I take no choices from the Formans."

"Same here," said Sian.

"And here," I surprised myself by saying. I'd never before defied my parents on an issue of such importance.

My father shook his head. "Even if the war ended tomorrow, I can see that you children are changed forever, just as Katinka is."

We took Katinka into the forest and dug a grave, lining it with pebbles. We then laid down a blanket before placing my sister in to sleep. My mother shut one of her eyes, my father the other, and everyone in camp sprinkled a handful of sand over her, again and again until together we filled in the hole. My parents sprinkled the first two handfuls and the last. In that way, they buried a child for the ninth time in their lives.

Back at camp, Maruk laid out his map and studied it while most of the rest of us ate. My parents conferred to the side, nibbling occasionally on pieces of meat as they talked. I saw how after more than a hundred years together they were two heads, two hearts, two bodies, and one soul. When one died, the other would.

My father walked over to where Maruk studied his map. "Maruk, you've recently come of age, and these are extraordinary circumstances, so I must allow you to make your own decisions. But your mother and I have decided to return to see whether we can negotiate, and we would hope that you would take care of your brothers and sisters at least until you reach the hotlands."

"No, you can't go!" I said. "I saw your ghosts in a dream." That gave my parents pause, but I could see they'd made their decision.

"There are twenty Ba Mirada clan members still alive here, including you children. They'll take care of you, and you must take care of them. I don't think I can do more for you than to try to end this absurdity."

"Mother!" I said.

"Where one spouse steps into danger, the other must follow," said my mother.

When my mother spoke in that tone, her mind would not be changed.

The events of the day had caused the shattering of our family. I went off to the forest to pout with Artie. I believed from my dream that my parents would die. Beyond that I held no beliefs.

Artie licked my face and hands with his huge dry tongue. He placed his paw in my lap and fell asleep. I, too, fell asleep, leaning over with my arms around him. I awoke to the sound of Maruk's voice calling my name. It seemed far away, part of my sleep, until I shook myself and saw how dark the forest had become.

"I'm here!" I said.

In a minute he rushed from the trees and hugged me. "You scared us all. Why are you hiding?"

"I fell asleep."

"Listen, we're all searching for you. I have to take you back to camp.

"I'm ready," I said.

"There's something else first."

"Go on."

"Sian and I are leaving soon for the Soom Kali border."

"What? They're nothing but barbarians there. You'll get killed."

"As you've seen, I could get killed as easily in my own sector."

"But your family is here."

"My new family will be where my wife and I make it."

"And your old family?"

"Always first in my heart. But a Bakshami cannot always act as his heart tells him to. In that respect, we're well suited for war."

"You're not the Maruk I grew up with."

"I cannot live a life of peace in the midst of a war. I might as well lie down and let the sun beat me to death. I have a responsibility to my fate. Grandfather wrote me that I would live someday in the Land of Knives."

He gestured behind him, and I noticed Sian's tall

form standing in the near-darkness. "We'll arrive in Soom Kali before you reach the hotlands."

"But Maruk," I said. "If you leave, I'll..."

He took my head in his hands and kissed me gently on my forehead, and still more gently on my lips. "You'll be okay. I make my own prediction. You must stick with Jobei and Leisha, and the three of you will flourish together."

"This is all my fault."

"How can any of it be your fault?"

"I don't know...I should have given you my knife. Then you would love me enough to stay."

"Mariska, Mariska. You've always known I longed to travel."

"But that was only a fantasy. Now your own sister is dead and you decide to leave with a strange girl."

"Katinka's death had nothing to do with my new wife. You must respect Sian as part of your family."

"I still blame myself for your wanting to leave."

"You must stop it," he said sharply. "There is no time for blame in war, only for responsibility. We must all fight for our future now."

"I'd rather die! I want none of the future, and if you had any sense, neither would you."

Sian held out her hand to me. "Come. Your parents are leaving tomorrow. You must spend time with them."

I turned away. But whereas before Maruk had always indulged my petulance, now he led Sian away with no further word.

I walked toward the camp when they were out of sight. I felt jealous of the girl, who in truth seemed

the glass mountains

brave and warm, worthy of my brother.

At camp my parents had already packed up everything they needed for their trip to Forma. They planned to go to bed early but for now listened as the other parents talked of their plans. I happened to sit next to Tarkahn, and while the others talked to each other, he spoke nonstop to anyone who happened to listen.

"It's true we could have tried to negotiate," he said, "but how can you negotiate with someone who is holding a gun in their hand when you yourself are holding only a jar of sand in yours, for isn't it an act of foolishness to think you can talk sense into someone for whom sense is the same as death, because you see in Forma if you pause to use your sense you won't be alert enough to see that your enemies are catching up with you, and in a place like Forma everyone is bound to have many enemies, sort of like in Soom Kali, don't get me wrong, of course the people of Soom Kali are equally barbarians, but at least they have style and flourish...and in any case, the hotlands are the spiritual center of Bakshami, and if we must die on the way there, then so be it. But to remain here doesn't make sense to me. We must visit the hotlands to know whether our sector is to live or die..."

"If all Bakshami commits suicide by going to the hotlands, then our sector that we claim to love will certainly die," said Maruk. "I may not accompany all of you as far as the hotlands."

While they argued over what to do, I went to sit by Ansmeea's youngest daughter, Ansmeea the

Small, who'd stopped sobbing and whose eyes had swollen so that they formed tiny hills with slits in the middle. I brushed my hand through her brown hair, which felt so thin and fine it wasn't like hair at all. Hair was something strong and beautiful, but hers was soft. I liked the way it stuck to my fingers like the webs of woodbugs.

"Your hair's so soft," I said. I wondered whether that had insulted her. "I like it."

She paused. "It's like my mother's was."

"No one else possesses such hair; therefore you should feel blessed."

Even through her slitted eyes I could now see a hopeful puppy kind of look. "Do you think?"

"My grandfather always said such things. Every time we complained, he said we should feel blessed we had mouths to complain with."

"Your brother saved my life, but not the lives of my whole family. Is that a blessing?"

"Not today, but in time you may see it is." I tried to remember what else my grandfather had taught me. "Grandpa always told me not to let too much time lapse between what I thought and how I acted. Otherwise I might end up doing only one or the other. So you thought about Maruk's warning, and then you acted by running. My grandfather was very old, so he must have known something. You followed his directions about thinking and acting. No harm could come of following my grandfather's words."

"I don't share your blood and don't share your convictions."

"But my convictions are the same as everyone's."

"I've lost my father to the viruses of Bakshami, my mother and one sister to the Formans, and another sister to your brother. Your convictions are a speck of sand among millions of specks of sand."

"You can be the sister of my sisters and brothers and me."

She looked away shyly and said simply, "No." Then she got up and walked away to sit near a group of people, probably of her clan. I felt stung but didn't dwell on it. Like many of us, she would be of age soon and must make her own decisions.

Because no one had slept much the night before, most everybody had started getting ready for bed. There wasn't enough bedding for all the families—or remnants of families—but we tried to divide everything equitably. I ended up with one tattered covering to share with Leisha. The grownups had come to no decision on what to do tomorrow. The only decision for now was to try to sleep as much as possible.

I'd slept in the forest earlier and couldn't sleep now. We lay unusually close together tonight, and I felt comforted by the sound of a hundred friends breathing. Tarkahna had lost two of her seven brothers. Even from across camp, I could make out her labored breathing. I hoped she felt comforted by the sound of Tarkahn mumbling in his sleep. Apparently he didn't dream of the present, but of the past. All his mumblings concerned his toolmaking business back in our old village. I hoped my parents, too, dreamed of the past now, so that at least they would savor one more night of happiness before embarking on what would certainly be a hellish and lonely journey back. Two people and two dogs, alone in the sand. Meanwhile, unless events dictated otherwise, I would be headed for the hotlands. I would probably be of age before I would know whether my parents failed or succeeded.

My mother rustled, and I saw her dark form slip out from under a sheet and come to sit by us. I'd slept so soundly during the walking that I'd never been wakened by her coming to make sure we didn't die in the night. But somehow I'd known she'd continued this personal ritual of hers. Usually my mother was a person who held her back straight, but tonight her back bent into a weird shape and her head rolled from side to side as she stared straight ahead.

"Mother," I said.

"Mariska, what are you doing awake?"

"I took a nap earlier. I'm tired, but I'm not tired."

"You speak like an elder—full of contradictions."

I got up and leaned on her and felt her arms around me. As I huddled against her I noticed that the elder and her daughter, though much older, were huddled in the same way. "Mother, you have to promise that if you need to you will not hesitate to kill anyone in your way."

"Mariska, it hurts me to hear you talk that way. Children should not speak of killing."

"I'm only saying if you must."

"You must not worry about me but about Jobei and Leisha. Maruk may not be with you for long."

"He is abandoning me, as you are."

She ignored that. "You must watch out especially for Jobei. Jobei's heart is as big as the sun. There was a time in Bakshami when a heart like that needed no extra protection, but that time passed last night. Will you promise never to leave his side?"

"I promise I will stay with him as long as to do so makes sense."

"Then you are saying you will not promise."

My mother did not scold me the way she once might have if I defied her. Instead she held me quietly, and as half-night approached she began to talk, almost the way Tarkahn did.

"There are two things I want to talk to you about. One was brought to mind by my conversations with Ansmeea. She talked often about her late husband, who died at the peak of her love for him. She once left home for her husband. Having made that sacrifice for him embittered her. So even as she loved him more and more, bitterness tainted her love. As time passed their marriage grew more complex rather than more simple, as my own marriage has. I would wish a more simple life for you. I also have a favor to ask you. My own mother taught me that you should do everything you can for your children, but that once one of them dies, as is inevitable, you must think first of your live children, then of the dead one if there is time. I loved Katinka as much as I loved anyone in the world, but now I have to think of you who are left, and only after that's taken care of can I take a moment alone to think about Katinka. Perhaps that moment will never come, so I hope that before you have your own children you'll take the time to do what I may never have the opportunity to."

"Are you saying you'll never have a moment's rest again?"

"I look at the future and don't see where rest fits into it."

"Shall I rest for you, too?"

"If you think of me sometimes, and of your father, yes, perhaps you can try to find a restful spot inside of you and reserve that spot for us."

"I can make my whole heart restful if you want."

"Just a spot. We will try to return soon, but remember that as time goes on you'll have feelings for many people to fill your heart, but if you would just promise a spot for your parents, I think that would be enough to make me feel during the next couple of cycles that the walk is not unbearable."

"I promise that, and more."

"No more is necessary."

When I woke it was morning, and my parents had already sneaked off.

My brothers, sister, and I went to the edge of camp and gazed into the horizon. All day we said things like, "They've passed the old camp now," or "They're probably taking lunch now." We sat together until evening, and then we returned to camp.

In camp, I furiously beat sticks together all night, learning rhythms I hadn't even known existed.

And in this way another evening passed.

•

part (three)

For the next few days I had a strange sickening feeling that was not only love for my parents but disbelief at their departure. At moments that night I wished I could learn to hate them, for though hate was new to me it already seemed familiar. The moons shone through the sparse trees, like certain metals before polishing. Damos was not quite full, but you could see the faint outline of its full form. I watched the sky and comforted myself with the knowledge that my parents watched it, too, and thought of my brothers, my sister, and me.

That night I heard a sound I'd never heard before, that of Maruk and his new wife having sex. They did it almost noiselessly, but I knew what the soft sounds meant. In the background Tarkahn mumbled, and the elder crabbed on, her voice alternately pleading and berating, full of both wishes and bile. Jobei, Leisha, and I slept close together, Jobei shivering and hugging me so that I could feel his soft penis against my leg, and feel his chest heaving with sadness and fear.

The next morning Jobei and I got up early and hurried to the outskirts of the forest, to maintain a vigil at the last place we'd seen our parents. Jobei told me that given the choice between possibly ending the war and keeping our parents with us, he would have chosen keeping our parents. Of course there was no such choice. But sweet Jobei felt himself dishonored because he knew that if there *had* been such a choice, he would have made the "wrong" one.

Every day someone suggested the hundred of us remaining should leave the lake for the hotlands. But there was always a reason not to. For instance, we needed to dry more furrto meat, or we needed more furrto hides to make water carriers out of. Other reasons we decided not to leave were that it was too hot, or there was a possibility that it would be too hot, or it had been so hot the day before that we hadn't rested well.

When the memory of our parents hurt less, Jobei, Leisha, Maruk, and I spent the days practicing our rhythms, and in the evenings after dinner we would go off to our separate projects—Maruk and Sian to obsessing about adventure, Leisha to compulsively memorizing jokes that the others in camp could tell her, Jobei to tidying up and helping anyone who needed it, and I to daydreaming for hours about what my parents might be doing at each moment I daydreamed. Maruk counseled me to stop my daydreaming if I ever wanted to amount to anything. He said my body was becoming unattached from my soul, and that wasn't the way of a Bakshami. So I started to pursue whatever occurred to me on a certain day. I'd work extra hard on my rhythms, accompany Jobei on his helping rounds, listen to Tarkahn or the elder lady, or train Artie to accomplish ever more complicated tasks. I would also watch Maruk for long periods. I saw in his face something I'd never seen before, a coldness that had once been mystery, an aloofness that had evolved from his anger.

the glass mountains

My parents had made us believe we were the center of the world. Now I was forced outside my selfish world, and so I noticed people in a new way. I'd known Tarkahn my whole life. But here in camp I noticed much that I'd never seen before. For instance, in spite of all his talking, he was a good listener. I'd known he was polite and that when someone else wanted to talk, he would lower his voice so that others could hear. But I didn't know he lowered his voice so he, too, could hear the other person. And unlike most people, who can only either talk well or listen well at any given moment, he could be thinking hard about what he was saying while at the same time thinking hard about what his interlocutor was saying. It was quite a talent.

I also watched Ansmeea sometimes. I noticed how she grew angry over the slightest provocation, often even over circumstances—which couldn't be changed.

The elder lady intrigued me. She actually seemed to have the seeing and knowing powers, but she was cunning. I suspected she'd denied her powers so she hadn't had to make the trek alone to the hotlands years earlier, only to come back before her death. My grandfather had muttered something once about her being a cheater, but we'd thought he was just being cantankerous. Whenever she spoke, which she did often lately, the elder lady never segued gracefully between subjects. Instead she leapt wildly from subject to subject, so that it was said only the very witty or the very witless could keep up with her in conversation. She and Tarkahn had formed a friendship.

He respectfully called her Elder, and she disrespectfully called him his childhood nickname, Tak-Tak.

"Now the secret to training your dogs well," he might say, "is that you have to press and rub them softly near their genitals, because in this way they learn that they can trust you..."

"Tak-Tak, pervert," the elder would reply. "I knew it even when he was a boy."

"...well-trained dog is one of the foundations for survival in the world..."

"Pipsqueaks! I'm surrounded by pipsqueaks!" the elder would then exclaim. Next she might pounce through the air with surprising and thrilling agility and land right where I would have been sitting if I didn't move. "So what if a spouse's habits annoy you! For example, maybe he makes chewing noises after he drinks water, yes, that's very annoying. And maybe he doesn't smell so good, I can see where that might be a problem. But maybe he also works hard. Did you ever think of that?" She would grab her head with both hands, as if her head pounded with pain. "Oh, when I think of the time I've spent worrying over fools!"

And Tarkahn, who'd been mumbling in a respectful and appropriately soft voice, would jump in. "The subject of fools is always an interesting one. There are many questions, like whether a fool is a brave person with no common sense, or whether a fool is a person with common sense and no courage. Which one is the bigger fool is a question that..."

And so on.

As a new season approached, the air became no cooler, except perhaps only slightly at night. We didn't miss any of the blankets that had burned in camp. Yet some people said that as long as winter neared we ought to stay at the lake, because it might get uncomfortably cold after dark or it might start to rain as we traveled. These people said we should wait until we were sure it wouldn't rain much before resuming our trip to the hotlands. But the opposition said that when winter ended the others would say we should wait until it *started* to rain. The rift grew between those wanting to stay and those wanting to leave, with those wanting to leave becoming more and more frustrated. We held a vote, and staying won out. That's what I voted for. But one evening, those who wished to leave called a meeting at which they announced they planned to depart the next day. All who wanted to come should come and all who wanted to stay should stay. "If you're coming, be ready at sunrise, because that's when we're leaving."

And because the rest of my family chose to go, I left, too. That's the way war is. Yesterday's decision means nothing as circumstances change. As the sun rose the next morning, about sixty of us set off. Fifteen belonged to the Ba Mirada clan. We took enough water but not enough food to last us until the next lake, but we hoped to run into game along the way. As we left, Tarkahna and I stared longingly at the camp. But it was time to leave.

Despite her protestations, the elder was tied to a sled and forced to come with us to the hotlands. But she'd said the sled hadn't been constructed that could take her where she didn't want to go, and on the fourth night she disappeared, never to be seen again. I tried to remember how many people had disappeared from my life, but I couldn't count them all. That, too, is how war is.

Maruk left in the middle of the night eleven days after we started off. I had been begging him to stay and threatening to follow him. But the day before he left had been a brutal one, astonishing in the hallucinatory viciousness of the heat. I could barely keep my head up as he kissed my cheeks and ears over and over, whispering that he was going to Soom Kali for adventure, and then on to Artroro to raise a family. A family, indeed! It did not matter to me in the slightest if I died, or lived to raise a family. And yet there was something in all of us that made us go forward. On the same day that Maruk left it was as if he had already left so long ago the memory had faded. Whenever I felt Maruk creeping into my heart, I felt too tired to walk. So I put the sorrow out of my heart. Love became secondary to survival. I would not have thought it possible that anything might be more important than my honored brother; but I would not have thought many things possible that had already come to pass.

The following days fell into a rhythm of walking and resting, hunting and eating, drinking and beating sticks together. We'd left any remaining drums in camp, so we had only the sticks we found to play rhythms.

We didn't know whether the war still raged behind us, or whether Forma had taken over. We knew that, if war continued, those Bakshami that had remained in their villages had died. I thought about my brother and parents each night before I went to sleep, and sometimes if we had the energy Tarkahna and I played rhythms on sticks and prayed for our families. Prayer in Bakshami was aimed at the wisdom of the world. You could pray to the sky or to a rock or to the sand, for the wisdom resided everywhere, one had only to make oneself heard. So Tarkahna and I prayed to the noise our sticks made and tried to devise increasingly elaborate noises and rhythms in order to please the wisdom in our sticks.

Every night I combed through Artie. Everyone else thought I spoiled him and that my spoiling would turn him bad, but I knew that wasn't possible. He hauled more than any other dog, and he deserved to be treated with respect. The hair of some of the dogs had grown matted and infested, which amazed me; back in our village owners had taken great pride in their pets. Children were taught to groom first their dogs and then themselves before going to bed. I thought of what Cray had said about remembering our kindness and thought he would be disappointed.

He would be disappointed, but he wouldn't hold our behavior against us. It's hard to express the fatigue we all felt. Every hour of every day we felt tired. We felt tired when we woke up and while we walked and while we took breaks. Even when I slept there was the feeling that the sleep wasn't quite deep enough. In Bakshami the annual heavy rains could beat you down, while the dryness sucked the life out of you. We'd actually been hoping to encounter heavy rain, as we would have gotten at this time of year back in our village. Sometimes I even hoped for a life-threatening storm, because the monotony of each dry day seemed like a greater threat than a storm, no matter how big. I wanted to feel something again, to miss my parents and Maruk and Katinka. But I was too tired.

Though nothing horrible happened, this part of the trip was in certain ways worse than the previous part. The tedium of walking overwhelmed us at times. I felt I wanted to bury my head in the sand and suffocate myself to escape the tedium. When, half-starving, we reached the second lake, we collapsed in it with the dogs. One man was so tired his head fell under the water and he didn't bother to lift it. Jobei helped him lift himself.

This lake was smaller by far than the last, and now there was no question of settling down. No one saw the point of staying. We found the discards of a previous group of campers—goods that probably had grown too heavy to carry. Mostly the previous group had left behind glass bottles, probably using furrto skins instead as water containers. Bakshami was a culture of glass: unbreakable glass, breakable glass, colored and clear glass, sand glass and rock glass and glass woven into threads. But during the last month when we'd been famished, we'd taken to chewing on our furrto skins. So the skins, in addition to being lighter than the bottles, doubled as food during a pinch. At the new lake we trapped furrtos for both food and new water containers.

We'd started cutting our hair short and shaving

the glass mountains

the dogs to get rid of the fleas, but at the lake we let our hair grow again. One family announced the mother was pregnant. They started to build a dwelling, and another family began a dwelling of their own. But except for Ansmeea and a few especially weak children, our bodies had grown into the walking. We moved with less grace but greater strength than we once had. As exhausted as we were, we still held hopes for the future, and we knew there was no future at this little lake. It wasn't large enough to support a village even a small portion of the size of my old town. So, eventually, forty-nine of us left.

This time as we walked Jobei's face thinned and grew gaunt. He retained his sweetness, but Leisha grew sullen and quiet. She didn't care about mimicry or jokes anymore. Sometimes Jobei would try to perk her up by asking her to tell him jokes or by making up jokes to tell her. And Tarkahn's previous constant talking had devolved into a nonsensical muttering that grew quieter and quieter until one day he moved his lips but no sound came out. I don't know which day that happened—it happened so slowly the change had seemed almost natural, and I could scarcely imagine a time when he'd expressed himself with vigor.

We gave Ansmeea an extra ration each day, but she continued to wither away until we didn't understand how she stayed alive. Her brown hair had gotten bleached from the sun even through her hood, and her skin, which formerly held tinges of sky blue, turned pink like her mother's had been, so that she looked less and less like a Bakshami. She no longer walked; Artie carried her on the sled every day.

Now and then we'd come across skeletons, but most of them appeared old, from before the current troubles. There were a few, however, that appeared more recent. If there was no food we chewed on these bones for sustenance.

Not long after the previous lake, we came across a camp that had been decimated much as ours had been. The ashes hadn't yet been incorporated into the landscape, and a sickening sweet smell lingered. The thought that we could be killed even this far into our trip disillusioned all of us, and one man, who'd already lost his will, lost his life as well at that. He simply looked at that decimated camp and he lay down, the life gone from him.

We didn't even bother to play the rhythms. I lay awake until half-night staring into the sky and listening for the sound of humming. Once I looked around and saw the faces of my compatriots under the bright moons. All of them had eyes wide open as they stared into the sky and listened for the humming. I don't know when the others fell asleep, but when I next woke the midday sun hung hot above camp. Usually, we woke before sunrise. Several other people still slept, and more appeared to have just arisen. After that we lost the meaning of what we did. That is, we no longer thought of the goal of reaching the hotlands, we just knew that every day we walked. Walking was what we did and walkers who we were. Except for Jobei, who retained his sweetness, we grew to have no other personality except our personality as walkers. When I opened my eyes I saw the sand on which I walked, and when I closed my eyes I saw myself walking on the sand. It grew too tiresome to hold my head up as I walked, so generally I watched the feet of the person in front of me.

Time passed in this way. A baby was born, but he died. Otherwise nothing much changed. At every lake, one or two or more stayed behind so that finally only thirty of us remained. Surprisingly, Ansmeea survived. We felt no sense of triumph at our achievement. We were nothing more than insects.

One of the lakes at which we'd expected to replenish our supplies turned out to be nothing more than a puddle, and we kept ourselves alive by drinking our own urine. We were trudging along in our zombielike way one day when Tarkahn suddenly exclaimed out loud, "Look, look!" It was the first time we'd heard his voice in months, so rather than look at what he pointed to with his finger we first looked at him, at his sunken face and twig of a finger. Then, across the flat expanse of sand, we saw a glimmering sliver like our silver moon Damos rising over the horizon in the evenings. It wasn't Damos; it was the crest of Mount Artekka, the highest peak of the fabled Glass Mountains. I thought then that I'd never seen anything so intoxicating and beautiful as that sliver of shining hope, as that picture of our future rising over the horizon. And for the first time in months I felt emotion. I felt I loved Jobei and Leisha and all my fellow travelers; I wondered what had happened to my parents and Maruk and hoped I might hear news of them soon; and I remembered my home, and what a sanctuary it had been not only against the sun and heat but against all types of worry and cruelty as well.

We fell to the sand and kissed it, thanking it for letting us get this far. We walked with new ardor for the next few days, our mood elevating as the mountains before us rose higher. The mountains reflected sunlight, and at times the heat neared the unbearable, even for people used to great heat. But we couldn't be stopped now. Our supplies had run low and we'd cut rations by a third, yet our energy grew rather than diminished. During the day Tarkahn's voice rose to a snappy mumble, and he began to talk in his sleep again.

His talking heartened me on the one hand, because it showed his spirits were rising. On the other hand, his talking saddened me, because he talked about the recent past, and the recent past was gone. The recent past had not yet turned to dust and blown to the hotlands to become a part of the Glass Mountains. The world in which I had been raised was in limbo.

2.

The Glass Mountains had always been and would always be. They contained everything and everybody that had ever existed in Bakshami, except whatever had been destroyed in the recent past. Here I myself would come to rest, after my bones had turned to dust.

As we walked I could see nothing but glass around us, reflecting the heat until my blood seemed to boil inside me. The mountains weren't smooth, except in places. They were ragged, occasionally like prisms, and they weren't really glass but a type of quartz. Clouds of dust occasionally covered the sky above them.

At night, however, the dust settled and the temperatures dropped. The stars shone all around. While in daytime I was surrounded by a thousand blazing reflections of the sun, at night a million reflections of the stars glimmered around me, and I knew the meaning of paradise.

On the fifth night after Tarkahn had spotted Mount Artekka, we reached the Glass Mountains. The night was clear and the moons reflected endlessly off the surfaces of the mountains. We continued to walk at night, to try to get through while it was a little cooler. I felt amazed that any outsiders had successfully made this trip, but then I remembered that many had died on the way to the hotlands, and many others had traveled with entourages—servants and numerous dogs per person. Most had traveled from another direction.

When we couldn't go any farther we slept for a few hours and rose before sunrise to continue. It took several days to get through the mountains, and the only reason we made it was because without our knowing it our will had grown stronger during our long trek. Tarkahn was the first through, and from my place in the middle of the pack I could hear him talking, "There's the village we've all heard so much about, it doesn't look like much to me, I don't know what the fuss is about, our village was bigger than that, but on the other hand I don't know that I was ever as glad to see our village as I am to see this one;

that is, I felt a deeper love for our village, but I can't really say I felt excited every time I saw it; but in any case I do feel disappointed..."

I, too, felt disappointed looking down the sweeping valley and seeing a village so far away it looked like a dollhouse, and an empty one, too, since no people walked the paths through town. I'd thought we were closer and that the village was larger. But when I first saw a person leaving a building my heart beat in my ears and I felt dizzy. I could see then that it was not a dollhouse spread before me but a real village, one where I might soon live, and one where I might soon hear news of my family. Mountains ringed the village, and two miraculous lakes shimmered. So far as I knew, this area was the most unlevel in Bakshami. I'd never seen lakes in a valley before. The effect inspired me and filled me with love for this village. Of course it wasn't paradise by any means. Dust and sand swirled over the houses just as it did over all Bakshami, and the dwellings were modest even by the standards of my people.

We kept walking, and as night began to fall we saw people come out to light lanterns in front of their houses, and more and more people began to walk outside, going from one building to another. We watched as crowds began to fill the paths. Someone said that those were not houses at all below, but saloons.

"What's a saloon?" said Jobei.

"It's a place where you'll never go," said an uncle sternly. But it turned out the uncle was mistaken, for a few days later, hungry, out of water, we walked thirty strong, with forty dogs, into the first door we came to. Though the sun blazed, when we passed through the door the inside was as dark as my house used to be at night when lit by candles. The saloon's builders had added just a few windows, and heavy drapes of a type of fabric I'd never seen hung across what windows there were. Surprised by the drop in temperature and nervous to have arrived, I felt a slight but unusual chill. Only a few people sat at tables scattered about the large room. Hardly any of them looked Bakshami to me.

"Can I help you?" said a man's soft voice from the bar.

"More villagers running from the Formans," said a voice with disgust. "How many more are there to be? A man like me can take only so much." The speaker was neither male nor female as far as I could see, and perhaps wasn't even human. "What are you staring at?" he snapped at me.

I stepped back and tripped over Artie, causing laughter throughout the room.

"Hayseeds!" the speaker exclaimed.

I'd never before heard the word he used but felt sure of its intent.

"That one shivers as if she's cold!"

The man with the soft voice stepped into the path of some light coming through the drapes. He was a slight Bakshami man with his head shaved bald. "Lokahn processes the refugees. He's at the biggest saloon, across town."

"How many more of us are there?" said my uncle.

"Thousands, we don't know what to do with them all."

"Where are they all then?"

"Asleep. Why get out of bed at this hour?"

"But it's almost midday."

"Exactly my point."

"Well, what about the war?" said my uncle. "Give us some news, man."

"What about it? The Formans wiped out many villages. They're trying to reach the hotlands through diplomatic channels. Their diplomats flatter the Soom Kali with new gifts and brilliant new compliments. But we're safe here. The Soom Kali are too smart to want the Formans as neighbors."

"Hey, hayseed," said the person who'd insulted me. "Take a bath and come back, I may need a servant." Tarkahn mumbled, perhaps in reply.

"What will happen?" said my uncle.

"The Formans are marching through all of Bakshami, destroying villages until the elders give themselves up and come to Forma with their riches."

"Then this is about riches."

"It's about a thousand years' worth of accumulated riches, and about servants for the Formans."

"Bakshami should make good servants," said the insulter. He pronounced it "backshammee" instead of "bahkshahmee." "They're hard workers and they don't like a fight."

The man with the soft voice smiled at us. "Talk to Lokahn."

Tarkahn's mumbling sounded insane, and he began wrinkling his nose, clearing his throat, twitching his eyebrows, and blowing out his cheeks as he talked. The insulting man looked at Tarkahn and

the glass mountains

shook his head sadly, as if there were just no hope for Bakshami.

Before we left I turned to the man with the soft voice. "Excuse me, sir, why do you work here?"

"Every generation of my family all through history has worked here. I've never been outside the hotlands. Where else should I work? I'm serving my sector here." How provincial, I thought, until I realized that before the war I'd traveled little myself, and probably never would have moved from my village in my lifetime, just as my parents had never moved.

We walked across to Lokahn's, where a man groaned when he saw us and said, "What, more? Bevia! Bevia. More refugees." He walked off mumbling, "Why must I be in charge of them?"

Lokahn, like the soft-spoken man, didn't act like any Bakshami I'd ever seen. For one thing, both of them had shaved their heads though neither were rebels. And when Lokahn's wife appeared, she, too, had shaved her head. She swept brusquely into the room and because she looked forceful and solid, when she stood on a table her presence hushed us all. "Sit down and listen, we haven't all day. Here's the arrangement we've made. The elders will give you all the jewels you can carry, and you can try to get out of Bakshami to resettle in another sector. If you wish to stay here, you must help dig wells. The elders claim there are great reserves of water if you dig deep enough, even here in the molten center of the planet. Oh, save us all from destruction, you're covered in fleas! Get to the baths now, all of you, before you infest my saloon." She pointed toward the back of the saloon, and we went through some doors to a hot spring, where we bathed with our dogs until our skin wrinkled and the water grew thick with fleas. The dirt and old skin fell off my body in chunks. In the drying-off room I saw my reflection for the first time since we'd left my village. My face, formerly round, now formed an oval, and my eyes, formerly gray-black, had turned pure black like Maruk's. They were also dull from months of hunger and fatigue. My skin no longer shone as it once had, and my limbs were lean and muscular, like the limbs of Maruk's wife had been. I was scarcely younger than Maruk had been when we left the village.

After our baths Bevia started work in the saloon, and we wandered through the village. The village had come to life. Since the elders didn't care if their patrons brought money or not, all manner of kings, politicians, robbers, and scum crowded the streets. The kings did bring jewels and money for the elders in case it bought better service, and the politicians pretended to have money or not, depending on how they perceived where the advantage lay. In the saloons, a robber might sit next to a king, and a moral man next to a woman who would slit your throat on a dare. All they shared was wanting advice from the elders. The elders never turned anyone away without giving them as many answers as they wanted to as many questions as they had. As a result some people got addicted to knowing all the trivia of their futures, staying for years asking ever more trifling questions.

I even met one lady who'd once spoken to my grandfather Samarr years earlier.

the glass mountains

"Why don't you leave?" I asked.

"I have so many questions," she said. "Sometimes I think there isn't enough time to have them all answered." She glanced up at the sun. "In fact, I have an appointment with an elder now." She rushed away.

Another day I saw a lady who moved across the sand as gracefully as a Bakshami. She'd covered her hair and half her face with veils, and an entourage attended to all her needs. Lokahn said she'd served as queen of a tiny monarchy I'd never heard of. Her husband had gone off to war with another tiny monarchy nearby and hadn't returned. So she'd traveled to the hotlands to ask the elders what had become of her king. At first they all refused to answer her question, but finally an old woman told her that her husband had returned from war not long after she'd set out for Bakshami. Finding her gone, he'd waited and waited but then had fallen in love with a princess from an adjoining sector. So now the queen didn't know where to go or what to do. She belonged nowhere. She wandered around from saloon to saloon covered in veils.

That night as I lay in a bed of the softest fur I'd ever felt, I looked out the window at the stars glistening with such clarity off the mountains that they seemed to inhabit the glass rather than hang in the sky; and I thought about how, way beyond those mountains, a queen had walked for longer than any of us to learn her husband's fate. And about how even now, despite the war, more robbers and graceful queens, more politicians and ambitious scum, were embarking on the journey to the hotlands, pulled here by the elders as the people of my village had been. And I decided that had I been the veiled queen and had I loved my king, I would have done the same thing she did. I wondered whether the people of my village had made a similar mistake by coming here. But before falling asleep I saw the beauty of the stars shining through the swirls of dust above the village, and when I woke up I saw the sun shining through the Glass Mountains. Despite this beauty, or because of it, my heart filled with pain, and I wished Maruk could be lying there next to me, so that I could stroke his beautiful face as he dreamed happily of wars and knives and a violent world I could not even imagine.

3.

Later that week, after we'd rested up and feasted every night, sucking the marrow out of fresh furrto bones and eating dried fruit for dessert each night, Tarkahn called a meeting. We met in Lokahn's saloon, deserted because it was still morning. Some of our stomachs had grown as large as a pregnant woman's because of our overeating, and I myself never went anywhere without bones and fruit stuck in my pockets. Tarkahn said, "Now I don't know quite how to say this, because I love you all like I love my wife, which of course is not strictly true since I know my wife much better and we have a much deeper and more complicated love than I'll ever know with any of you, but nevertheless I do love you all, but that isn't the point, or rather it's only part of the point..." My head spun over his words, and when I recovered from my spin I found myself craving food.

"...and in conclusion I want to suggest that perhaps it's time for each of us to go our separate ways, since after all our numbers are small and our needs varied, and since regardless of what you people decide, my wife and I have decided to stay here and start having babies, since the answer to all the deaths the Formans have caused is to have more babies..." His voice grew softer then, either because of emotion or so that others could interject their thoughts.

Ansmeea, now of age to make her own decisions, said, "I've decided to stay as well. As a matter of fact I've found work at one of the saloons."

One by one, everyone, including Jobei, Leisha, and myself, stated a preference to stay. I felt certain my destiny lay in stuffing my mouth full each night, and sleeping soundly among the remaining people of my village.

Still, since we were there anyway, several of us decided to make appointments with the elders to get advice. The appointments secretary scheduled a morning appointment for Tarkahna and me to come together.

Sometimes patrons of the elders made an appointment and ended up with twelve or more spellbound elders explaining their fate; other times people made an appointment and ended up with just one seemingly indifferent elder.

The elders held appointments in a large, elegant building in the center of town, like the hub of wisdom surrounded by spokes made of saloons. The walls inside and out were pinkish rock. Outside the doorway stood worn statues of the mythological blue firebeast and the kind Soom Kali man who was the first settler of Bakshami. A crack ran through the torso of the firebeast, and the first settler's nose was worn down to a small mound. A man outside the door waved booklets. "Catalogues of the elders! You name the price. Descriptions of all the elders and their specialties. Love! Money! Hate! There's an elder to predict any aspect of your future. Power! Philosophy!"

Inside, about forty people sat, stood, or wandered around the waiting room. Some of them, including me, had brought their pets, and the room smelled faintly of dog. There were no chairs, so Tarkahna and I sat on the floor next to a nervous woman who kept rubbing and scratching her hands and a tranquil, almost sleepy man who stared straight ahead with a slight smile on his face.

"Have you come far?" I asked him.

"It's been so long I've forgotten," he said reflectively. "I arrived here a few weeks ago, but now I find I don't care what the answers to my questions are. I just want to find out how I can get out of here by a simple route. But I can't let any of these troubles bother me." And he returned to his smiling.

The woman to my left was reading a list of what I assumed were questions, but they were written in a language I'd never seen. She appeared to have hundreds of questions.

Someone called our names: "Mariska Ba Mirada and Tarkahna Tarkahna."

We got up and giggled as we followed the appointments secretary. He led us into a large room with several elders, but most of them were playing some game at a table. There were no pieces that I could see on the table, so I couldn't be certain of the nature of the game that absorbed them. Every so often they would laugh. One old woman paced back and forth. We directed our questions to her.

"What is my future?" Tarkahna said.

"That question is too vague."

"What will happen to me tomorrow?"

"That question is too specific."

I spoke up. "I want to know what has become of my brother Maruk. And of my parents. Please try to be as specific as possible."

"What?" the woman said. "You say you're in love!"

"No, that's not what I said at all. I said—"

"I heard you. But let me ask you something. Why must everyone ask me such questions, the same questions over and over, with the same answers? I don't mean to offend you, young lady, because you seem very nice, I'm sure you're quite upstanding. But I feel I'm asked over and over again to break people's hearts. All manner of people, people you wouldn't even believe had hearts, the lowest of the rabble that infests the earth with its violence and its selfishness comes in here, and lo and behold, these people have hearts. These sin-encrusted people have hearts! And they come in here asking me to break them. Why not ask me how you can find happiness? Why must everyone ask me how to find what is sad in their lives?"

"Those are my questions, please," I said firmly.

"In Soom Kali with a young lady, tomorrow you will do nothing special, both in Forma, one half dead and one a slave, and some good and some bad."

For a moment Tarkahna and I couldn't get straight in our head which answer went with what question. "One half dead?" I finally murmured. "Can you be sure?"

"No," she said simply.

"No?"

"No. This isn't science, you see. But you can be certain that the happiness in their lives lies behind them now."

"But what of the war my parents had hoped to end?"

"Haven't you girls had enough answers for now?"

I felt angry. "We've walked a very long way, and with all due respect those others are sitting there playing some silly game." The others looked at me with surprise. I needed to control myself so I wouldn't yell at an elder. My parents would not have wanted that. But my efforts at control caused my arms to shake and my breath to catch in my throat.

The woman grew gentle and took me in her arms, making me feel peaceful. Her bony arms around me had an almost soporific effect. "Dear girl, I can't see everything. Neither can the others. It doesn't matter who you speak to or how many. We only work in groups to keep ourselves amused while we hear the same questions over and over, day after day." She smoothed my hair. "You've become a young woman. I know for you the death of a parent is monumental.

I myself lost my parents when I was around your age. That's why I was chosen to talk to you. We're not without sympathy.

"But listen to my advice. I'm not asking you to forget your parents. On the contrary, I hope you dedicate your life to them, as I did to mine. But let me tell you both something. Out there in the stars you stare at every night, beyond the dust that sweeps across the fields, beyond the wars that have killed one million Bakshami, you will find you are capable of amazing yourself. It's easy to be amazed by the world, the world is an amazing place, but it's rare to be amazed by yourself and what you're capable of and how much your heart can hold. Go and think about it. It's hard to turn down a life like that." She pushed me toward the door, holding me just a moment to say urgently, "Don't turn down that life."

All the elders watched as Tarkahna and I departed. When we walked through the waiting room, the veiled queen stood in a corner with her entourage. Everyone stared at her. But she stared into space, her face full of silent pain.

Someone who'd just come from an appointment collapsed on the floor in grief. He must not have been the first person to collapse after leaving the elders, and the receptionist calmly showed him outside.

I walked dazedly toward the saloons with Tarkahna. One parent half dead, maybe, and one a slave. That meant both alive. The sun's rays, diffused by the day's heavy dust clouds above the mountains, made the saloons look soft and especially hospitable today. We walked into the first one we came to. There were just a few people inside drinking, each person seeming lonelier than the last. I stood there, the loneliest of all. Tarkahna was a quiet girl, particularly considering who her father was. We sat deciphering the elder's remarks in the lonely saloon. Few people visited the saloons before midday, but I'd heard they filled up steadily all afternoon until they became full of carousers at night before emptying out again when the sun rose.

"Some good and some bad, what does that mean?" I said.

"As much is true in the life of anyone."

Tarkahna watched with fascination as a couple fornicated on a table. "Have you ever seen such a thing?" she whispered.

"No," I said. "But who cares? I don't even know them."

"But, well, it's interesting. It will be you someday, you know."

"Then it would of course be interesting to me. But pay attention."

The bartender was a tall, nondescript woman who kept wiping with a rag at the counters, chairs, and floor. One couldn't keep the doors forever shut, but at the same time even if the doors to a dwelling were never opened, dust and sand would creep in somehow, covering the floors and counters and becoming caked on everybody's oily skin.

"Excuse me," I said.

"Yes?" She didn't look up from her wiping. "Would you like a drink?"

"Yes, both of us would. To help us think."

the glass mountains

Tarkahna and I giggled as the woman brought us drinks. "And how will you pay for this?"

"I thought drink was free to native Bakshami."

The bartender walked away damning the traditions.

We had one drink apiece and then fell asleep on the table. When I woke up I was outside a different saloon and facing the refugee camp where I lived. We had set up camp behind a dune, never a safe place since dunes could migrate quickly. But in this case the elders had told us to set ourselves up near the dune and dig as deep as we could, and then we would find water. So every day the refugees dug with dilapidated equipment belonging to the village.

Tarkahna lay beside me unconscious. The paths had become crowded.

"What a gift," said a woman passing by. "To see two novice Bakshami girls intoxicated. Have another one, girlies, on me."

I tried to speak. "I didn't realize..." But I felt nausea engulfing me and closed my eyes. "...What were you saying?" Everyone in the world seemed to be laughing. I thought I heard millions laughing. I smiled weakly.

Someone took pity on us. "Which camp are you from? I'll help you back."

"I think I'll stay right here, actually. In fact, I've decided most definitely to stay right here. Thank you for your assistance." I closed my eyes and was asleep in an instant. I dreamed of trying to breed with a succession of strange but compelling men. But they were compelling for bizarre reasons, like lack of a limb or an extra eye. My loss of control with these men alarmed me even in my dream. When I woke up the paths teemed with revelers. At that moment, drunk and sick and surrounded by what appeared to be equal numbers of honest people and scum, I drunkenly dedicated my life to my parents. "I'm dedicating my life to my parents!" I shouted into the noise of the crowds. I would seek to redeem their suffering. And in making that decision, I somehow changed not just myself but the world that lay around me. Suddenly I had to admit there was something thrilling about the crowded paths.

Everybody on the paths tonight seemed either to know each other or to be introducing themselves to others. Lanterns burned outside each saloon, and whenever a door swung open I heard the sounds of voices laughing, talking excitedly, or fighting. Every so often, another novice Bakshami would collapse in the dirt. That's why, after a while, nobody paid us any mind: Here and there the ground was spotted with Bakshami. I was nothing special.

It all reminded me of a debauched version of the holiday season in Bakshami, when each family in a village cooked food and set it out on a table in front of their house, making sure the table always stayed full. My family and I would take turns cooking or wandering from house to house, eating and drinking.

The wind blew up a cloud of dust, and many of these outsiders to Bakshami covered their eyes and exclaimed what I assumed were curses in their native languages. Sometimes the air in the hotlands cooled

the glass mountains

off considerably at night. On that cool night, sitting there in the dirt surrounded by people from all the varied lands of Artekka, I got my first whiff of what the elder had spoken of, and what I realized my brother Maruk had felt every day of his life. Though I mourned the despair of my parents, I also felt amazed by myself, by the thought that Mariska Ba Mirada, from a tiny village in a provincial section of Bakshami, whose parents had left her and destroyed their lives, should have come to be sitting here in the dirt in what seemed like the center of the world. I felt amazed by my power—I could leave this place and save my parents! I could do anything I wanted. I did not even know where Maruk was, and yet I felt his mind and heart become my mind and heart, his power become mine.

4.

I sat for nearly an hour, watching the parade of patrons to the elders pass. Most wore versions of sweeping Bakshami gowns, but with accessories that exemplified the tastes of their homelands. Some wore our simple gowns with gaudy jewelry, others wore gowns in grays or beige rather than the colors native Bakshami wore. Still others tied scarves around their necks, or wore animal-hide hoods and pink shoes.

When the novelty of watching the parade passed, I pulled Tarkahna home. When I got to her family's tent, Tarkahn became angry at me for the first time ever.

"What has happened and what have you two girls been doing? *You*, Mariska, whom I once held in esteem as the daughter of the mayor and whose mother sat on the interclan council, though what the council actually did I still don't understand..."

I staggered away, waving to him as he chattered in amazement. The refugee camp reminded me of the camps we'd stayed in on the way to the hotlands, except that on the outskirts of this camp families had already built houses, with more being built all the time. The excitement of the saloons still filled my mind, and the camp struck me as drab and static. Everyone staying here had taken a chore or a job. I'd chosen to care for dogs. Each night people's dogs lay outside their tents until I came by, and I attended to the ones under my care. Every night I carried around a lantern and first checked their feet for thorns or tears. I loved dogs' feet, the way they possessed human qualities like toes and yet were completely alien. But of course I loved everything about dogs. They were the bravest, most hard-working, most uncorrupted of animals.

After I checked their feet I combed their hair with flea combs, and I checked their eyes for signs of disease. But tonight I went right to my tent with plans to go immediately to sleep.

I was surprised to find Jobei awake. His beautiful kind eyes stared at me not as if I'd just walked in but as if I'd just finished saying something that had injured his feelings.

"You stink," he said.

"I was out late."

"You have been to a saloon."

"I went to see an elder."

"And then to a saloon."

"Yes, yes. But let me sleep."

"I went to the elders today as well."

"What did you ask them?"

"How to end the war."

"What did they say?"

"They said the war may never end."

"What? Of course it must end. If nothing else the Formans will kill everyone outside the hotlands and then desert Bakshami. Surely they won't spend more time here than they have to. They're bullies, but they're also cowards. The weather will destroy their morale. They won't stay...I'm sick," I said. He turned over and didn't speak again to me, not that night or for many nights afterward. I tried to cajole him with treats and by taking special care of his dog, by tickling him and by begging for his understanding. His anger upset him so much that for several days he couldn't get out of bed. And I knew why he was angry. As he lay brooding in bed, I had come to a realization: I wanted to be amazed by myself, and I could not amaze myself here in the hotlands.

So Tarkahna and I decided we must leave.

We dreamed of traveling out of the hotlands with anyone who might be leaving in the next couple of cycles, a thief or a saint, whoever was departing soonest. With the war, passage probably would be more difficult, and there was only one direction we could go in: to the east, toward Soom Kali, the Land of Knives. That was where Maruk had gone, and where I would now go. Within Soom Kali's border lay a narrow strip of land much like Bakshami, dry and forlorn. Because this strip of land was sparsely populated, I thought it would be easy for me to walk through there and into Mallarr on the other side, and then on to Artroro. From there I would pay someone to fly me to Forma, where I would find my parents, assuming what the elder had told me was correct. Seeing all these people who'd come to the hotlands from all over the planet, and knowing they possessed the courage to make the trek here and leave again, I knew I could find the courage as well.

Our departure came more quickly than we'd expected. We'd figured that with the war only a few people would be venturing forth. But living in the hotlands was like being trapped in a fire for many of the restless patrons of the elders, and fourteen sunrises after we'd decided to leave, a large group of people who desired Bakshami guides said they would leave with us. It didn't matter that we'd never traveled in the section they planned to walk through. They just wanted a real Bakshami.

Lokahn arranged for us to receive the promised jewels, though the sum turned out to be substantially less than promised. Apparently, no one ever took the elders up on this promise, so no one knew the truth. The truth was, there were far fewer jewels than the legends made one believe. Jobei, when he learned I would leave, mercilessly shunned me. So did Leisha, not because she was angry, but because she perceived that she and Jobei were a team now.

Tarkahna and I would be traveling with a queen, though not the one whose heart had been broken. On the night we planned to leave, we slept outside together, since both of our families shunned us. Both families held me responsible for leading Tarkahna astray. But she had been glad to depart. Like me, she saw no future for herself in the hotlands.

We sat up, too excited to sleep, and laughed over the practical jokes we would play, like collapsing the queen's tent and training her dogs to obey only us. Like all Bakshami, Tarkahna and I had the idea, even knowing better, that there were two places in the world: Bakshami and outside Bakshami. Until we left Bakshami's borders, everything would be the same. In the silence while we tried to fall asleep, however, we each retreated into our private fears.

Not being able to sleep, we walked with our dogs to where Ansmeea now worked. The paths weren't as crowded as they'd been the other night, but there were still a large number of people around. Many of them were the hard-core salooners, as they were called, and displayed weapons around their waists for all to see, and brought servants to carry the jewels with which they gambled in the saloons. Outside the saloon a small crowd had gathered around three frisky dogs, two males and one female, and someone was taking bets on which of the males would copulate with the female first.

"Look at the Bakshami's dog!" someone exclaimed, pointing at Artie.

"I'll bet you any amount that dog can beat out the other two."

"He doesn't gamble," I said. I planned to breed Artie as soon as I settled down. But this wasn't the place.

Inside the saloon where Ansmeea worked she was flirting with the person who'd called me hayseed my first day in the village.

"Ansmeea," I called.

She reluctantly came over. "What are you doing out at this hour?"

"I couldn't sleep. I'm leaving the hotlands tomorrow."

"I heard you were talking about it. Where are you going?"

"Soom Kali to find Maruk. Then I'm going to find my parents. After that I'm going to breed with an Artroran muscleman and bear many strong children."

She gazed at the person she'd flirted with. "You'll die before you get that far. Why not just breed with a fat man with lots of money? Aren't you tired of walking?"

"I'm tired of the sun. I want to go somewhere it rains. What do I need money for?"

She stared at her dainty feet, shod in shiny black shoes such as I'd never seen. "These were a gift from him."

"That's a man? Are you going to breed with him?"

"I don't know. Do you think I should?"

"No, I don't like him."

"I know, neither do I. And he doesn't like me, either. I guess we're just bored."

"Why don't you come?"

"It's rumored that once Forma takes over for good, there's going to be all manner of modernization going on here. People will be able to fly to the Glass

Mountains instead of walking. So why leave when the world will soon come to me?" Ansmeea stretched and yawned. "I don't mind being here when the Formans take over. I'd like to see this village modernized. Then I can have a hundred pairs of shoes like this."

"You don't have a hundred feet."

She spoke in a sort of snarl. "You never understood anything but your own ways. I have to go." She walked off to join her friend.

Outside, the same crowd as before was trying to entice Artie to have a go at the female dog. "Hey," one of them said when he saw me. "What do you want for your dog?"

"He's not for sale." We walked off, with the crowd calling us names as we left. But we didn't care. We were leaving!

The next morning Jobei and Leisha were still asleep when I looked in on them. They looked so comfortable I thought about how nice it would be to lie down and miss my appointment with my traveling companions. Instead I kissed my brother and sister lightly on the lips and left a special present, one dried flower apiece laid down near their pillows, Jobei's flower red and Leisha's yellow. I'd found them in a garbage pail, but they were exquisite. I'd heard rumors of a garden of the elders, but I'd never seen it. I knew even if Jobei and Leisha were angry with me they would save their flowers until I returned.

Artie gladly let me attach him to my sled full of supplies. He needed much space to roam, and the village had grown crowded. He trotted ahead, pausing every so often to make sure I still followed. The rising sun, shining pink through the mountains, painted the dust clouds above and the sand below, so that everything around me blushed faintly with promise.

I waited out where the village met the mountains on the east side of town. The sleeping village appeared lovely lit by morning light, but for me the mystery and potential of the world lay elsewhere. I saw Tarkahn already awake and ready for a day of building—he and his wife had chosen a site for their new dwelling. They'd marked off an area about the size of their old one. I felt briefly wistful about the life Tarkahn and his wife would lead here, and about how different it was bound to be from mine. A few drunks wandered here and there, as well as a few people who were dressed up and carrying packages—no doubt full of jewels—on their way to appointments with the elders. The profusion of jewels in the hotlands made one wonder how they could hold their worth. But a lot of people took them quite seriously. Even I, not used to bartering with jewels, found myself eager for more and for both the protection and the danger I assumed they offered. Knowing my backpack and a package on Artie's sled contained jewels made me feel alert, watchful for whatever spirits, fools, opportunities, and flukes such jewels might attract.

I wondered exactly how many Bakshami had sought refuge in the hotlands. Out of twenty million Bakshami, not many had made it here. I hoped more had reached lakes and founded new settlements. We couldn't be sure what was going on in the various sections of Bakshami. In the old days what went on in one section was pretty much what went on in every section.

I did not think my country backward, but of course it was undeveloped in certain ways. But we possessed a highly developed sense of ritual and honor. Even for a Forman, some places and people must have been sacred and honored. Perhaps our people had that in common.

I remembered how my mother, ever practical, had told me that parents must always think of their children who are alive. My people, backward and impractical to the rest of the world, had always seemed—and still did seem—sensible to me. But our world had turned insensible. How could I think only of those of my compatriots who still lived when so many had died?

Our traveling companions still hadn't arrived as the sun began to turn yellow and its effects harsher. If they didn't show up I wondered whether we would have the courage to leave by ourselves.

Where were our companions? If they took much longer we'd lose all the coolest morning air. But finally I saw them, about fifty strong, a queen and her entourage. I was surprised to see that the queen's servants pulled her in a carriage, and that only three dogs, two of them ornamental, accompanied the group. I saw that, unfortunately, this lady wasn't open like the queen with the veils, the most graceful and tragic figure in the hotlands. Our queen had hidden herself in her carriage. We sat on a rock and watched the entourage. When they approached, a big pompous man in an ill-fitting robe hurried up to me. "Are you Mariska? Well, what are you waiting for?"

"I beg your pardon, sir, we were waiting for you." My words and attitude were polite, but he found my honesty impudent. I felt irritated that they hadn't prepared better for the trip. Their weapons wouldn't help when they grew tired of pulling the queen.

"You're sassy," said another. "But it's too late now. You'll come around. Let's go. We're late." He handed me a package. "You carry this, and be careful with it. It contains the queen's towels." To Tarkahna he gave a package he said contained ornaments for the queen's tents.

We set off between the mountains. Luckily, dust filled the sky directly overhead, blocking the sun somewhat as it rose. Nobody talked to me as we walked. In fact, the others seemed to make a point of walking apart from me. Many of the queen's entourage bulged with muscles, and one man pulled a load as heavy as Artie's. But none of them moved as well as Artie and me, and by midday my dog and I had pulled ahead. Tarkahna chose to stick closer to the others. It was hard to believe that if I walked out there in the hot sun, every day, I would eventually walk through Soom Kali and Mallarr and into Artroro, where I would lie basking in the sun instead of pulling my hood tight to protect myself from its rays. I felt well rested and well prepared for this journey.

Slightly after midday I heard calls, and when I turned around the man who'd first spoken to me earlier waved and yelled my name. I didn't want to walk all that way back, but decided it best to cooperate for the first few days, so I returned to him.

"You're a servant guide, not a servant scout. From now on you are to walk to our side, fifty measures to our left."

A servant! "My father was a mayor," I said. He rested his hand on a weapon at his side, and several others smiled at each other. "I demand to talk to the queen," I said, and everyone laughed heartily.

"Even I have never seen the queen. Get on with you. Fifty measures to our side." He and his cohorts took a threatening step forward, and Artie growled. To walk fifty measures would have meant going up a hill, but I cooperated. Tarkahna, who I could see had already become their pet, walked in their group.

"Come on, Artie," I said. We moved to the side and walked there for a few minutes, until someone called for a lunch break. Then I sat way to the side, sharing some dried meat with Artie while the others dined on fruit and breads.

This went on for days. I sat, slept, and walked far to the side, and assented when asked to do small ridiculous chores like braiding the favorite dog's hair and picking up skeletons if I saw them so as not to upset the invisible queen.

Having always grown up with my family bustling around me, it was a revelation to discover how easily I fit into the role of loner. And I didn't complain when we spent twice as much time getting through the mountains as my people had on the way in. Even on the plains the folly of the queen's entourage managed to slow us down. Each night while they spent an hour pitching spacious tents for the queen and her top aides, Artie and I sat alone eating, facing east toward our futures and only occasionally glancing to our sides to see the others struggling in the wind with their unwieldy tents. And they wondered why I possessed so much more energy than they. They thought me an animal because I never seemed to get tired. No doubt they also thought me a fool for playing the rhythms every night on small drums I'd gotten in the hotlands.

And yet even a loner likes something to feel disengaged *from*. So, much as I hated to admit it, the reason I occasionally glanced to my side was not to see what simpletons they were but to make sure they still walked beside me, and that I wasn't alone out there in the sweeping plains that could engulf me in an instant, eventually leaving in my place a small skeleton that would someday degenerate into sand.

part (four)

Though I never once saw the queen, every day as I walked I dreamt of escaping her and facing the trek by myself. Tarkahna was no longer speaking to me, so infatuated was she with the queen's pantywaists.

The more energy the queen's deputies saw I had, the more they gave me to carry, until finally I was their equal in fatigue each night. But the next day they would give me still more to carry. I already hauled the queen's towels, her perfumes, her hairpieces, and her best jackets. I carried them without complaint. When the entourage needed advice, I gave it. When no one asked for advice, I didn't speak. Even though I was a loner, I was too scared to go off completely by myself.

As we neared the boundary between Soom Kali and Bakshami—the landscape on one side of the border looking exactly the same as on the other—we saw the first people we'd seen since our departure. They stood outside a sand-colored stone building on which huge animals had been carved. There were several other buildings, these shaped like animals, as well as a building under construction. I'd never seen any Soom Kali before. Everything about them, from their clothes to their hair to their demeanor, seemed to be a manifestation of their strength. Their hair was as heavy as ropes and tied behind their heads, or cut short to show the shapes of their perfect heads. Rather than wear the loose flowing robes of my people, they wore matching trousers and shirts, with metallic insignias all around the collars. Their stretchy, uncomplicated outfits were designed for traveling with speed and power, just as Bakshami garb was meant for traveling with ease and grace. And the Soom Kali were tall and held themselves straight. The shortest one was as tall as my father, an unusually tall man. It wasn't just strength they exuded, but vigor. There was one woman whose face almost glowed with her power. Even knowing what barbarians they were said to be, I couldn't help but look upon them admiringly. Their strength had built an imposing outpost in the desert in one of the hottest areas of the planet. Forma, too, built outposts at its desert borders, but that sector used its servant class to do all the hardest work. The Soom Kali were famous for doing for themselves, and taking pride in what they did. They allowed almost no one to pass through their borders except people going to and from the hotlands. Anyone who joined their sector had to go through a lengthy period of integration, during which they were taught to be warriors.

A dog-faced man, with a long nose and furry face, seemed to be in immediate charge, but he also seemed to be trying to impress an enormous woman with her own entourage. He came forward and spoke with one of the queen's deputies, who then motioned us all together while the Soom Kali man walked away. From what I could overhear, the Soom Kali language was similar to Artroran—an irony since the two sectors had fought many bitter wars.

the glass mountains

"That gentleman would like to talk to you one by one. It's just a formality, as our warrants are in order," said the queen's deputy. "Here are a couple of rules I learned from passing this way before. Never talk louder than your questioner. The Soom Kali don't like that. And keep in mind, among these barbarians the penalty for a foreigner telling a lie may be death if the one to whom you lie is in a foul mood."

The dog-faced man questioned the servants one by one. When I neared the front of the line I could hear the type of inquiries he made. What is your name? Do you have currency or jewels with you? What are your allegiances? But I couldn't hear the answers. The interviews passed quickly. The man asked some of the servants only one or two questions. When he got to Tarkahna, though, he asked so many questions I thought my turn would never come.

When my turn finally arrived, he asked me to take off my hood. He scrutinized me. "It's rare to see a Bakshami servant."

"Yes, sir, though I'm not a servant, except a servant of expediency."

"What is your name?"

"Mariska Ba Mirada."

"Do you have any money with you?"

I stupidly hesitated, but said, "No." It seemed astonishing to me that after a life of never having or using money I now found myself willing to risk death for my jewels. I feared he might take them. I felt dizzy and hot.

"What are your allegiances?"

"To my dog and my family."

"What else?"

"I'm sorry?"

"I said what else. Please listen carefully as I'm growing bored."

"Well, of course I have an allegiance to Bakshami, though much of my sector has been destroyed by Forma."

"What makes you think I'm interested in your life story? What did you say were your allegiances?"

"My dog and my family, and Bakshami, of course."

"Where is your family?"

"I have a brother and sister in the hotlands, and parents in despair in Forma. I have a brother I adore living I know not where."

"Do you have any money?"

"No, just meat and water, both of which are running low."

"What's in your packages?"

"Towels and fine jackets for the queen."

"How did you come to be traveling with these people?"

"My friend and I didn't want to leave alone. Perhaps it would've been better, since we faced no real dangers."

"We haven't all day," he snapped. "What is your name?"

"Mariska Ba Mirada."

"What are your allegiances?"

I hesitated again, and I saw suddenly that the man's eyes were warm, kind even. My mind searched for a proper response. "My allegiances are to the queen."

"Do you have any money?"

"No."

"Good, and don't forget it."

He waved for the next person in line.

When the questioning ended, the man directed us into a building for inoculations. During the inoculation I felt only the smallest pressure on the inside of my arm, and I had a hard time believing the small pressure would protect me from disease. Because the medicine didn't take effect right away, the Soom Kali told us we would have to spend the night at the compound. But we could leave first thing in the morning.

The man in charge posted no guard at our section of the compound and simply told us we were confined to our rooms. But I could tell from his arrogant smile that he dared us to try to escape.

Just as Bakshami was a culture of glass, Soom Kali was a culture of stone and metal. Stone made up the furniture, beds, walls, and floors. All utensils were metal, and I watched out my window as dully shining metallic vehicles came and went across the sand. Occasionally one took off into the sky. Unlike the plain Forman ships, these vehicles possessed a majestic, birdlike quality. I remembered what everyone always said, that the Formans were simple barbarians, and the Soom Kali were barbarians with style. I admired their splendid barbarism. I also liked the way they complimented Artie. Some of them even made a special trip to my room to see the dog they said looked as if he should have been from Soom Kali.

At one point after dark the dog-faced man came into my room. He exclaimed admiringly over Artie, then sat himself on a chest.

"I am visiting some of you tonight to let you know that several soldiers and I will escort you through Soom Kali and to the Mallarr border. What do you and your friend plan to do next?"

"I'm going to Forma to save my parents."

"By yourself?"

"Maybe with my brother. He came to Soom Kali with his wife. He may be integrated by now for all I know."

The man nodded. "I thought you said you didn't know where your brother was. Let me give you advice about my sector. Although we don't care anything for your money, we do not care for liars. Do not lie to me again, or I may not be so lenient next time." With that, he got up and left the room.

The next day I left with the queen's entourage and a contingent of Soom Kali soldiers. The terrain, though harsh, wasn't as unmerciful as the terrain of Bakshami. The ground was harder and less sandy, therefore easier to walk on, and the sun didn't seem to be constantly on the verge of defeating me. Trees sprang up here and there, moister and taller than the trees of my sector. At night, the rising moons brightened the looming animal shapes behind us.

One of the queen's dogs got sick, so I combed the dog and massaged her limbs. The queen's deputies wanted to throw the dog away; instead, I gave her extra water and food, and she became my dog. She was one of the entourage's ornamental dogs who'd fallen out of favor and become a working dog, and because she was sick she became useless to them. She slept between me and Artie nightly, a slender black dog, big yet dwarfed by mine. Every night she slept close, often with her jaws resting on my shoulder.

One night she licked me face, and I awoke to see a deputy killed, exactly the way one of the other deputies had warned me about—his insides turned outside while he screamed. All because he had stolen from a Soom Kali soldier. She licked me again, as if to say, Don't worry.

The stars had never seemed so bright, so full of the same life that pulses in a tree or an animal. I saw the familiar stars upon which I'd gazed all my life, but there was nothing in them to tell me I was special. I felt certain that my grandfather had erred, and that I would never find guidance. I kissed my poor sick black dog. I don't know how the queen's deputies chose such a graceful but susceptible dog to haul heavy loads. This dog might be capable of getting across the sand with no load, but she didn't have the stamina to work hard in the desert. I was surprised she'd made it this far. I kissed her again, on her soft ears. In Bakshami we didn't consider ourselves elevated above our dogs. Without humans, the dogs would survive easily, but without dogs, our life would become harder still. We felt the dogs helped us out of generosity, and we felt indebted to them.

Everything in the world was so far away at that moment. My destination, my home, my family, the stars, my future, my birth, and even my death. Nothing was close to me except the dogs and the wretched ground on which I slept. I felt like a child floating out in space, surrounded by warmth and brightness but not close enough to touch any of it. Toward the Bakshami horizon I saw the long sweeping clouds like the blades of knives. I felt for my own knife under the sand near my head. I planned to sleep with it within easy reach for the rest of my trip. I could feel in the air that outside of Bakshami it was best to keep a knife nearby.

We set off each morning before sunrise. The Soom Kali were excellent walkers. For the first time in my life, I could see sky at a horizon instead of the dust clouds that encircled Bakshami. After a while I saw only traces, almost like ghosts, of the same type of clouds at the horizon behind me.

I called the new dog Shami, or "fire," for the flame-shaped orange-tan spot on her chest. Other than the flame and touches of white on one paw, her fur was black. Still sick, she moved unsteadily when she walked, but her natural grace soon took over, and she kept up with Artie and me if we walked a little slower than usual. She didn't carry anything, so even in the heat of midday she still had energy to walk. As she improved, I saw how willful she was and why she'd ended up getting the whippings that had no doubt contributed to her sickness. When I called her to me she ran away, and when I wanted to be left alone, she pranced like a flame around me, playfully kicking loose dirt at my feet to entice me to chase her. Dirt increasingly comprised the ground. I'd been waiting eagerly for this to happen, but now that the moment of solid earth had come my feet seemed to hit the dirt with a jarring thud, and I began to see the advantage of soft sand under one's feet. Still, there was something to be said for solid earth. It made me feel that I was really somewhere, instead of in the middle of nowhere, in the desert.

When we set up camp at night, I felt pleased with the progress we'd made. Perhaps we would get to the Soom Kali-Mallarr border sooner than I'd expected. Rather than getting weaker, Shami became invigorated by our swift progress. She barked at Artie, begging him to play, and he looked happy. His happiness made me realize that he'd been unhappy for quite some time now. When she felt especially good, she tormented the deputies by stealing their packages when they weren't watching.

As for the dog-faced man, he made pets of Tarkahna and me. Tarkahna had never liked talking, but now she and the dog-faced man carried on long conversations throughout the night. With the Soom Kali in charge, Tarkahna tried to befriend me again, but I would have none of it.

As soon as I got ready for bed, both dogs pawed and scraped at the ground, and then immediately lay down and fell asleep. Shami, a delicate-looking dog, groaned long, deep-throated extremely indelicate groans in her sleep. She'd been groaning this way for as long as she'd been sick, and I figured it had to do either with a pain she felt from her illness, or a pain she remembered from her whippings.

I ate liberally most days, and fed the dogs liberally as well. Several times I'd caught sight of furrtos running in groups, and a couple of times I'd seen larger animals I didn't recognize. So there was plenty of food for our trip. The landscape would never be better than rigorous—that's one reason the area remained un- derpopulated—but compared to parts of Bakshami a rigorous landscape was a blessing. Most of Soom Kali was said to be as lush as the whole of Artroro, so few cared to settle an area like this. In fact, Soom Kali had once tried to sell this strip of land to my country. I wished we'd bought it. But the elders had refused, saying we shouldn't give profit to warmongers like the Soom Kali. My people feared the Soom Kali and their warrior ways.

The different landscape affected me, made me see that the determined character of my people was brought to the fore by the land. Now I felt that same determination, but something else too, an alertness that I rarely needed traveling in my country. Dur- ing the nights the alertness turned to fierceness as I dreamed of plunging my knife into a faceless Forman's chest and exulting in the feel and sound of the plunge, and in the smell of Forman blood. In my dreams the Forman flesh offered only slight re- sistance, like an overcooked root. I awoke after these dreams in triumph, invigorated, eager for another day of walking.

Except for a mild dust storm, the land didn't change for days at a time, and when it did change, it was only to rise a bit, then fall a bit. We eagerly noted the rising and falling, happy for any change. I liked this new feeling of alertness. It was a new taste on my tongue, something tart and fresh, like the taste of junyi leaves we used for spice, a touch sweet, but it sent fire through my veins. If even just this small change in the landscape could affect me so, I wondered how I would feel surrounded by greenery and waterfalls. When we stopped for a lunch break the dogs frisked like puppies. Shami, agile and calculating, darted in and out to bite Artie's legs. Artie, on the other hand, was fast and muscular but perfectly straightforward. Shami always knew in advance what he would do.

We walked in high spirits. I'd never traveled over such amenable land before, land where I might find a lake or at least a creek even in the driest-looking area, and where dinner could be caught almost nightly. The Soom Kali loved Artie and the speedy Shami, and because they liked my dogs they liked me, too. And I think they admired the two young Bakshami girls who had set out on their own. They didn't say so, but I felt it. On the other hand, the queen's stuffy entourage bored them.

Rather than try to preserve the meat, we ate fresh whatever we caught. I'd never lived so luxuriously, with a steady supply of fresh food and water.

There were problems. My legs, built for sand, sometimes felt strained on the harder ground. And around the lakes mosquitoes buzzed in such numbers that from far away the air looked gray. Watching one gray cloud fly toward me, dampening the sun, I feared for my life. From close up the mosquitoes' noise made a constant even drone, not like millions of tiny insects, but like a single large one. They descended upon the dogs' eyes until the dogs screamed, and I, myself beset, could do nothing to help. I started leaving the dogs behind while I went to the lakes alone, my face and head covered with my gown as I peeked out. Apparently the mosquitoes fed on the furrtos, which seemed particularly skittish and red-eyed around the lakes.

Because of the mosquitoes, I never bathed at the lakes, just filled my water containers and hurried away. For a while I entertained a notion that I would find a way to make use of the mosquitoes, cook them or something and sprinkle them like seasoning on my meat. My mind, with nothing else to keep it busy, devised plans to overcome the mosquitoes. I fantasized about setting fire to the forest around the lakes, and burning all those insects. Or of constructing a sticky trap out of tree sap. Maybe I could dig a huge hole and throw furrto meat down below, and when the mosquitoes flew in, I'd bury them in dirt and sand. It was all fantasy. I realized that like the sand and heat of Bakshami, the mosquitoes could best be overcome by accepting them.

When we neared the Mallarr-Soom Kali border, the dog-faced man—named Panyor—and Tarkahna spoke ever more earnestly and urgently each night. I expected to see more magnificent stone buildings, but instead, one night shortly before we stopped I saw in the distance a section of wall. It was a tall straight stone wall, unadorned, worn only a little in places, and pausing at a forest before stretching into the distance. There were a few buildings as well, maybe to house border soldiers.

We stayed near some bushes, the dogs sleeping touching me as they always did now. During each day they frequently looked up at me with adoring faces, and I adored them back. I wanted more dogs.

the glass mountains

Still, I was glad Shami hadn't gone into heat during our trip—puppies were the last thing I needed.

The ground now was nearly hard, and I could see that in one direction there was a village. I couldn't stop myself from wandering over to stare. I protectively dragged my things closer to the village while the soldiers who'd accompanied us watched curiously. I'd never seen electric lights before; they were only a rumor in Bakshami. There hadn't been any at the outpost on the Bakshami border. Each house was like a miniature fortress or castle, the huge ornate doors covered with carvings. At each door, a lamp hung to the side. The sight was so beautiful that I couldn't believe people slept inside at night, instead of outside where they could see their intricate doors and their amazing lamps swinging in the wind, throwing shadows on the ground, on the steps and on the watching stone faces. Those lights and their shadows made me feel that everything in the world that I could possibly want existed in this tiny village.

I ached to knock at one of those doors, to talk to another person, even to one who would wish me dead. Watching the dogs prance together, seeing how the company of another dog had lifted the glumness from Artie—an invisible gloom, the kind I never realized he felt until it was gone—had filled me simultaneously with joy and loneliness. I envied Tarkahna's new friendship and even envied the queen's entourage.

I became aware that I was being watched as I sat alone, admiring the village. Far in the distance, the dogs played silently, capering beneath the stars.

"Nice dogs," said a bored voice.

A young man sat next to me, not handsome exactly but of such confidence as to seem almost insolent. This confidence took my breath away. In Bakshami he might seem immoral. He smiled, not at me but at the dogs.

"Have you bred them? I'd like a good puppy."

I looked around, scarcely believing he talked to me. "I don't speak Artroran so well like you," I said uneasily. I worried he might be trifling before he harmed me.

"Your accent isn't very good," he agreed.

"Have you been watching me?"

"It took you a long time to realize."

"Why didn't you show yourself?"

"To anyone else, I would have been showing myself. Your eyes and ears are as weak as an old woman's. The whole camp sees us." I looked back, saw the soldiers smiling with amusement at us. One of them said something to him in Soom Kali and all the soldiers laughed. He laughed, too, suddenly warm. "Look, I don't mean to insult you. What are you doing out here? You're so small. You're like a doll."

"In Bakshami I'm rather tall. Not terribly so, but rather."

"You're in Soom Kali now, little doll."

"You, on the other hand, would be the tallest person in my old village."

"Me? I'm only average." He stretched like an animal. He looked wistfully toward the wall. "Where are you going?"

"To Artroro first."

"Artroro," he said scornfully.

"They're the most powerful sector on the planet. Why not go there?"

"They're not so powerful," he said.

Such insolence! "I've heard, anyway, but I've never been outside Bakshami before."

"Are you going with your dogs and your packages? You should keep a better watch on your things."

"What do you mean?" I noticed suddenly that one of my bags was gone.

"Relax. I'm going to return it. I just wanted to learn more about you. I don't want your precious jewels. Of course if you wanted to give me some jewels, I might help you get to Artroro."

"Why not just steal from me?"

He genuinely seemed to be thinking that over, then he smiled brightly. "Because I like you."

I felt quite taken aback. First I wanted to hit him, then I felt drawn to him.

"What are you thinking?" he said. "You have a funny look on your face."

I spoke shyly. "You could have a puppy if you wanted."

"Is she pregnant?"

"No, I meant when and if she has puppies."

"I don't accept promises from strangers." He picked up a lock of my hair. "So this is the fabled Bakshami hair. It's dirty, but otherwise it's very nice. I like strong things."

Artie and Shami finally had noticed the young man and ran over growling. The man put out his hand so they could smell him.

"They like you," I said. "Usually I would have to restrain Artie."

"I'm good with animals...What are you going to do in Artroro?"

"I'm going to hire a muscleman to take me to Forma, where my parents are in trouble."

His eyes flashed hatefully for a moment. "The Artrorans have been attacking us once a generation for as long as anyone can remember."

"That's because you don't pay them freedom fees. Why not just pay them and have a little peace?"

"Our freedom can't be paid for."

"Do you live in the town?"

He nodded. "I work at the border with them—" he nodded at the other soldiers— "but I'm on leave now."

"The town is so inviting."

"How can a town like this seem inviting? All the towns on the edge of the desert are barren like this. But I have to stay. I'm an only child and my father has been dying for three years."

"Where's your mother?"

"Dead. Murdered by an Artroran."

"I'm sorry. Many of my people were murdered by Formans."

"If it's any comfort, the Formans take many prisoners for servants. I have heard that many Bakshami refugees have become servants to Formans."

"Do you think my parents suffer?"

He hesitated. "No." He was rubbing Artie's stomach as my dog smiled and waved his hind legs helplessly in the air, a child being tickled. "I've never seen such a big dog."

"That's what everyone says. He was the runt of the litter. That's why I chose him."

"Why choose the runt?"

"Because see what happens when you do. You end up with the biggest."

He seemed to think that over, and he nodded. "Are you hungry for fresh meat?"

"Yes! Do you have any?"

"I can catch some, and we'll cook it at my house. We have to hurry. The soldiers will let you enter my town, since they're my friends. But you need to leave by morning with them. No one can stay at the border more than one night without integrating."

He called out something to Panyor and then easily picked up my load. "We'll leave the sled here. Take it from me, no one wants it." We walked past the town to a small woods, where we sat quietly on some rocks. "Don't move," said my new friend. I realized we hadn't exchanged names yet.

"What's your—"

He cut me off with a quick stabbing motion. We sat quietly for quite a while, so close I could feel the warmth rising off his body. It made me lean in closer, to feel more of his warmth drifting against my face. It was like when I was a child and would cup my hands, trying to catch rainwater, and I would rue the water that fell between my fingers, and eagerly drink the water I caught. He moved suddenly and I heard a whoosh through the air, the noise almost simultaneous with a tiny cry perhaps twenty measures away. I jumped up, immediately worried for the dogs. But they stood right next to us as surprised as I was. We all ran toward the cry, to a large dead furrto with a knife through its small head. There was surprisingly little blood, which I commented on.

"You have to hit them through a certain spot toward the back of the head. That way you can be sure of killing them with as little blood as possible. All the nutrition is in the blood."

It seemed preposterous that he could have aimed so carefully in the near darkness, with only the light from the sky and town filtering through the trees. I myself possessed good night vision but could barely see five or ten measures away in this forest.

"Hurry," he said.

We gathered my things again and moved through the town, stopping at one of the lovely lamps. The ornate stone door was perhaps one-and-a-half times as large as the entrances in my old village. He pressed his hand against a metal plate on the door. Then he opened it and we entered.

"What is that thing?" I said.

"You mean the lock? You don't have them on your doors in Bakshami?"

"No, what does it do?"

"No one can get in except me and my father. Here where so many foreigners pass though, we must be careful. This quiet town has seen many murders. Come on."

The high ceilings curved slightly, not quite domed, but more curving than simply slanted. The ceilings hadn't been carved, but many of the items in the house had been. He turned on an inside lamp, and light danced off the metal vases and boxes arranged throughout the stone room. I'd never seen such beautiful metalwork. One box was covered with shiny blue metalwork almost like lace. When I touched it, I heard soft metallic bells from within the box. They played a childishly simple rhythm, but the effect was pleasing. "My father made that for my mother before they got married. He was the best metal- and stone-worker in town before he got sick."

"It's very beautiful." I studied the other items in the room, and thought about how much Jobei and Leisha would enjoy playing in this room full of beautiful strange things. Two stone beasts guarded the immense doorway to the next room. The beasts looked so real it was as if they'd been turned to stone, not carved. And some of the rocks glowed almost like metal, so that I needed to look closely to distinguish metal from stone. Embroidered cloth pillows lay on each chair. Even without touching them, I could see the softness in the cloth. "Are all the homes here like this?"

"We own beautiful things because of my father, but there are striking homes in every village. But come into the kitchen. My father will sleep for a few hours more. He sleeps most of the day. Shortly before I go to bed, he likes for us to talk until I'm sleepy."

We walked into the kitchen, the walls of which were lined with all manner of knives. I could see where my brother Maruk would fit in easily with this culture of knives. Someone had hand carved each one. Some possessed carved faces, others a series of faces, others faces with bodies, others animals. There were trees, flowers, insects, anything you could find in nature. I took out my knife to show him.

"I sleep with this each night," I said.

"What for? I can see you don't know how to use it from the way you handle it."

"Someone once told me that surprise is more important in war than skill."

"That was no doubt someone who had never fought a war."

"Can you teach me?"

"There'll be a price."

"What price?"

"I haven't decided yet."

"I think I have a lot of money."

"Yes. I've counted. But let's eat. We can discuss this and other matters later."

He took out some kitchen knives and adroitly skinned the furrto while I peeked out back and saw what appeared to be human skulls sitting on a low wall at another house.

"Those skulls out there look human."

He raised his head briefly. "Huh?" he said absently. "Oh, those, that's correct. Human."

"Whose are they?"

"People killed in war by my neighbor."

"Not Bakshami?"

"Of course not. We have never been at war with Bakshami." He smiled, and I felt fear of him, that he could smile over a subject like skulls. And yet I myself had chewed on human bones I found in the sand.

"If someone were trying to integrate into Soom Kali, and this person failed, might this person's skull eventually end up in a line on such a fence?"

He looked at me strangely. "Of course not. What a question. We feel no triumph when someone fails to integrate."

He pressed a button, and a cross of fire lit up. In a moment the delicious smell of fresh furrto cooking filled the air. My friend fried all manner of vegetation and starches with the meat. And in this way, in this kitchen of knives with a fence of skulls beyond, I came to eat the most delicious meal of my life.

My friend's name was Moor-Ah Mal. He was one of the best knife throwers in the Soom Kali army. After our meal he put me in one of the rooms in his large dwelling and told me to bathe while he spoke with his father. He told me he got dispirited thinking about his sick father too much, which happened when he spent too much time at home. Yet the only thing that lifted his spirits was the time he spent talking to his father. "And watching you," he added reflectively to me. "Every night after my father fell asleep I used to sit up in my room, thinking about his pain and his impending death. Sometimes I don't sleep at all. When I discovered you it took my mind off my father for the first time in three years."

He was blunt, like many Bakshami, but his bluntness made me shy.

He left me alone, and I sat with the dogs. Feeling both out of place and immensely satisfied, I explored the bathroom, where water poured out of the faucets without benefit of a pump, and I took a real bath for the first time since I left the hotlands. There were many pretty things in the bathroom, but they all had an aura of age about them, and an aura of having once belonged to someone else. The embroidered linens gave off an exquisite aroma hallucinatory in its vagueness, and the carving on the soap was slightly worn, as if someone had used it just once or twice. On a counter lay a beautiful silvery comb with eyes painted on it, and in the prongs I found a single pale orange hair. Moor's hair was very dark brown, almost as dark as a Bakshami's; perhaps the comb had belonged to his mother. The lamp in the bathroom reflected off the window as I pulled a wet dead flea out of my hair. I felt the weariness of all the walking in my past, and also the weariness from whatever walking might lie in the future.

I got in bed, where huge stone beasts rose on the headboard behind me, and I remembered drowsily that I ought to bathe the dogs, or at least fill up the bath for them. But they had fallen asleep, and as the room darkened with night I slept also.

2.

I awoke to the sounds of phlegmy coughing and spitting. The sounds came from the room. A man's tall, wasted shadow blocked what little light reached through the crack in the curtains. I didn't close my eyes, but neither did I move. After a long while the shadow moved with some difficulty out of the room. I didn't hear the dogs breathing, and I jumped out of bed.

The dogs' absence panicked me. I always knew

where they were, and they were rarely out of sight. The coughing, phlegmy shadow man hadn't shut the door all the way, so before going outside my room, I laid my ear softly against the crack where the door met the cool stone wall. At first I heard nothing, and then I heard the muffled voices of two men. When I pushed the door open, the dogs greeted me from the other side. They licked me passively and then settled in as they had been. Now I could hear more clearly Moor's voice, probably talking to his father. That must have been his father who had come into my room. Now it was my turn to spy on him.

I followed the voices down the hallway, my feet falling on the stone floor. The hallway stretched before me, the voices growing louder with each step. At the final door I stopped.

First I heard Moor, speaking in a hybrid of Soom Kali and Artroran. He seemed to be asking whether his father needed another blanket.

"No, it's warm tonight," said a raspy voice.

"Did you see her? Was she still asleep?"

"Yes. Maybe she isn't well," said the raspy voice. "You should wake her up."

"She's just tired. I feel very alert to her. I think I would know if she was sick."

Moor's father spoke sharply in Soom Kali. Then, "Kill her and eat her dogs before you fall in love."

I couldn't make out anything for a while, and then Moor spoke the words "brave" and "lucky."

"Brave and lucky. That's a good combination, I admit. But it doesn't explain why you want to help her."

"Because she's come all this way. I can't find the words..."

There was a long silence. There was an intensity to their silence as there had been to their speech. The silence and speech were, after all, between a dying father and his son. Maybe it was Moor's intensity that prevented him from discerning my presence despite his excellent hearing. Then the raspy voice spoke. "Have I kept you here in the village too long, Moor? Will you help the girl escape as you wish you could?"

"I'm glad to stay here with you. But in return can you understand that I plan to help her? I don't believe she can find her parents without my help. It's harder than she realizes. Her bravery won't change, but her luck might."

"And are you so powerful that you can control a person's luck?"

He spoke sharply to his father for the first time, but I couldn't understand what he said. He continued sincerely, without the sharpness. "The borders are dangerous today. If Forma declares war on Soom Kali, the borders will grow more dangerous still."

"War has been a constant since as far as even I can remember. The presence of war doesn't change the borders. If she got this far, she can get farther."

"Why do you resist me?"

"Because I have no wife, no brothers and sisters. I have only a son. And my son wants to help a foreigner from a sector whose people don't have even the courage to fight their own wars. And you call her brave. If she's so brave, why does she run from protecting her sector?"

"You should see her standing up. She's about my age, but she's the size of a child."

"If you want a child, have a child." But he spoke with resignation this time, and a sort of fatigue such as I had never heard anywhere, his voice wasting away just like his body. "I have some influence left," Moor's father almost whispered. "Perhaps I can get you out of your army commitment."

There was more silence, and I understood that they were both in despair. I sneaked back to my room and pulled the drapes open. It couldn't have been very late because here and there people still walked outside, huge strong people with knives hanging by their sides. Once I suspected someone was looking straight at me, and I froze, such was the power in that gaze. The Soom Kali were legendary for their savageness, and yet my friend Moor seemed as gentle as anyone I'd ever met.

The door knocker tapped softly, and Moor called my name. "Mariska? Are you awake?"

I pushed open the door. "Yes, I was just looking out the window."

He peeked out with annoyance and pulled shut the drapes. "I could get in trouble for having you here."

"And what would happen?"

"You might have no more trouble ever again."

"Sometimes I've wished for that."

He stepped into the room and lowered his voice. "You must take these rules more seriously. They have ways to make you feel they're killing you once each day for a thousand days."

"But what would happen to you?"

"Trials in Soom Kali can result in only two outcomes: death or freedom. I would be free but would have to go through the trouble of the trial."

As he spoke I again felt the heat radiating from him, and this time I seemed to be absorbing it, my face growing so flushed I felt I should look away. I turned my head toward the closed drapes. "Nobody could see me," I lied.

"You should be more careful just the same," he said gently.

He'd caught more fresh meat, and we ate another sumptuous meal. The dogs, too, ate like kings. Moor had taken them hunting earlier while I slept. He said they learned very fast and deserved good meals. After our meal he sat across from me and showed me how to hold a knife, so when I held the knife, it felt like an extension of my hand. "Most people like to hold it here," he said. "But I like to hold it this way." He moved his hand almost imperceptibly. It was quite a science, holding a knife. "I once knew a man who liked to hold the handle even when he threw his knife. It seems impossible, but he was actually a passable knife handler. So in the end you must find your own way. But you must start out the right way. If I teach you nothing else, at least you may be able to protect yourself."

"Can a knife protect me from my future?"

"A knife can change your life, at least in my sector."

So while he worked around the house I sat in that kitchen of knives and practiced holding mine. I moved my hand up and down the blade and the handle. But still the knife felt alien to me.

When Moor finished with his chores he took me for a walk in a forest. Later in my travels I saw other fine forests, but at the time this grove in Soom Kali was the biggest I'd seen. Even this close to the driest parts of Soom Kali, there was a sense of moisture and life in this forest. In Bakshami, even the lakeshores and woods seemed dry and devoid of any life but for the life of the ubiquitous fleas. Here, the moisture of the trees and the heat I felt emanating from Moor made me feel something there was no word for in Bakshami, but what I later learned to call bliss. In Bakshami we might feel a serenity as we sat at storytelling in the warm tranquil nights beneath the clearest sky on the planet, but I had never felt bliss before. In the same way, I sensed that Moor had never felt serenity. We shared with each other a tumult in our hearts—that pain I was born with was his pain as well.

I touched his arm as we sat quietly in the forest. "How long has your father been sick?" I asked.

"For three years. The doctors told him he would die several times now. It's a degenerative disease. It taunts him. A death this slow is the worst kind."

"As if there were a best kind."

"Old age, of course. In Soom Kali only four in ten die of old age. Two in ten are killed in skirmishes with Artroro."

"In Bakshami many children die of dust viruses. But we have no wars."

"You fight no wars, perhaps, but you have them anyway."

"Is it true the only reason Forma doesn't invade the hotlands is because Soom Kali forbids it?"

"It's true. We don't want Forma as neighbors. We have no love of Bakshami, but we liked a neutral country next to us. We were willing to let others pillage your towns and bomb your refugees because we didn't really care what happened to your towns and refugees. But if they destroy the hotlands, they destroy Bakshami. And as I said, we liked your people as neighbors. We always took for granted what good neighbors you made. Now we see how neighbors who can't protect themselves can prove troublesome."

"You talk about my sector as if it were an object instead of a living thing."

"Many times in our history foreigners have betrayed us."

The dogs chewed on sticks a short distance away. I remembered that I hadn't played the rhythms since the day I first spotted the wall. When I'd traveled with the queen, I tried to practice the rhythms almost every night. The sound of something so familiar gave me comfort on those still nights when there was no noise at all except for the breathing of the dogs, my own breath, and the rustle of my hair against my ears. The rhythms are the first thing a newborn baby hears, and the last thing a Bakshami soul hears before relinquishing the body at the death ritual.

In the forest Moor and I practiced throwing our knives a few times. He said my grandfather had given me a fine knife, with admirable carvings and some valuable jewels in the handle. "It's weighted nicely, too," he said. He took the knife from me and threw it

the glass mountains
149

at a tree I could barely see. I heard the thunk as it landed solidly in the wood. I practiced at a much closer tree. He also showed me how to change from holding the knife to throw at something far away and holding it to stab something closer by. He said that the knife should seem to have a life of its own as it changed positions in your hand. Indeed, he could change grips from handle to blade with such speed there seemed to be no movement in between—one moment he held the blade, the next the handle.

As we walked back to Moor's house, I practiced manipulating the knife, but a couple of times I dropped it. I didn't think it was the Bakshami way to hold knives and have wars, whereas the Soom Kali were born with war in their blood.

It was very late, and only one person walked across town. Moor told me not to stop, and we hurried our steps slightly to reach his house.

"Don't you have any easier weapons to protect yourself with?" I asked in the main room of his house.

"I have a whole room in this house devoted to such weapons."

"And yet you use a knife."

"The only thing winning a battle with a weapon proves is who has purchased the finest weapon. A knife, unlike those other weapons, is a part of the person and proves who is the best warrior. We use the other weapons in wars, for convenience."

With his rangy appeal, and his face full of insolence and pain, he looked like a young warrior who already had fought in many wars. And he said he'd already fought in a few battles with the Artrorans.

Like the Soom Kali I'd seen at the border he possessed a power that I couldn't help but admire. I decided I should try to breed with him before I left. He wasn't an Artroran strongman, but I doubted those Artrorans could be any more powerful than Moor. Perhaps they could lift more at one time, but they couldn't possibly boast the same combination of strength and agility that the Soom Kali seemed to possess. I felt quite intoxicated.

"Maybe we should breed together," I blurted out.

He smiled insolently. "In time," he said. "I'm tired now. I haven't slept at all for a day and a half." He turned around and walked toward my room.

When we arrived at my room he studied me seriously. "But I'll sleep in your bed with you," he said. I felt my face grow hot but agreed. So Moor and I undressed and got in the huge stone bed together. After feeling all that heat coming from him, I expected his body to be warm, but it was surprisingly cool. I can't say that it was unusually cool, however, because I'd never held a naked body next to mine before. I put my arms around him and held him firmly and rubbed my skin on his and rubbed my hands on his skin. My feelings of discovery and need and bliss coalesced into something physical rather than emotional, so that the more I had these feelings, the more I rubbed my skin against his. I felt every part of his body I could from top to bottom, and when my feelings of discovery and need abated I settled into bliss. When he fell asleep and I felt how hard the muscles in his arms stayed even while he dreamed, I experienced the illogical feeling that more than all the things I wanted at that moment I wanted to protect him always. At that moment, I would rather have protected him than go to Artroro or see my brother or even, I'm ashamed to say, than save my parents. The feeling was completely illogical and completely overwhelming. So I slept all night with my arms around him, and when I woke up he had left.

I luxuriated in the bath and then wandered into the kitchen, where breakfast awaited. Moor had laid out breads and fresh meats and left some sort of note that I couldn't read—I could speak Artroran fairly well, but could barely read it. With nothing else to do, I wandered through the dozen or so rooms of the house. One large room was for metal and stone work. On a huge slab against the wall someone had carved a beast, and on a table sat several gorgeous metal vases almost as tall as I was. Everything seemed oversized except a series of delicate bracelets with the same lacy quality as objects in the main room.

Moor and his father had stored their weapons in the next room. What can I say about this room except that there were a hundred ways to kill an enemy in there? As I came out I heard grunting, apparently as Moor's father got out of bed. He seemed to fall to the ground with a thump and I hurried to him.

In the light he was even frailer than his shadow; at least a shadow in the dark appears to imply substance and a type of incorporeal potency. But this man seemed to have so little potency and substance that I couldn't speak for a moment, only stare. He was as tall as his son but weighed perhaps half. He stared back at me acidly.

"If you've come to help, then help. If you've come to stare, then leave."

I grabbed hold of his arm—he was nothing to lift—and helped him back into bed.

"I heard you moving around and was going to check on you," he said weakly. He closed his eyes and rubbed one of them with a clawlike finger. "If you've stolen anything I'll have my son kill you. He likes you, but I'm his father."

"I'm sorry. I was curious."

He regarded me acidly again. "You don't seem so brave to me. My son has got it into his head that you're courageous."

"I left Bakshami with just a friend."

"Bakshami, don't tell me about Bakshami. Even without your wretched country, the planet has all the sand it needs. Your country is just overkill." His mood suddenly changed, and he looked at me with light in his eyes. "Tell me, did my son leave you some meat in the kitchen?"

"I've eaten it. Can I look for more for you?"

The light in his eyes dulled. "No, damn him, he's hidden it. The doctors say I can't digest meat, and he gives me the same revolting roots every day. That's what's killing me, I tell you. You must promise to sneak me some meat, young lady, do I have your word?"

"I don't think I should. I can ask Moor—"

"Don't ask him, curse you. I thought you were brave! You must sneak me some meat! So what if I die? What's a life without meat anyway?" His eyes grew desperate. "If you lived as I do, you, too, would beg."

the glass mountains

"I'm sure Moor doesn't want you to suffer. I'll speak to him if you think that would help."

"I stay alive only because I want to see my son again each day, not because he follows doctors' orders and denies me meat. I love my son and couldn't bear him going away, but frankly neither can I bear him staying to take care of me. Every time he's gone I think of meat. Despite my weakness I search the house for where he might have hidden meat. I told my son to kill you and use the dogs for meat," he mumbled. He closed his eyes and began to breathe laboriously.

I sat in the only chair in the room, the chair in which Moor probably sat as he spoke with his father. He told me he stayed up all night with his father occasionally. Hard and straight-backed, the chair was probably disagreeable to sit in for even an hour, let alone a night. Still, as time passed I could see how the chair supported my back without making me sleepy.

The air passing in and out of the lungs of Moor's father seemed to hit all manner of phlegm and disease. I got up to open a window and while I struggled with it I saw outside how simple the village was despite the ornamentation of the doors. Even without benefit of the sparkling lamps to entrance me, the houses appeared inviting. The lamps swung in the breeze, knocking with pings against the stone doors. This simple village beneath the striking blue sky possessed a storyteller's quality. It reminded me of my old town, a place vivid in my memory but long since destroyed.

3.

The breeze from outside was a delight, touched with a sweet coolness I'd rarely felt in daytime air. Moor's father groaned in his sleep. I thought of Maruk and Sian going through integration and couldn't imagine how they could integrate without losing their minds from the tension that must press forever against their temples. To act like someone you were not might be an adventure for a while, but after time when you started really to become who you were not, what then? From then on, your life would be nothing but suffering.

The cool fresh breeze cleansed the air in the room. It started to make the room seem like someplace one might come to live rather than a place one came only to die. Moor's father didn't seem to notice. His face as he lay there was swathed in a bitter sleep, and because his mouth fell open bits of white-flecked drool fell down his cheek to the pillow. Now and then he made a sound like a dog growling, and I would not have been surprised to hear him bark. Here was a man, I believed, who had spent his life hating others, and I wondered why Moor loved him so. But as the afternoon passed and I watched that angry face that knew no peace, I came to see that there was little in the world more heartbreaking than the deathbed of one who has never been happy, or who has become bitter, or who has hated more than he has loved. So perhaps Moor's heart was breaking for that reason. I also knew that between a parent and a child explanations existed for things that outsiders found inexplicable. There were no murders in Bakshami, but I knew that within families even in my sector there were reasons for love, and sometimes reasons for murder. Not excuses, just reasons. So Moor's heart was breaking for some of those unfathomable reasons that exist between parent and child.

For now, the only way I could think to protect a strong young man who scarcely realized he needed protecting was to sit in his place at his sick father's bedside. My back grew sore and the difficult breathing of Moor's father started to oppress me. And in this way I learned something of what Moor's life had been like for the past three years.

"What are you doing in here?" I hadn't heard Moor enter. His voice sounded poised between surprise and annoyance.

"I heard your father fall and came to see him. Then I just sat here."

He went to close the window. "It's freezing in here."

"So it is. My arms are full of bumps."

His annoyance began to fade. Now he was just confused. "But why did you sit here in the cold like this?"

"I don't know. It did occur to me once or twice that it was cold, but for some reason I couldn't get up. I wanted to sit here as you did."

Moor's eyes softened now. "Let's talk elsewhere," he said gently.

He took my hand and led me to his room, a large, almost majestic chamber with walls, floors, a table, and a bureau of sparkling, polished rock. He smiled at me.

"I know it's grand, but my parents made it for me when I was born, so I've always stayed here," he said. "But how was my father?"

"He slept most of the time."

"I mean how was he to you?"

"He told me he'd advised you to kill me and eat my dogs."

"I don't like dog meat."

"How lucky for me."

"You *are* lucky. But sit down. I want to talk."

I sat on a couch embroidered with shiny metallic thread. The fabric felt as smooth and soft as glass, and the cushion as soft as fur but with a springy quality about it I'd never encountered.

"The soldiers are moving out now," he said. "You can't stay or some stickler for the rules may want to dispose of you. The army pays the guards bonuses for any foreigners caught here without going through integration. Once foreigners are caught, the soldiers are free to dispose of them in whatever way they choose. I myself have witnessed twenty-six such disposals in my lifetime."

He seemed so professional now, as if helping me were somehow his job.

"Can't I stay for just one more night? It's so comfortable here."

"The integration laws are the strictest laws in the sector."

"I haven't told you something. My brother and his wife came to Soom Kali. He may be trying to integrate. I would like to see him."

"If you see him, he will surely fail his integration."

the glass mountains

"Then he will be forced to accompany me to Forma."

"Should not your brother make his own decisions? If you love him, you must let him integrate without your interference. It is a harrowing process."

"I don't mean to interfere." I fell suddenly to my knees in tears. Moor did not move. "I'm scared," I said. "I cannot go on alone."

Moor lifted me gently to my feet. "You will not be alone."

I stared at him. "You?"

"Yes. Otherwise you travel alone. Your friend Tarkahna is being romanced by Panyor."

"The dog-faced man!"

"He's a good man."

"He has been fair," I agreed.

"Tarkahna will start the integration tomorrow."

"What? At every step she has abandoned me whenever she could."

"You could integrate, too, although I don't think I would like you as much if you did."

"I'll never integrate."

He nodded with approval. "Just as I thought."

"I've never been alone, but it can't be worse than everything else I've seen."

"There is nothing worse than loneliness. I have heard it said many times."

"What is your price to accompany me?"

"I haven't decided. For now you must leave some of your jewels with my father."

"And you will leave your father?"

"It was his idea. He'll probably buy meat with

the jewels you leave behind. But that must be his decision."

"But he said you should kill me."

Moor laughed. "Yes, that would be his first choice. But I think you remind him of my mother."

"Did he love your mother?"

"In his way. He became twice as embittered when she died. That was a type of love, I suppose."

"But you? Why will you do this for me?"

His eyes flared. "For the adventure first. And for you second. Maybe someday, you'll be more important to me than the adventure. But the yearning for adventure has been with me since I was a boy, and the yearning for you has been with me for just over a day."

"I see the Soom Kali make love differently from Bakshami. Here you believe in frankness, while in my sector the time of romance is the time of lies. It's an extension of our tradition of storytelling. You tell your partner ever bigger and bigger lies, like a kind of ritual. But eventually the lies become truth."

"Don't expect me to act like a Bakshami. I offer what I offer."

"Of course. I only say that it's better to start out with lies that become truths than truths that become lies."

"That's nothing but a Bakshami tongue-twister."

"And what is it that you offer?"

"To risk my life for yours. Isn't that better than a ritual of lies?"

He seemed hurt, and my hand, moving of its own volition, stroked his cheek, feeling that surprisingly cool skin capable of emitting a type of heat I'd never felt. "I would not want you to risk your life. And I do prefer the truth. The reasons for the romance ritual have always been a mystery to me." That wasn't entirely true. In fact, it was the sort of lie that was a part of the romance ritual, a ritual that didn't have to make sense.

Moor and I didn't have much time and went to get his bags, which he had already prepared. When we were ready we went in to talk to Moor's father together. His father lay awake in bed, propped up against cushions. The opulent cushions made him look even more insubstantial than he was. There was only the one chair, but Moor sat at the foot of the bed. Seeing them together for the first time and observing their ease with each other, I felt like a trespasser in their world. I knew that Moor's father was probably feeling the same way about his son and me. But I also knew he was wrong. I knew he could control his son's destiny with one word: Stay.

But he didn't speak that word. He asked rambling questions about my life in Bakshami, and about my family, and made rambling remarks about his wife's uniqueness and courage. When his father got tired, Moor signaled me to leave.

"Wait," said Moor's father. "Son, did you tell her that there was a time when I was the strongest man not just in this tiny village, but in half the land? My military career was the pride of my family, and all the generals begged me to join their personal troops and enticed me with promises of homes and money. A man as strong as I brought prestige to a troop. I wouldn't want her to think I was always like this."

Moor's father began coughing uncontrollably while Moor held his hand.

"Can I help?" I said.

Moor shook his head. "The doctors say there's nothing to it but to wait until the coughing passes." Moor's face was a mask now. I knew he'd endured many such fits.

I winced at the worst coughs and hummed to myself to cover the sounds of a man dying.

In a few minutes, Moor's father continued as if nothing had interrupted.

"My wife hated the army. I couldn't admit that I'd started to hate the army as well. My son will have a different life with you. So Mariska, I give you permission to take my son. I might not see him again."

"Father, if I thought I'd never see you again I wouldn't leave."

"You can believe whatever you want. I'll die when I want to." He spoke with pride. "I'm sick of doctors telling me when I will or won't die, and, frankly, I'll be glad when you leave and I get some meat in my stomach." He spoke as if he meant what he said, his eyes blazing with the strength of his appetite for meat.

"Moor, can we not leave him with meat?" But there were things between them I did not understand, and Moor refused. With bowed head he knelt at his father's bed, just as I had knelt at my grandfather's tomb. His father seemed barely conscious as we left.

"Moor, you don't have to come. I'll be fine, I can feel it." Another lie, since I believed as he did that I would probably die without his help.

"I don't want to join the army and spend my life currying favor with the generals and killing foreigners."

"Maybe you could be a general yourself."

He savored the thought, but then he shrugged. "Then others would try to curry favor with me and I would order *them* to kill the foreigners." He reached out suddenly and touched my face, and ran his hand down my neck and over my breast where my heart lay. "You're so small, little doll. But your heart is strong. I can feel its beat."

"I'm strong," I said.

He laughed but didn't reply. Then he pointed to his pack. "Can you lift this, little doll?" The pack was as heavy as a hundred big rocks. I couldn't budge it. "I know women your age who could pick that pack up with one hand," he said. "I speak seriously. Don't overestimate yourself, or underestimate yourself either. You've been lucky so far, but if I'm going to travel with you, you must see things for what they are. Otherwise it will all become a nuisance to me."

"Ah, the frankness again. I guess that's supposed to mean you love me."

He laughed again. "As I said, don't overestimate yourself."

"I might say the same to you."

He studied me for a moment before taking my face in his firm hands and kissing me: my closed eyes, my cheeks, my temples, and my lips. His strong hands held a gentleness that even my parents had never shown me. And with those strong hands and gentle kisses I knew he now controlled me more than my parents and all the rituals of Bakshami ever had. When he finished kissing me I took a stunned step back and fell over my pack to the floor. He pulled me up and shook his head. "How do you expect to breed with anyone if you act like that?"

I shot him a look that returned his arrogance. "Naturally, my mother has told me how to breed. Do you think I'm a child?"

He laughed. "Everybody breeds, even the fools," he said. "But I can assure you, their mothers aren't there at the time."

"Than how do they know what to do?"

He laughed again. "At least I won't be wanting for amusement on this trip."

We loaded up the dogs, and he went into his weapons room to decide what to take. When he came out his jacket bulged slightly and his face was hard with the decisions he had made in his roomful of weapons.

I felt scared. "Who are you expecting to meet? You said you preferred a knife."

"I do prefer knives, but others may not."

Somehow, as we passed through the door, I felt certain that his father lay awake in his room, knowing for only the second time in his life what it meant when a hard heart broke. That was something my mother once had told me about. "Keep your heart soft," she said. "It will break more often than a hard one, but each break will mend after a fashion. Once broken, a hard heart never mends." Because she was a practical woman, she'd spoken not philosophically but with mild sternness and the air of one teaching a simple fact of life. And then I realized that I had not thought of my parents all day, the longest that I hadn't thought of them since we parted at the lake.

The lamps pinged against the doorways, seeming to announce that all was well inside, and visitors welcome. I was not a visitor, I was a foreigner. But the village was lovely!

"Let's stay just one more day," I said. In his wavering eyes I saw that I held power over him, too, just as he held power over me. I leaned toward him. "One more day, please! I've traveled so long."

"It isn't possible."

"Make it possible."

"I cannot change the laws."

"Tell your friends to let you. Would they do that for you?"

"No doubt."

He relented as easily as that, and when the others left we were not with them.

The day passed quickly, as Moor showed me more about knives and we cooked ever more delicious meals. I enjoyed sitting with his sick father, as I had not had a father myself in so long. As soon as night fell, Moor said we must leave, and this time he didn't listen to my entreaties to stay. He'd decided we must now leave at night, since we had broken the integration laws and mustn't be caught.

So we moved with stealth through the forest that half a day earlier we could have passed through openly. I don't know how much time passed as we hurried through the forest. Because of our urgency, time passed differently among those trees. I could see, hear, smell, and think twice as much now as I ever could in the same amount of time. After a while I also felt I could sense Moor's soul so well that I was no longer following nor he leading. Instead we moved like two arrows shot from the same bow.

The cool air on my face exhilarated me, and the sense of shared perception with Moor, the sense of moving with such skill toward the same target, thrilled me. As soon as I had these thoughts, I regretted them and promptly tripped on a stone. Moor seemed to be turning to pick me up almost before I'd begun my fall. He righted me, whispered, "Watch out" so that his warm breath comforted my cheek, and resumed his course all in one smooth flow, like the movements of a dance ritual.

After that my skill returned but seemed to require greater concentration than before so that my mind grew more tired than my body. Moor pushed on. He saw my fatigue, however, and sat with me on a fallen log. Feeling his arm around me, and feeling just as clearly his protective alertness, I felt both comforted and as if I were failing him—after all, I'd vowed to myself that it was I who needed to protect him.

At one point he paused, and though I could hardly see his form in the dark forest, I thought he held up his hand to silence me. I could feel him listening, feel him gazing into the distance with his sharp eyes. "They'll have guards patrolling the forest tonight as no one is scheduled to be leaving. A friend of mine is stationed here. He got promoted recently," he added proudly. He paused. "That would have been my life eventually."

"Perhaps we'll meet your friend and everything will go smoothly."

"My friend would kill me, and perhaps you, too."

"Then how can you two be friends?"

"We've known each other since childhood, but if we meet tonight he will have his duty to the army and I my obligation to you and my desire to live. If I see him first I'll kill him first; if he sees me first, he'll kill me first—if he can. But you're the real catch, not me. So I hope you're lucky tonight and that your luck protects us. Even as I risk my life, I find I have no desire to suffer for you. I seek to aid you, not to die."

"I had no idea we would be in such danger. What difference should one day make? Why did you let me stay?"

There was a long pause. "I don't know, when you asked...But it was a mistake, certainly."

For a moment his voice sounded so stricken it was as if his eyes could penetrate the trees, and see his father lying at home, and see himself making his first wrong decision after a lifetime of making correct decisions. He fell into deep contemplation, quickly, the way a person might fall off a cliff, but then just as quickly he shook himself out of it. I turned in the direction of Bakshami, but my eyes couldn't penetrate the trees. Shami barked. But it was only an animal scurrying through the trees.

"Quiet," I snapped. I needed to repeat myself three times before Shami came to attention.

"She's no better trained than that?"

"I didn't raise her."

"Something is wrong," he said. "If we get separated, keep going east. Is that clear? No matter what happens, go east. Can you feel which way east is? You must be able to feel the way."

"But where will you be?"

"I hope to be with you, but it may not be possible. And one more thing."

"Yes."

"If there's trouble keep only your knife. Don't worry about the pack on your back. Whoever is chasing you will probably be able to move more quickly than you and will certainly be stronger, so you'll need every advantage. If there's trouble and the dogs are with you, don't bother about them. Because whoever is chasing you won't care about the dogs. Nobody gets promoted for capturing dogs, even Bakshami dogs. Are you ready? It's not far to the border." I felt stuck there, my legs heavy and metallic.

"If they catch me will they let me integrate?" I said.

"That choice will be gone if they catch you. But they won't."

"Now I feel Tarkahna is the lucky one for having made a different decision."

"You're lucky, too, but your luck will have to carry you someplace different. Remember what I said about seeing things for what they are. If you can't do that, we're going to be wasting a lot of time, and maybe wasting our lives here tonight."

"I'm ready. I just got scared for a moment. I'm

going to find my parents."

We hurried into the night. Such was my alertness that my confidence rose, and I felt as if I were invisible and soundless.

Even I could hardly hear the sound of my footsteps as I moved across the dirt. Fear gave way to the exhilaration of the adventure. The air was dead tonight, and such sounds as I heard clearly came from the area closest by, from the dogs or myself. Moor was so quiet I knew he was there only from instinct. I tried to concentrate on knowing which way was east. Now and then I needed to readjust my direction somewhat as Moor guided me along.

The forest's darkness shocked me, like no darkness I'd ever encountered. The difference between opened eyes and closed ones was barely perceptible. At times I thought closed gave me an advantage because it heightened my other senses. I concentrated on going east. The border is east, I said to myself with every step. The border is east.

I'm not sure how much time passed. But suddenly Moor grabbed my arm and pulled me mercilessly through the forest, half dragging me. Branches ripped into my clothes and skin, and I felt blood falling down my face. And I could hear something chasing us. I released my pack and stupidly tripped over it, almost bringing us both down. The noise of my pack falling sounded like an avalanche to my ears. I clutched my knife tightly, but it still didn't feel like an extension of my hand.

"Run," said Moor, and suddenly he was not with me any longer.

There was the sound of quick movement through the forest, but I kept east. I repeated "east, east" to myself like a ritual chant. The sound of movement wasn't getting any closer to me, but farther away, and when I heard a bark I realized it was the dogs running. If I could catch up with them, I would feel safer. Bits of moonlight filtered through the trees now, and my eyes devoured the light. I still seemed to be moving in the right direction. I knew whoever was giving chase, if indeed anyone was, was more adept at moving through this forest, meaner and stronger, but I did not believe that person could outrun me. Moor might have thought otherwise, but I knew my speed and grace to be considerable. And yet someone was gaining on me.

I hoped it was Moor. I continued to run, I hoped, east.

Unbelievably, before me I saw dim light, and I knew I approached the Mallarr border. Moor had said the Soom Kali respected the border because the Mallarr were clients of Artroro. I crossed the border as several Mallarr soldiers looked on with amusement. "Hey, girlie, girlie," they called out in high silly voices. They laughed but then came to attention, and I turned to see a Soom Kali man standing at the border behind me.

"Mariska," he said. "I'm Moor's friend. He's hurt. You must come back and help him."

I walked back toward the border as the Mallarr soldiers hooted. "Crazy girlie, first she runs out, and now she returns!" But I didn't cross over.

"Is he badly hurt?" I called out.

"It's his leg." He saw my hesitation and continued. "But don't come after all. He asked me to tell you he loves you and to go on without him. I can show you where he is if you wish, but he wanted you to leave him."

That sounded true to me. That would be exactly what he would want.

"Put down all your weapons and go in front of me," I said.

He set down one weapon, but I saw a knife in his belt, a knife he no doubt used better than I used mine. "That's right, I don't blame you for doubting me. You're a smart girl. No wonder Moor loves you so very much." He took several steps away from me with his hands up, and his mouth stretched into a disarming smile. His smile was quite beautiful. I took one step over the border, and he took a step back. This man did not seem so strong, so fast, or mean.

The man stepped back once more, still smiling. I relaxed a bit and had scarcely loosened my grip on the knife when his smile turned into a sort of grimace. It was amazing how the slightest adjustment in his mouth changed his gorgeous smile into something almost like a contortion of his lips. He did not grimace at me, however, but at Moor, who had just approached. The Mallarr soldiers fell silent as knives flew through the air, Moor's knife hitting his target in the heart, his friend's knife hitting Moor's leg, and my knife arcing uselessly to the ground.

For several moments Moor and I stood there. Dark liquid trickled from Moor's friend.

There was nothing but silence, or else the ringing in my ears drowned out all noise from outside. Moor reprimanded me. "I said don't stop going east. He might have killed you."

Moor was staring at his friend. "Forgive me, if you can," I said.

"For what?"

"For having caused you to kill your friend."

"I haven't killed him." The man on the ground groaned softly, and Moor kneeled to examine him. "But he's going to die, I'm certain of that. His heart is cut."

His friend groaned louder. "Kill me, please. This last favor I ask you."

"Forgive me," said Moor.

"All forgiven, friend."

Moor stabbed the man through the heart again, wincing just slightly, and then cleaned off his knife with leaves. "Pick up your knife," he said shortly. His friend didn't move again. His clothes rustled in the wind like the dead leaves around him.

"How old is he?" I asked.

"My age. We were born within a day of each other."

We walked quietly back over the border, Moor limping. The soldiers walked toward us.

One of the soldiers stopped us with a gesture. "The girl is Bakshami," said the soldier, "but what are you? You look like a Soom Kali to me. You're not allowed in this country without a warrant, Soom Kali."

"He's Bakshami," I said. "I know he's very tall. Everybody made fun of him as a child because he was so tall." The man looked at me with amused disbelief, and I realized that a reckless lie might do more harm than the truth. But I couldn't stop myself. "It's true," I pleaded.

"I know it's not true, so don't lie until you learn how to do it. But I have no desire to make a scene. Making a scene sometimes costs a life. Probably it would be your life, Soom Kali, but it might be mine. I've witnessed that taking a life means little to you. Making a scene also sometimes prevents the earning of money that might otherwise have been earned. In Soom Kali at least they know how to take care of their soldiers. But a soldier's pay is low here."

Moor opened my pack, which I noticed for the first time he carried, and pulled out a single gem, one of the smallest ones. The soldier's eyes lit up. Moor handed the gem to the soldier, who bowed slightly and walked away with the gem in his pocket. When the other soldiers crowded around the one with the gem, he ignored them and continued walking. They looked toward us, but Moor was already pulling me away.

We walked just out of sight before he collapsed and opened up his own pack. He took out a metal container and spread foul-smelling ointment on his leg. Then he tied a piece of cloth around his thigh. "It's nothing. I've been injured worse many times." Perhaps I looked as aghast as I felt, because he smiled cockily and lifted the leg of one of his pants. Several scars marred the skin. "The Soom Kali learn how to use knives by using them." He pointed at one of his scars. "My friend also gave me this scar. We played often as children, and even then we were almost evenly matched."

"I tried to make the knife become a part of me. If it had I might have killed one man to save another. In my sector no one kills another person."

Moor nodded with understanding and stared back again toward his home, stared in that way that made me believe he could see through trees. I noticed for the first time that his jacket no longer bulged with a weapon. He seemed terribly vulnerable.

"Where is your weapon?"

He checked his jacket distractedly. "Gone," he said simply. There was something inconsolable in his eyes, and I knew it was I, flirting with my own power over him and causing him to ignore his own good judgment about staying an extra day, that had brought that look to his eyes. In the distance were only a few tattered buildings. We huddled into some bushes and sat quietly. I slept on his shoulder and dreamed about the past, about the round leaves of tansan trees dropping to the dusty ground, and about the circles of dust that surrounded my sector. As I'd once dreamed about being a woman, I now dreamed about being a girl full of longings to leave those trees and that dust. And when I woke up I was a woman, and the trees and dust of my childhood lay far away.

·~

part (five)

Mallarr was a small, corrupt monarchy that served as one of the buffer sectors between Soom Kali and Artroro. Because Mallarr had aligned itself with Artroro, Soom Kali dealt cautiously with it. The Mallarr government supposedly allowed no Soom Kali in their sector, but because of the corruption of almost everyone in Mallarr, we easily found someone to fly us to the Artroro border. Moor wanted to get as quickly as possible to Artroro, where we hoped to lose ourselves in the crowds. He was worried about his friend's death. Soldiers were accorded great status in his sector, and the murder of a soldier meant almost as much as the murder of a prominent leader. The killing joined Moor and me closer together, but I hated being tied together in this way. It was as if my whole life—past and future—were now colored by this killing. I would not have blamed Moor for hating me, but he did not. He took responsibility for his friend's death, just as I did. But at the same time he possessed a coldness that I knew all warriors possessed at times. He hired us a plane, and I saw nothing in his eyes but coldness. I knew he would not let me use my power in this way over him again.

I'd never ridden in a plane before. I'd never seen so much green at one time. Hills covered most of the land, rivers twisting through the valleys. Moor had visited Mallarr with his parents years earlier, when it was Soom Kali and not Artroro who sponsored this monarchy. Nothing had changed much in the land-scape since then, but he found the people different. They were less corrupt when Soom Kali had spon-sored them. Moor said that he found his country one of the least corrupt places he'd ever been.

"How can a country that violent not be corrupt at some level?" I said.

"What I mean is my people keep their word. My friend gave his vow to uphold the orders of his com-manders, so he had to kill me if he could. I said I would try to get you over the border alive, so I had to do so. The Soom Kali are a violent people, but they're not without honor."

We talked loudly, above the plane motor. Every so often I felt nauseated by the ride and needed to lie back and close my eyes.

"How was your mother killed?" I asked him after a silence.

"A brief war between Soom Kali and Artroro broke out while my mother visited Mallarr. Artroro attacked the village where she stayed, and she got killed."

"How could your father have helped if he'd been there?"

"The presence of another person always changes what occurs. It could have been anything. Perhaps they would have been out for a ride at the time of the attack, or perhaps they would have stayed at a differ-ent village."

When we landed in Artroro, we told the airport guard that we were tourists; he let us through imme-diately. Despite the wars Artroro often found itself in, the Artroran border was open. The guard petted

Shami on the head, and several people smiled at us. My travels had torn and dirtied my robes, and I truly looked like the hayseed I'd once been called.

There were so many different types of people it was hard to say just what a native Artroran looked like. Moor said the Artrorans were almost as tall as the Soom Kali, but huskier. I saw several people who met that description. I also saw several Bakshami, graceful black-haired people in native gowns. I felt so excited I waved to one, but he only glanced at me with surprise and hurried on. I waved at another, and she, too, seemed surprised, but also amused. Moor, who until recently had struck me as exotic, seemed almost normal among these strangers. He'd gotten his knee bandaged up properly in Mallarr, but blood had seeped through the bandage. Even that made him fit in—I saw a couple of people with bruises on their faces, another with her arm in a brace, and another with blood seeping through a bandage on his neck. A number of these strangers carried themselves with the same confidence that bordered on insolence that I saw in Moor. In this way I saw that he was not as unusual as I'd thought, and yet I continued to care more and more for him.

Since Moor could read Artroran, we could follow the signs to a place where the thunder of planes and ships crushed my eardrums and the crowds of people shouted and cursed and laughed with each other. Moor told me that the planes looked older and were less maneuverable than the sleeker ships.

The air held an astonishing amount of humidity. The humidity clung to my face and gave my skin a moist sensation that I couldn't tell if I liked or not. There was something voluptuous about it, like the heat that emanated from Moor and made me aware of my skin and of the heat in my own body.

"Nobody has dogsleds here," I said. Instead people used what I'd heard Moor call motorsleds, and ships and planes like the ones I'd seen in both Soom Kali and Mallarr.

"Bakshami exists in the dark ages. I camped in Bakshami once with my mother, but we didn't get very far. The conditions there were so awful we didn't want to go on."

I listened to the loud, grating noises around us and looked at the people pushing to get from here to there while opposite them others pushed to get from there to here. "Are these conditions better?"

"I have no love of this sector, but, yes, to me, these conditions are preferable." We needed to speak loudly to hear each other.

Somewhere in the back of my head I knew there was much here I would like to gawk at, but the noise oppressed me, and all I could think of was how much I wanted to leave. "Let's go," I said. "My ears hurt!"

He led us directly into a huge crowd, where the noise grew louder still. I pressed my hands over my ears as we pushed through. Every so often, Moor would turn to see whether I followed, and I noticed his eyes shone—these crowds and this noise excited him. The air was so wet that my skin and clothes had grown damp.

"Why doesn't it rain?" I shouted.

"It will!" he shouted back.

Finally we reached the end of one crowd, but there were still crowds all around. Moor suddenly seemed to spot something he'd been searching for and rushed forward to grab a man next to a vehicle that looked like a halved, somewhat flattened sphere. It was similar, but with less flourish, to a couple of vehicles I'd seen in Moor's town.

"Why travel in these when they could fly?"

"Let the skies remain sacred," said Moor, crying out above the din. "There are sectors like Forma that pass few rules restricting the number of people in the air. In Soom Kali we prefer to see clouds in the sky, not ships. The same is generally true of the people here."

The man he'd grabbed shook his arm away in what seemed like feigned anger. "What, you hold on to me while you give her a lesson in philosophy?"

"We need a place to stay," Moor said to the man. "Can you take us to the nearest village? How much would you charge?"

The man regarded us with amusement. Everyone seemed especially amused by me and my dogs. "I could take you for free just for the laugh, but then I've already had my share of laughs today. Therefore the charge would be high."

The man was smaller even than me, and I'd never seen a man so round about the stomach. The sight had disoriented me so much that at first it had occurred to me that maybe he wasn't a man at all but a pregnant woman.

"Never mind," Moor said. "I see someone else who can help us." He peered over the top of the man's head. I rose on my toes but didn't see what he saw. He hoisted his pack and signaled me to come with him.

"Perhaps a good laugh is worth something after all," said the man. "Therefore the charge would be moderate."

Moor said, "That motorsled I see over there is larger than yours, and the driver seems eager for company." His heavy pack remained positioned on his shoulder.

The round man again regarded me and my dogs, this time letting out a huge belly laugh. "They're funnier than I realized! An excellent laugh is worth a lot in a world like this. Therefore the price would be low."

Moor threw our things into the motorsled and hoisted the dogs in. He and I climbed over the edge and squeezed into the tiny vehicle. Artie sat closest to the man. We sat for several minutes while the driver fiddled and the motorsled groaned and coughed.

"It sounds like it's dying, not coming to life," I said.

But the groaning and coughing ceased, and we lurched forward while the driver pressed a button to make the motorsled scream shrilly in warning to pedestrians. He himself shouted constantly, "Are you crazy? Get out of the way. Do you want to die? No, then move, you ass!"

Moor comforted Shami, who trembled in her seat.

Artie sat placidly. We moved through throng after throng, but finally we broke through and I could see a breathtaking view before me, flowers everywhere, in the trees and along the paths and in the hair of men and women. The heavy air captured the scent of the flowers and coated my skin so that when I sniffed my arm, the smell seemed to rise from me as well as from all around me.

Many people walked the paths. "Why do so many people walk when they could drive?" I said. It was a variation of my earlier question about why people drove rather than flew. But having never encountered so much technology before, I found myself enamored of it.

"There are advantages to walking that don't have to do with speed," Moor said. "Technology is for finding expediency, lack of technology is for finding grace."

"When I settle down I plan to buy ten different motorsleds and alternate them according to my mood."

The man ignored us and talked to Artie. "Where are you from? You're a nice-looking dog, very handsome. You remind me of my brother, who is the opposite of me, a muscular fellow. We have different fathers, and as a matter of fact we have different mothers as well. All right, you've found me out, he isn't my brother at all, just a neighbor. A very handsome man."

"What powers this thing?" I said to Moor.

"It has to do with gravity and magnets, and also with the power of the sun. My interest in science has always been minimal."

The man turned to look at us disapprovingly. "And what of your other interests? When I was your age I already had ten children as healthy as dogs," he said. "Where are your children? Left them at home?" He didn't wait for a response. "Let me tell you a story that may help you. We kept two pheasant once, a male and a female. The male always tried to mount the female. He tried to knock her down and do it, he tried doing it with her beak and with her eyes and with the feathers on the back of her head. In frustration she tried jumping on top of him. They just couldn't figure it out. Finally she sat down on top of a rock and pretended it was an egg. Every day she sat on that rock, waiting for it to hatch. Through the most intense heat wave in my memory, she sat on that rock instead of hiding in the shade. One hot day we went outside and there she was, diligently atop her rock, dead. She made a fine supper for my family but that's not the point. The point is, if those pheasant had been able to talk to the mother of my children, everything would have worked out. If the two of you would like some advice, she has a knack for it. We knew a couple who tried for half their lives to have children. After one talk with Lederra, bazoom, they started to have so many children they could have started a village of their own. Lederra's a genius on such matters. We ourselves have nine children."

"I thought you had ten," I said.

"Did I say nine? I meant eleven," he said.

"We'll have twelve," said Moor. "And our pheasants and dogs will have forty."

The man laughed uproariously. "Then you must sell me some of your pheasants and dogs. They sound like good breeding stock."

the glass mountains

We passed a monstrously muscular man with a face as grotesque as the beast carvings of Soom Kali. The driver stopped and sent his siren blaring to catch the man's attention. "Sir! Sir! Please, if there's ever a fight you're on my side!" The man tolerantly nodded his beastly head in acknowledgment. The motorsled stalled, and the driver fiddled some more before we got started again. He turned his head halfway to talk to us. "You have to be prepared in this world, and get your friends straightened out *before* a fight starts. As a matter of fact, you look like quite a strong young man yourself. You're on my side, too." He paused the motorsled and turned to grab hold of Moor's hands and kiss them. "I'm at your service, my name is Penn. Remember, we're all friends now, in case there's ever a fight. It's to your advantage. I'm not strong, but I'm sneaky and handy with blunt objects."

"Do many fights break out?" I said.

"All the time. I myself have never been involved in one, but as I said, it's best to be prepared. You're like me, you must learn to make yourself handy with whatever objects are at your disposal. A sneaky weakling can be a powerful ally, indeed."

"I don't like to think of myself as a sneaky weakling."

He laughed. "Lederra could conquer such as you without use of her hands *or* her feet! She would just push you over, smash you with her head, and be done with it!" He pondered that and laughed some more.

"The strongest will makes the strongest soldier," said Moor. "She's Bakshami. Their wills are hardened by the sun."

"Indeed, I know many Bakshami myself. Sneaky weaklings with wills of rock."

"My brother and his wife are as strong as any Soom Kali," I said defensively.

"Then let them be on my side, too!" exclaimed Penn.

We arrived at the village, which was almost as crowded as the airport, and Penn dropped us off at a place that he said was the cheapest inn in town. "You did want the cheapest, didn't you? If you want the best, I can help you with that, too. Something in between?"

"This is good," Moor said. "How much do we owe you?"

"I'll take one of your dogs here if you're short of currency."

Moor handed him a tiny gem, one so small it was barely more than a speck.

"What is this, I can hardly see it," said Penn. He squinted as he moved his head in and out from his hand.

"This is the low price I promised you," said Moor. "As you well know, it's a higher price than most would pay you for the same ride."

"You've taken advantage of my good nature, but I'm willing to give you another chance." He handed us a small metal plate that contained a few symbols on it. "This is my contact card. If you need a ride in the future, let me know."

We stood aside with the dogs while Penn drove off. I examined the metal plate. "What is this?"

"You don't know? You stick it into the contactor

and he answers on the other end. He'll pay the minimal cost."

"Oh, my brother used to tell me of such things. My brother knew everything about Artroro and what a paradise it is."

Moor didn't respond. I looked at the world of flowers around me and thought of how I'd made it to Artroro, the most powerful sector on the planet, the sector of Maruk's, and by extension of my own, dreams. But instead of strongmen, each more amazing than the next, I saw crowd upon crowd of people who blended each into the other.

Moor pulled on my arm, and I rushed to keep up.

2.

We walked into a decrepit wooden reception room. A woman with hair as pale as her pale skin pulled back her lips and bared her teeth and gums in an attempt at a smile. "Need a room? We're almost booked up, but we have some very nice accommodations left. Four of you?"

"Two," said Moor.

"Two and two dogs. That's four."

"Then the dogs will sleep outside."

"What if someone steals them?" I said.

"Whoever steals these dogs will have their hands full," Moor said.

The woman never stopped smiling. "They can sleep in the room for only a small fee, if the lady would like. They can sleep outside for a smaller fee, if the gentleman would like."

"We'll pay the larger fee," I said.

"Ah, the lady is new to Artroro. Perhaps she would like a tour."

"They'll sleep outside and we won't pay," said Moor. "We'll pay only for a bed for ourselves."

"Ah, the gentleman has visited Artroro before. In that case, perhaps he would like a driver to show the lady the sights. We can provide that as well."

"Just the bed," said Moor. "And a private room."

"A private room! That changes everything. In that case, the dogs won't be bothering other customers. So I will be able to charge you the smaller fee I'd promised you for having them sleep outside. Only now they may sleep inside for that same low fee."

"As I said, they'll sleep outside. They're used to it."

"Moor," I said. "Everyone here seems anxious to possess and acquire. The dogs must be safe."

The woman leaned over the counter to me, so that her face was so close to mine she became blurry. I instinctively leaned back, but my feet remained stuck where they were. There was something hypnotic about the fervent greed in her eyes. Never had I seen anyone so completely focused. As she exhaled, her clammy breath filled the air I breathed. "I must tell you, the price I'm talking about is a pittance. I can see you're a lady whose heart would break if something happened to her dogs. A most generous and kind-hearted lady. You can save yourself a great deal of worry by paying a pittance." She leaned even closer, so that I could feel the hairs on her nose brush the tip of my nose. "When I say a pittance, I mean it sincerely. If your friend here cares for your feelings, he will understand." Her eyes glanced at Moor.

I knew she was a swindler. Still, what she said made sense. I turned with annoyance to Moor. "What about my feelings?" I said.

He took my arm and pulled me aside. "I think I should handle all negotiations for a while."

"But my feelings," I said. "She said that if you cared about my feelings, then, ah, what did she say?"

"No one else who sees you sees Mariska, as I do. They see a young woman whose only purpose in life is to provide them with fees and jewels. They see someone as easy to rob from as a ground crawler is to step on. The dogs will sleep outside."

"Then I will sleep outside with them."

"If that's what you wish."

"I don't like all this frankness after all. I would prefer more lies in this supposed romance. Perhaps rudeness isn't the most efficacious way to begin a friendship such as this."

"The dogs must stay outside."

"I've slept outside many times myself. I will sleep outside tonight. If you want to join me, you're welcome."

"The Bakshami have a fine strong will, but couldn't they put it to better use? The woman has no morals."

"She may have no morals, but what she says is true. For a pittance we can make sure the dogs are safe."

"I can assure you that knowing how badly you want this, she'll charge more than a pittance. I must insist I do all the negotiating from now on."

"Not where my dogs are concerned."

He angrily returned to the woman, who still hadn't stopped smiling. "We've decided the dogs will sleep outside."

Her smile collapsed momentarily, but then it became even more expansive. "Good, good, dogs belong outside, I don't want fleas in my rooms. I was only worried about the young lady. As a matter of fact she reminds me of my daughter, and as such, I can make some extra efforts on her behalf. For complete payment in advance you may keep your dogs in the room for free."

Moor paid her a fee. "Where is the room?"

She shrewdly but very quickly glanced at the small payment he'd handed her. "The best room available is the one for you. I tell you it's the best! Out and turn left. The room has a blue door."

"And how will we open the lock?" said Moor.

"Lock! We have no locks. There is no danger. We're not like some other establishments which I won't name but which are located just down the street from here. You've chosen your accommodations well." Someone else walked in behind us. "Welcome! Please. Tell me how I can help you. The best room for you?" With one of her hands she shooed us away, never taking her eyes off the new customer.

Moor brought the dogs into the blue-doored room. Something scurried across the floor, and so many bugs climbed up one wall it seemed the wall was alive. The bed slanted precariously to one side and also down at the head.

"Wouldn't it be better for us to sleep outside?"

"It isn't allowed except in certain areas."

"How can it not be allowed to sleep outside?"

"Because those who make the laws prefer that you sleep inside."

"Such absurdity!"

We sat on the bed, each feeling great annoyance with the other. Now and then a bug would lose its footing and fall from above. A bug fell beside me, and then crawled over my leg before falling off the bed and to the floor.

"What did we pay for this room?" I said.

"Next to nothing."

"It's worth less."

"Anything less would be free."

"It's worth less even than that. Why don't they pay us?"

"Good idea, perhaps you *should* negotiate for us next time."

There was a silence, and then he rubbed and pushed at his eyes and temples and took big breaths of air. I thought he might cry if he could—but he could not. I put my small hand on his large one.

And there in that infested room, with the blood rushing to our heads and the bugs dropping to the ground with soft pings, Moor and I copulated repeatedly in the same avid way I'd witnessed among animals. For me this uproar between my thighs was something new, something I had not known existed despite all my mother's teachings about breeding. At first Moor conducted himself with the same mix of responsiveness and harshness with which he lived, and it seemed to me that this was all something he'd done as often as he'd thrown a knife. But after a while, with my legs wet and sticky and my lips raw from the harshness of our kisses, I knew there was much about this—about me—that was unlike anything even Moor had ever known. In our lovemaking he became not more experienced, but more innocent. At one point pain rose from inside of me alongside desire, but the pain was a part of the ritual of first copulation, the way, when the first of their parents died, some Bakshami would play the rhythms all night, until their fingers blistered from holding the sticks and the noise reverberated in their heads and their fatigue made them clumsy. The next day, exhausted, they nevertheless would feel deeply satisfied that their parent was really and truly dead, and that after this tragic yet inevitable departure from their daily lives the world had somehow righted itself again. Without the ritual there would be no feeling of rightness. So toward the end of our lovemaking, with every time Moor moved within me, the pain increased, and at the same time I emerged from this pain with a feeling of profound satisfaction and a sense that my insensible world had started to right itself.

When Moor fell asleep I rubbed against his skin as I had the other night, with a new sense of discovery based on my new experiences. I also felt the way I did when I petted my dogs most evenings and marveled at what wonderful dogs they were and at how lucky I was to have them. Though they were supposedly my slaves, each night when I combed them free of fleas I vowed that I would be their slave for as long as they lived. Being their slave had made each of them mine. We had opened a passage between us through which our desires, our dignity, and our trust might flow. Tonight Moor and I had opened the same passage between ourselves. This made the dogs seem less important, and made it easy for me to see the wonder rather than the hopelessness of this room of moving walls.

Moor had barely slept in the short time we'd traveled together. Holding his body I could tell he slept deeply now and that he could hear no sounds from the waking world except those heard through the filter of dreams. Perhaps the soft rustle of thousands of crawling insects sounded like the tinkle of tree leaves in the distance, and perhaps the occasional angry shouts from outside were the calls of desire he'd heard such a short time ago.

Within my sleepiness I felt an excitement that wouldn't let me sleep. To be here, in this place, was not to achieve bliss but to achieve an enchantment of my soul that paradoxically felt still and clamorous at the same time. In this gloomy room that should have been a place of sadness, I clung to Moor and wished we could stay in this village for a long while, exploring Artroro by day and each other by night.

Finally I fell into a deep dreamless sleep. I began to rise out of it with an awful feeling similar to one that used to come over me as I was growing up and going through a period of intense dreaming. I would think, If I don't get up now, my brother (or my sister, or my parents, or Artie) will die. Now I felt I had to get up or Moor would die. I felt as if I were suffocating. My sleep felt like chains I was trying to break free from. I awoke with a jerk and sat up immediately. Night had fallen, but electric lights leaked into the room with a sort of dead quality, an unnatural quality. This light was trying to mimic daylight but couldn't.

The shouts from outside had died down, and the inn had grown so quiet I could scarcely believe that throngs had crowded the village paths earlier. I went to the window and pulled aside the drapes. The view was obscured somewhat by a smoky quality to the window. I tapped the window, but it didn't ring as glass did. The electric lights cast a queer and exotic luster on anything reflective outside. Shadows fell unnaturally, colors lost their vibrancy, and the unliving and the living seemed hardly different at all. The lights that were situated low enough threw shadows up rather than to the ground, which was the natural place of shadows. And the trees seemed more lifeless than during the day; on the other hand, the buildings seemed to possess a mystery I associated with life. These awful lights! They lit up not just the walls but the corners, not just Artroro but, seemingly, the sky above the sector, as well.

"What do you see?" Moor had gotten up and spoke from the bed.

"I see silence."

Moor stretched his back and rolled his neck. "Stuffy in here. We should get out, take the dogs for a walk, and maybe get something to eat."

"Let's go hunting."

"It is no hunting culture. We can buy food some-where."

"Who would be up at this hour?"

"The innkeepers. They lie down but never sleep deeply in case a new customer comes."

He got up and pulled on his clothes.

"My clothes are conspicuous because they're so worn," I said.

"Not just your clothes but your expression of in-nocence and curiosity."

"Someone once called me a hayseed."

"All right, we'll buy you new things tomorrow."

I got dressed while he took my place at the win-dow. Neither of us spoke while he gazed outside.

"In my country we honor the quiet as the source of life," said Moor.

"I would have thought your people would honor war as the source of life."

"It's because of our many wars that we honor the quiet. The lack of noise, the stillness that accompa-nies it. The lulls between battles."

He let go of the drapes and opened the front door. "Bring your valuables with you. The lights burn all night in this sector for a reason."

I called the dogs and we went out into the cool humid air still thick with the scent of flowers. The dogs sniffed excitedly and rolled in some grass. The queer, exotic luster from the electric lights touched Moor's hair and eyes and made him seem like a magi-cal thing, and also made me feel shy when he looked at me. We walked quietly to search for food. At the innkeeper's room we found perhaps a dozen people sleeping on chairs, on blankets on the floor and on the sofa.

The smiling woman lay in a semi-enclosed area with her eyes shut and mouth twitching, as if from the daily strain of smiling. Her enclosure, I supposed, provided better accommodations than that of the people sprawled around the room, and yet seeing her in her enclosure, on a small bed behind the bureaus and tables where she worked, made me feel sorry for her in a way that I didn't feel sorry for the others. For added to the indignity of her accommodations was her loneliness, and added to her loneliness was the strain of hiding it. People did not suffer in this way in Bakshami.

"Perhaps we should let her sleep," I said.

"She would welcome the extra money of selling us food."

"She thinks she would welcome us, but that sort of welcoming has more to do with habit than with joy."

Moor touched my face, the first time he'd touched me since our lovemaking. The touch made me wait avidly for anything he might say. He could persuade me of anything.

"Let me wake her up," he said gently. "I'll make it worth her while."

"May I wake her then?"

"Of course."

I studied him for a moment, at the unlikely mix of gentleman and warrior in his face and demeanor. I knew the same mix existed in his heart. It was his responsive quality, the quality that made him wait patiently for anything I might desire, that ruled at this moment. I entered the area behind the tables and bureaus where the woman lay and touched her shoulder softly. She laughed and mumbled to herself.

"Please forgive me," I said, shaking her this time.

She sat upright, her smile erased, and in its place a look of suspicion and, improbably, faint terror. But then the smile seemed almost to leap upon her face again. "Forgive you, darling, but what have you done?"

"I've woken you from your dreams. My friend and I were hoping for something to eat."

The fervent greed lit up her face again. I liked seeing that better than her improbable terror. Maybe she felt sheltered within her greed, just as I'd once felt sheltered within the naiveté that was fast dissolving. The woman stood up. "Whatever it is you wish I can give you. If you prefer meats I offer those, and if you prefer fruits I offer those as well."

The saliva under my tongue increased and felt warm in my mouth as she spoke. "Fruit for me," I said. "But my friend likes meat, too."

"Fruit and meat for both of us," Moor said. "And some meat and bones for the dogs."

"The price is high for a good meal at this hour," said the woman. "But I can throw in some bread for free."

"We must see the food first before we pay," Moor said. "But if the meal is good, we'll make it worth your while."

"I was reluctant to wake you," I said.

I regretted my words immediately. I could see through her smile that my words had made her think of a way she could take advantage of us for more money. My way of being considerate no longer worked.

Moor, seeing the same, spoke up. "But I myself was not reluctant," he said.

We waited in the small crowded outer area while she left for our meal. While Moor stood at the curtainless window, I sat on the floor and listened to the variety of snores in the room. All the sleepers lay on top of packs, probably the packs that contained their funds. And I noticed, too, that several had awoken and watched us warily. Moor, the woman, and I had talked in low voices, so I was surprised we'd woken up so many. I returned the stare of one man, thinking to make him turn away, but he continued to glare until I myself looked off. Artie placed a huge paw in my lap and moaned softly.

"Are you hungry?" I whispered. "Food is coming." Shami sat to my other side, smiling mischievously but sweetly in the way she often did.

The food the woman brought was passable at best, and my sympathy for her had started to wear thin. But I let Moor pay her the generous fee he'd promised me, and we went outside to eat. We sat on the ground outside our room. The dogs chewed happily on their bones, sucking out the marrow with loud slurping noises, and when they finished they sat at attention to our sides, begging us with their eyes for food. I gave them each a piece of bread and two pieces of meat. Despite its mediocrity, Moor and I ate the food hungrily. I found I enjoyed eating mediocre food in the cool air under the supernatural light.

"What should we do tomorrow?" I said.

"I have a friend in Artroro who is indebted to me. We'll look for him. We must find passage to Forma."

"Is your friend Soom Kali?"

He nodded. "He encounters much prejudice but has managed to make a life for himself."

"Why live here among some of Soom Kali's greatest enemies?"

"Who understands you better than your worst enemies?"

We finished eating in silence and returned to our room, leaving the door open to alleviate the stuffiness. Moor found a couple of flat rocks outside and slipped them under the head of the bed to balance out the slant. We'd started to get ready to go back to bed when Moor urgently motioned me to be still. "Quiet!" I told the dogs. We all three looked at Moor. I could hear the grating voice of the woman who'd checked us in.

"Of course the man was rather rude. He seemed to think I might cheat them! The young lady seemed decent enough despite her dishevelment. We have a high class of residents here. We're not like some other places I won't name. I had no idea they'd murdered a soldier. I only let them have the room because—"

Moor quietly closed the door and gathered up our pack with the currency. There was a flimsy-looking door in one wall, and he leaned hard against it until it fell open. We rushed through and found ourselves in another room with a woman pointing something at us. Moor smiled charmingly.

cynthia kadohata

"You don't want to hurt us, just as we don't want to hurt you. We're only passing through." He threw her a jewel and we rushed through, the woman pointing her weapon and cursing us.

On the other side of the inn there was another inn, and we ran around that, and kept running through the mazelike paths of the village until I had no idea in what direction the original inn lay.

3.

"Do you know where you're going?" I finally asked Moor.

"Yes, I'm going away from the inn. I don't know what I'm going toward."

We walked all night through the village, and well before morning we passed through town and into some flower-covered hills. We slept in bushes, and when we awoke I felt ravenous, and ridiculously optimistic despite what had happened the night before.

The sky shone less blue than in Bakshami, where there were no motorsleds and few machines, but I'd never seen such clouds, huge white swollen masses that threw shadows on the hills encircling us. The flowers were every shade of pink and red, so profuse they often blocked out sections of the green hills entirely.

"How can they catch us in a country so crowded?"

"There are many who'll see us and report for a price. To kill a soldier is a severe crime in both sectors. Luckily even severe crimes are soon forgiven if you're fortunate enough not to get killed for them."

"Then we can trust no one."

"There are people who check the listings for criminals every day, in case they're fortunate enough to spot one and claim a reward." Moor spoke patiently.

We walked past the next town and into the next. At the contactor machine Moor stuck in the card that the taxi driver Penn had given us. It was getting late, and the streets had already begun emptying out. The night lights had resumed their queer luster.

"This is Moor. The Soom Kali man? You gave my Bakshami friend and me a ride yesterday with our dogs." He rubbed his forehead. He looked drawn and exhausted, not just by the tension of the last few days but by the weight of responsibility for me. I had sometimes felt that same weight with my dogs. "Yes," he continued into the speaker. "But we need your help. We need a ride to a town quite a ways into the sector, and we need the ride now...The price is fifty thousand peroxes in jewels...No, it's not negotiable. As you well know, that's probably about what you'll make in the next fifty days, and that's if you're lucky." He rubbed his head again, kneading his fingers into his temples. "Penn, Penn, you talk too much for me right now. Please say yes or no. My head is throbbing."

Penn agreed to come pick us up and bring a good meal with him. In general, we thought, we should keep to ourselves, so we wanted to avoid the food vendors. We looked around the town we found ourselves in. It was even seedier and more crowded than the town we'd first stayed in, and without the sense of bustle. Instead many of the inhabitants moved disinterestedly through the paths, only glancing at us occasionally. An exception to this was a woman who maniacally ran up and tried to put a sort of half-robe around me. Her arms enveloped my waist.

"Does the lady need a gown?" she asked. "I have a blouse, too. Oh, how flattering the gown looks. And I have another just like it for the gentleman. Sir, it will flatter you every bit as much as it flatters the lady. Oh, what a handsome couple you'll make."

"I want to fit in," I said to her.

"Oh, dear lady, how you will fit in when you buy some of my clothes. People have often said to me, When I wear your clothes I feel I fit in as I never have before!"

The woman was about my size, with a quickness in her hands that was startling to watch as she whisked out her shining fabrics and enwrapped me.

"Nothing too bright," said Moor. "And something she can move fast in. Her knees and legs should be protected. Perhaps trousers would be best."

The woman threw up her quick hands in delight. "How lucky for you. Look what I have." She drew out a pair of dark trousers that she held against my legs. The woman swooned with delight. "Oh, how lucky, how lucky. These will fit perfectly. And many have said to me that these trousers excel at protecting the knees."

"Will I fit in?" I asked Moor.

"Will you fit in!" the woman exclaimed. "My dear, you will fit in so well no one will be able to tell you from anyone else. You will fit in so well you will all but vanish. Even now, just holding these up to you, I say to myself, Oh, how she fits in."

the glass mountains

"This is how much I will pay for the trousers and a blouse," said Moor.

The woman hardly glanced at the money, but like others I'd seen she seemed to catch all with her glance. "Try them on, my darling lady, see what I mean. Then we will discuss price. We needn't discuss price when the lady hasn't even tried anything on."

I put on the new clothes, and again the woman appeared faint. She slapped her hands to her head and threw her head back like the most advanced drummers in Bakshami, after they'd been playing intensely and were reaching their climax. Even as a cool breeze blew, sweat fell from the woman's brow. She grabbed a passer-by and pulled him over. "Does she not fit in well? Why, she almost vanishes into the background!"

The passer-by grunted and mumbled "Very nice" and pulled away.

"Oh, how your precious knees will be protected in these trousers."

Moor held out even less money than he had to begin with. "The blouse doesn't please me. But we're in a hurry, here's your money."

He took me by the arm, and we rushed off, the woman calling after us, "But sir, what about you! I have something that will feel like clouds against your knees. You will fit in so well you will not be able to find yourself in a reflection."

"Where are we going now?"

"Penn told me he'd meet us behind a certain inn in this village. Ah, there it is, with the large green sign."

We sat in some bushes behind the inn. I admired my trousers and compared them to the heavier trousers Moor wore. "Yours protect your knees better than mine," I said. "But I do fit in, don't I?"

"You're starting to sound like that woman."

"Is everyone so eager to make money here?"

"Yes, this is your paradise. But the land is lovely."

"The people don't look like I expected. They're smaller and less strong. But they do have a sort of grace, or agility, particularly with their tongues."

"The woman is not a native Artroran. Neither is Penn. In the outer villages live many immigrants. Later on we'll see more Artrorans. Believe me, they're a strong people. But some of them are growing soft," he added with a touch of disdain.

"What makes softness such an evil to you?"

"If your body grows soft, how will you defend your home sector?"

"If your heart grows hard, how will you care enough to protect the home sector?"

"My heart might turn to steel and I would still protect my home." Hearing his proud voice and seeing his fierce eyes, I knew that this was true. I felt a flush of shame to remember that the Bakshami could not protect themselves. But how could *I* protect my home?

Penn's piercing siren filled the air. He stopped in front of us and called out with irritation. "Hurry, you didn't tell me you were fugitives. I've already been questioned once today. The price for this grows every moment. Most drivers wouldn't do this for any price."

"As you well know, any driver would do it for a

the glass mountains

201

price," said Moor. We got into the motorsled. "It becomes tiresome to speak of the price of this and the price of that all day and all night. Isn't there anything else you can talk of while you drive, Penn?"

"We must get these things straight. I cannot waste my time when there isn't an adequate fee involved," he said. "For a price, however, I can be induced to waste the rest of my days."

His cheerfulness had diminished greatly since the last time I saw him, and in his eyes I saw the same grasping focus as the woman at the inn, but I also saw the same flinty courage as Moor possessed. The group of us would make a formidable opponent.

"We're going to Clasmata," said Moor. "Did you bring us food?"

"Clasmata! Do you know how far that is?"

Moor closed his eyes and suddenly looked sick. "I have to sleep," he murmured. "Save me some food."

As I ate the food Penn had brought us, I felt the same greedy focus toward the food as I saw in his eyes when he looked at us. The more he drove, however, the more relaxed he became, and his natural cheerfulness returned.

"Have you pondered the story I told you the other day?" he asked me. In the fields surrounding us I saw all manner of animals as colorful as the bountiful flowers. "The one about the pheasants? I was speaking to my woman Lederra, and telling her what a fine young couple you were, and she said she would if you wished be willing to talk to you for no price at all. See, your friend is wrong when he says only money dominates my mind. For no price at all my fecund Lederra can tell you secrets that will bring you babies beyond your wildest dreams. Conversely, she can tell you secrets that will bring you no babies for the rest of your life." He laughed heartily. "Of course, having no babies is easy, even you know how to do that!"

I stood up in the motorsled. I'd never felt the wind on my face in quite this way before. I could hardly breathe or open my eyes. The wind whipped loudly in my ears and I couldn't help smiling. When I sat down again I felt especially cozy, knowing how hard the wind whipped all around me.

"What a job you have!" I said to the man, leaning forward. "It's wonderful. To think this exists while others suffer."

His face lit up at the chance for more conversation. "It's dangerous, young lady. As a driver I meet all manner of mean, insane people. Once a day I meet a robber. One day I met three. They were delightful people, if you ignore their line of work."

"You're fortunate they didn't rob you."

"Of course they robbed me, but I don't hold a grudge. If I did, where would I be? Sitting here full of grudges. And as I said, all three were delightful. Two were a nice couple like you and your friend. You two don't plan on robbing me, do you? I've been robbed once already this day. If you plan to rob me, come back early tomorrow instead. I won't have much of value with me so early, but I'll be tired and off guard. By the end of the day I'm mean and alert."

"We don't plan to rob you. I like you," I said.

"It isn't a matter of liking me, who wouldn't like

me?"

The scent of flowers made the air seem thick and hard to breathe. And with all the bustle and colors around me, I began to wish for stillness and the quiet beauty of sand. Penn talked on. "As a rule I don't hold grudges, but I must tell you that every now and then I am tempted to hold a grudge against certain of my neighbors. The ones I'm thinking of cheated me during a business arrangement. You're not going to cheat me, are you? They owe me money, and I told them that in the interests of fairness I'm going to take it off the money I owe them. So don't cheat me. I've been cheated enough in my life."

"How can your neighbors owe you if it is you who owe them?"

"Money is a complicated thing, young lady."

"But between two separate entities, only one can owe the other money," I persisted. "If you both owe each other money, then either the debts cancel each other out or one of you owes more than the other, in which case the one who owes the most is the one you would have to say owes money. Do I make myself clear?"

"An interesting perspective, and I assure you I'll give it serious contemplation when I get home."

"But can you explain your point of view?"

Penn, driving carelessly, almost hit someone hurrying across in front of us. He paused the vehicle and leaned out the window, "Watch where you're going, you brainless father of whores!"

"You frigid son of murderers!" the pedestrian shouted.

cynthia kadohata

"Frigid! I have twenty children, you ugly son of dogs!"

"Half-blind driver of petty thieves!"

"What! Insult my passengers? I'll speak with you no more, sir!" Then they both giggled and saluted each other before Penn drove on.

"Did you know that man?"

"What man? That was no man, that was an animal." He laughed, tooted his siren and waved at the man we'd left behind. "You have to keep your tongue sharp in this business. I practice sharpening it with whoever will practice with me."

"It seems in Artroro a tongue is the most important part of the anatomy."

"Another interesting perspective! I'll contemplate that later as well."

"You yourself just said you need to keep your tongue sharp."

"Once said, the moment is past, young lady. We must move on to more important details. Tell me, who do you two run from?"

"I'm afraid you'll have to ask my friend, Moor. My name is Mariska, by the way. Moor understands these things better than I."

"You understand these things well enough to avoid my question."

"Tonight while you contemplate what I've said, I shall contemplate what you have just said."

"I risk my freedom by driving you to Clasmata. Have I not the right to know why you run and from whom?"

"Perhaps your freedom will be better served by

not knowing."

He laughed. "Son of a blue-bellied beast! You're right, it will be better served. But my curiosity will not. Ordinarily I don't make it my business to know my passengers' affairs, but the two of you have opened wide my sympathies. So confide in me, and I promise you you'll reach your destination safely."

I looked at Moor, who still slept deeply. I liked Penn. He struck me now as not so much greedy as happily and unabashedly opportunistic.

"In the act of protecting ourselves, it seems we may have inadvertently caused someone's death," I said.

"Who would not give you the right to protect yourself?"

"We were protecting ourselves during the commission of a crime, at least by Soom Kali's laws."

"Ah, no offense to your sleeping friend, whom I swear to you I respect and love as if he were my own son, but the Soom Kali are insolent warmongers. Then I take it you murdered a Soom Kali?"

"A soldier."

"A soldier! What? You ask me to drive you to Clasmata without telling me you've murdered a poor innocent soldier who was only doing his job and whose death for all you know has left a family of ten to starve? I will speak to your friend Moor the Soom Kali as soon as he awakes. The price as quoted to me is entirely insufficient."

"You just said we had the right to protect ourselves."

"And I meant it. I don't fault you, I only say the price will not do."

"Perhaps you're exaggerating your case."

"What? And now you accuse me of exaggeration. Young lady, you've wounded me even as my own children wound me when they don't live up to my expectations."

I thought that over, and then laughed.

He grumbled to himself. "Moor will hear of this," he said.

We drove quietly along for a while through the heavenly fields that now surrounded us. Every so often ships passed overhead, or vehicles passed us by. As evening approached I saw something I'd never seen before but had only heard existed: fog, the presence of so much water in the atmosphere that you could see the air. The fog blew across our path and over the endless fields as if it were alive rather than simply drops of water moved by the winds. These fog beings seemed to have a destination, and I looked at where they'd come from, and where they were going. In one direction night had nearly fallen, the horizon deep gray. In the other direction the sun had just passed out of sight and the fog diffused the sunlight and colored the air red.

I fell asleep and dreamed that Moor and I were light enough to ride this humid air that you could see. We felt the breeze against our cheeks as we floated on a wisp of fog, traveling from a world of darkness into a world of romantic light. I awoke to hear Moor and Penn arguing.

When I sat up straighter Moor looked at me balefully. "I tell you, it's not enough, sir," said Penn.

Moor said, "Then you must let us off at the next town, and we'll pay you for your troubles."

"Now listen to yourself," Penn said, suddenly conciliatory. "I would sooner drive myself over a cliff than abandon you." He turned around toward me. "I thought I heard you back there. Talk some sense into this young hothead, tell him how much I love him."

"He claims to love you like his own son," I said.

"Claims! What did I do to deserve this?" Penn said. "Oh, oh, the pain of betrayal is a great pain indeed."

"We haven't got enough to pay what you ask," said Moor, himself becoming conciliatory. "We have no desire to cheat you. But you ask the impossible."

"I'll compromise with you. I have fifteen children at home and my wife herself works day and night as I do. I can't take such a chance as you ask of me, but I will drive you as far as two villages over, and then you must pay me less than I ask but more than you think the ride was worth. Then I will return home, and you must find a new driver to Clasmata."

"All right," said Moor tiredly. "Drive us as far as you will." He turned to me. "Perhaps I've made a mistake. We should have just bought a vehicle. It would be less trouble." He leaned back and closed his eyes, murmuring, "But I was so sleepy I didn't think I could drive."

In front of us I could see the plains would soon end, replaced by prodigious hills. Night had fallen all around now. The fog had passed. I, too, closed my eyes, and this time dreamt somber dreams of capture and death. Another time I half woke to see Penn had gotten out and was talking on a contactor. I fell asleep again and didn't wake up until we'd reached the second town over, a town surrounded by dark hills. Moor and I got out with our pack of jewels and the dogs, and Moor paid our driver. Penn took my hands and looked at me with no pretense and an expression of such solemn affection I knew it broke his heart to leave us this way.

"Please forgive me, young lady. And believe me when I tell you that what you've paid me will do much good in my family. And believe me further when I tell you how fond I am of you and your hotheaded friend. But Lederra and I have a family of twenty-one to support and I can't put myself in danger. What would she do without me?"

"You mustn't feel guilty," I said. "My parents would have done the same thing, I'm sure, because of how much they loved us." The air was crisp now, and the moonless sky black. The lights in this town were the strange lights of the first town we visited, and not the warm lamps of Soom Kali. I knew how to read the word "inn" now, and saw several before us. "At least it won't be hard to find a place to stay." I saw shadows moving in the distance.

Before I could stop him, Moor had grabbed hold of Penn's arm and held his knife to the driver's heavy neck. "Tell me, what do you think you've done that we must forgive you for? Who is that ahead of us?"

"Well, as I said, just, I, leaving, you, here." I'd never heard him so inarticulate. Moor glanced furtively around. "Mariska, get the dogs back in, and yourself as well." He pulled Penn back into the vehicle.

"Moor!" I said. "He's done all he can for us."

"You yourself said to trust no one. I don't trust him."

"Surely no one does, but does that mean we should abuse his hospitality?"

"Where's your knife?"

"Here, but why?"

"You must hold it to his neck as you see me doing. I'm going to drive."

"Moor, we mustn't act like savages. I know you don't like him but—"

Moor switched off the motorsled's pale lights and turned the vehicle around, back toward where we'd come from.

"As time passes you'll see that a savage is not what you think it is," he snapped.

The path before us sloped downhill, and Moor let the motorsled move quickly by gravity down the slope. There were shouts behind us, and I turned around to see what seemed like an explosion of lights, vehicles, and people. Penn socked me hard in the face, and, yelling "Please forgive me," hopped out of the motorsled with his jewels and ours as well. He fell with a shout of pain and disappeared immediately in the night. The motorsled moved frighteningly quickly now. In the darkness I could barely see what came before us and could only hope that Moor kept us on course. I rubbed my aching eye socket. Moor turned down a side path, or what I assumed was a side path since I couldn't see clearly. Gliding down the invisible path this way made me strangely giddy. A white doglike creature sprang through the bushes and turned to watch us. The motorsled itself was so quiet I could hear leaves rustling all around me. Though I'd been taught that one must be ever ready to accept death, as I glided through the fog the only thought in my head was, "I love this life."

4.

Down, down, down. I hadn't realized how high we'd driven. At first I felt I shouldn't talk, shouldn't make any noise at all. I could barely make out the fields and bushes rushing silently by in the blackness. Behind us the black hill rose up and expanded as we descended. Above the very top of the hill a group of stars I knew well sparkled as I'd seen them do many times in Bakshami. Usually I hadn't stayed up this late, so I rarely saw them so high on the horizon as they were tonight.

"Do you know where we're going?" I asked softly.

"As is often the case when I'm with you, I know more about where I'm going from than where I'm going to."

"Are you angry with me?"

He concentrated on maneuvering the motorsled around a perilous twist and after that didn't talk at all. I hoped we would never reach the bottom of the hill and stop gliding in this way. At the bottom of the hill we would have to decide which way to turn, and I didn't think he knew. Logically, we would turn in the direction we'd been going before we got sidetracked. Before we reached bottom Moor stopped the motorsled near a cliff.

"We should get out," he said.

"Why not take this thing to Clasmata?"

"Too easily traced. No doubt they already know

exactly where we are and will be waiting at the bottom."

"How can they know?"

"Penn will already have given our pursuers the motorsled's electronic tracking number. They'll find us no matter where we go. If we steal this car now, we'll have Artroran soldiers as well as bounty hunters involved."

"Perhaps Penn won't tell them." But even I didn't believe that. "Why don't we remove this tracking device and continue on our way down?"

"Every device is implanted in a different place. I don't know where it is." We all got out of the motorsled, and Moor sent it down the path, where eventually we heard it run into the hillside. We decided to try to get around the side of the hill toward where we'd been going. So we turned and walked awkwardly in the blackness. We walked sideways along the slope of the hill, so it was hard to get a firm foothold. At some point we headed downward, and then we headed up the next hill. We climbed several hills in this way, and after a while I lost all sense of direction. Toward morning when it had begun to drizzle, we hid ourselves in some bushes to sleep. When we woke, fog moved all around over the green hills, and the pale gray sky grew brighter beyond the fog. At times the mist grew so heavy that when I held out my own hand I could see white trails caressing it.

Having both lost track of the direction, we didn't know whether continuing to walk would help or hurt our cause. Moor leaned back, and some of the tension left his face while he enjoyed the magic and changing scenery around us. "Sometimes the fog remains for days. Even with all their tracking devices and soldiers, the fog thwarts the Artrorans. In my country it is said that the fogs of Artroro keep the criminals in business."

"Since I am now a criminal, I approve of this fog. But think, you would have been a soldier chasing such as me in the countryside of Soom Kali."

"It's too late for me to be a soldier now," he said.

"How can one who aspired to be a soldier now aspire to escape them?"

"I would have been a just soldier and believe I am a just criminal as well."

"A soldier must follow orders first and justice second." The fog had grown heavier still. The dogs, sleeping down the way, passed in and out of my vision. Moor hadn't answered. "Do you regret that what you assumed would be your future has now escaped your reach?" I asked.

"No. No," he said.

"Moor." I touched his cool face. "I would not have let you come had I known the future. As a Bakshami I've no love of soldiers, but I would rather see you a soldier than pursued by one."

"And I would rather lie here beside you than see you pursued alone by soldiers, even just ones. But..." He rolled his eyes skyward, but couldn't see the sky. "This is so different than my life was. And what of you?"

"I was betrothed to the meat-seasoner's son. My own parents were glassmakers as well as leaders. I hoped to become a dog trainer."

He smiled suddenly. "All in all I like this turn my life has taken. Don't get me wrong. I would have been a good soldier. I'm not immune to the satisfactions of possessing power over others, nor to the satisfactions of standing strong as part of a group. But now in my life I will find other satisfactions instead."

"That's as your father wished." I immediately wished I hadn't mentioned his father, for his face hardened into a sort of rock, like the faces carved on his door at home. He sat up and studied the haze all around. After a while his face softened. And the softness in his face made me feel sad. I knew that because Moor helped me, his beautiful face would not know peace for a long time. We had killed his friend and had become fugitives.

He rose wearily.

"Perhaps we should walk now while the fog hides us. This fog is a gift that we should take and use. And then we must find new gifts."

The dogs rose reluctantly, and the four of us began walking. We judged the position of the sun from the way brightness was distributed in the haze. After more than an hour of walking, we were surprised to come upon Penn's motorsled, sitting like an illusion among the swirls of fog.

"We're lost!" I said.

"We were lost," he said wearily. "Now we're not."

"We should take this vehicle as a gift."

"Or a trap," Moor said. "But you're lucky."

Lucky or not, the motorsled refused to start. But looking out over the hills, it was hard to feel disappointed. The fog rose from the earth like silver evaporating. We walked all day without eating, and at night we slept in some bushes, huddled together to keep warm. When we woke up the fog still covered the area, and this time we walked straight down a hill until we reached flat ground. There was a village here, and Moor reached his friend on a contactor. I walked a bit with the dogs and returned to hear part of Moor's end of the conversation.

"Yes, yes, she knows that. After all, it's her parents...She has great talents in the area of walking, very strong legs, and in general she possesses excellent coordination...We would need to leave this area quickly...I'm not sure of our town. Wait, I see a sign saying Plima. Yes, there's another sign. The town is called Plima...All right, then, I'll meet your friend there and see you within five sunrises."

He disconnected. "What scheme have you committed us to?" I said.

"My friend has a standing offer to do business in Forma. He will take us there."

"What kind of standing offer? Legal?"

"We're in no position to ask such questions. Nothing is legal in Forma. You must walk on the left some days, and on the right others, depending on the law. My friend will send a driver here."

Once more I turned away in shame, for in truth I was afraid to search for my parents. The hate I thought I'd felt for Forma, as well as the courage I possessed in my dreams, now deteriorated into fear. "This reliance on drivers has already grown tiresome," I snapped.

He laughed. "You may walk." And then his face

the glass mountains

took on that responsive look again. "What would you have me do? Romance you as a Bakshami man would do? That falseness in romance offends me."

The fog began to lift while we walked to the next town. The walk seemed long, even to me. I was so sleepy and hungry that the fog seemed like part of a dream. When it lifted I saw everything was all too real. The town might have seemed quaint to me just a few days earlier, but now I saw betrayal in every face I saw. According to Moor, immigrants outnumbered native Artrorans in these outlying towns, and most of them struggled to make a living.

My eye still throbbed where Penn had punched me. Moor had not mentioned my bruise, even as I saw him studying it. Bruises were a part of battle, nothing more, nothing less. The fog had lifted and I looked around for soldiers. But we'd walked a fair distance from where Penn had betrayed us, and there was no sign here of our pursuers.

The friend of Moor's friend hadn't arrived yet, and we passed another night in the bushes. As I lay in the cold bushes, huddled up against Moor, I knew it was inevitable that I should go to Forma now that the opportunity had come to me. And yet I was scared. At every step of this new life I felt fear, just as in every step of my old life I had known no fear.

In the morning, our new driver was waiting for us at the far end of town. I could hardly walk I was so hungry.

"There he is," said Moor.

"How can you be sure? We must be careful who we trust."

"My friend said the driver's hair would hang in curls."

The man in the motorsled had long curled brown hair. He nodded to us as we approached and we climbed in wordlessly. When he drove off, we still hadn't spoken. He seemed more interested in the dogs than in us. Every so often he would scratch Artie in a seat near him, and a couple of times he turned to smile at Shami. I'd vowed to trust no one, but as a Bakshami I couldn't help trusting a man who liked my dogs.

Moor leaned forward. "How long is the ride?" he said.

The man bowed his head once quickly.

I leaned forward, too. "Do you like dogs?" I said, and he bowed his head quickly again.

Moor and I both leaned back. The man motioned us forward with his hands and pointed at his mouth as he smiled. Then he covered his mouth. "Are you mute?" Moor asked, and the man nodded.

As he drove I sleepily watched the landscape and soon realized that I was even more tired than hungry. That was the last thought I remembered before I woke up again. It was night, and the fog had drifted back in. The motorsled crawled along, the driver leaning forward. He'd turned on only the weakest lights. He sat right in front of me, but his outline was vague. I tapped his shoulder and he jumped, then laughed silently and nodded at me.

"I need to stop," I said.

He raised a hand in acknowledgment and pulled over while Moor opened his eyes sleepily. The driver gave me a lamp to carry and I walked out into the fog to pee. Though I walked just a few measures away, when I turned back I couldn't see even the form of the motorsled. I stood very still and heard someone walking not far from me, and when he stopped I called out.

"Moor?" My voice sounded small in the darkness.

"Coming." In a moment he stepped out of the fog and into my small circle of vision. I'd set the lamp down and could see nothing but Moor and the fog around us.

"How long is the drive?"

"It depends how many breaks our driver needs. I'm starving, so I hope we stop for food."

"Me, too. I'm surprised your friend didn't tell you he was a mute."

"I am, too. But I remember once he told me it was easier for a mute to keep secrets because by the time he has found a tablet to write down your secrets in order to pass them on, he has realized it's best not to betray you. And my friend has many secrets."

"How do you know this friend?"

"I helped him once as I am helping you."

"You helped get him out of Soom Kali?

"I hid him in our house when soldiers searched for him."

"Why did they search for him?"

"He killed his sick father."

"And you helped him when you yourself have cared so long for your own father?"

"I would never kill my own father, it's true. But my friend's heart was pure, that's why he could do it. I could never kill my father because my heart is not pure."

"I've never heard such nonsense."

"There have been many times I've wanted to kill my father because I was angry with him or tired of taking care of him day after day. But my friend never had such feelings about his father. He loved him dearly and never thought of killing out of anger or fatigue, only from mercy. So though my father, like his, has asked me to end his life by stabbing his heart, unlike my friend I could not do it. Because doing so would satisfy a part of me I am ashamed of. It's a small part, a part much smaller than the part that loves him, but it exists nevertheless. He has been cruel to both me and my mother at times, and despite his sickness I haven't forgotten the cruelty, only forgiven it." Moor spoke with a bitter sadness I'd never seen in him. But I admired how well he knew the darkness inside of himself as well as the light.

I stood on tip-toes and kissed him deeply on his lips. I wanted to erase the sadness in his voice, but the more passionately we kissed the more I felt swept up in his sadness until it filled me with my own. As a supposedly stoic Bakshami I didn't like to dwell on such things, so I kissed him harder and harder until the passion we felt erased all other feelings. But a new light shone on us then, and our driver stood smiling and nodding apologetically. He'd taken the dogs out as well, and the five of us returned to the motorsled.

Back in our seats, Moor asked about food, but the driver just showed us his empty palms. And so we drove for three more days, stopping each day so the driver might sleep in his seat while we wandered about and gave the dogs a chance to exercise. I don't know whether our driver sneaked food while we slept, but we ourselves didn't eat for the entire drive. Sometimes when we stopped the desperate dogs chewed on flower stems.

Moor and I would sit in the motorsled whispering to each other about food, scheming about how we were going to check the driver for hidden food, describing for each other what we would eat as soon as we found Moor's friend. One night as the driver slept we did check him and the motorsled, but we found nothing. As we were searching, we saw the driver watching us, but he closed his eyes again.

On the third day we entered the biggest city I'd ever seen; indeed, the only city I'd ever seen. Smooth towering buildings of metal, glass, stone, and wood stretched so high I feared one would fall on us as we drove among them. Ships flew across the sky, and on the ground the muscular Artrorans looked with mild curiosity at us as I hung out of the motorsled and stared at them. The buildings were as majestic as huge trees, with gigantic colorful banners rippling down some of their sides. Moor said the banners represented historical Artroran tribes, though there were very few people left with the pure blood of just one tribe. All the tribes had intermarried a long time ago, but the banners helped remind the populace of its origins and variety.

I couldn't decide whether to stare at the buildings or the people. The Artrorans, with their bulging muscles and shining eyes, were worthy competitors to the Soom Kali. They didn't seem as fast, as graceful, as the people of Soom Kali, but in a show of strength I would bet on an Artroran. Except for an occasional disdainful glance around, Moor looked straight ahead.

"You have to admit they seem very healthy," I said, trying to speak judiciously.

"They gain their health on the backs of the immigrants who work hard to keep this sector going and grow the food that builds their muscles. But how many immigrants do you see in this great city? None, at least not in this section of town. Not unless they're servants or contract workers."

"The Soom Kali don't tolerate any outsiders at all in their sector."

"We make our intentions clear. We don't invite them in only to abuse them. They know the price of entering our sector."

"Surely there must be some cooperation and affection between the natives here and the immigrants."

"Cooperation, surely, but such affection as exists moves in one direction—from the immigrants toward the natives. And it's more admiration and envy than affection." He pointed to one especially gorgeous building, built of stone with shining colored glass domes for roofs. "That was designed by an Artroran and built by immigrants."

We continued through the busiest part of the city and on to a ramshackle house down a dead end. Huge buildings Moor said were warehouses dwarfed the house. Our driver turned around, smiling, and indicated the house. I saw Moor, ever suspicious, fingering his knife as we walked up to the door.

"Hello!" he called out. "Zem! Are you there?"

"Come in," we heard a high male voice reply.

5.

Inside, piles of exquisite and unique items cluttered the floors and tables like so much junk. I was reminded of some of the items at Moor's lovely house. There were vases, paintings, bowls, embroideries, shoes, hats, furs, feathers, and a number of items I didn't recognize. Some of the bowls seemed not just to shine but to glow, and Moor said the metal came from another planet where anything was possible.

"What planet is that?"

"I don't know. Zem told me about it, but I've never been there. Maybe we can go with him one day."

Zem was an enormous bejeweled man with a slightly misshapen face and hands that made mine look like the hands of a baby. He tripped over a box as we came in, and the floor shook as he caught his balance. Artie and Shami growled at the three dogs that followed Zem into the room. The three were enormous, all almost as big as Artie.

"Moor! How handsome you look!" They hugged each other, Moor's arms barely reaching around Zem. Zem hugged me, too, and it was like reentering the womb the way he enveloped me in his warmth. "Mariska of the strong legs, how good to see you at last. Yes, yes, you do look strong. I know Bakshami have a reputation as hard workers, but I also know you've never been servants to any sector. So I hope you're able to take orders on my ship."

"We have no intention of being your servants," said Moor.

"Did I say servants? I meant companions and coworkers. We're all equal here. Let me rephrase that. This is my house but in my heart we're equal." He rubbed his leg where he'd tripped over the box. "The hardest work is only at the beginning when we load up. I need a great deal of provisions as I'm very fond of food."

He signaled to our driver, who'd slipped in the door behind us, and the driver left the room with the dogs. "He lives near Plima but comes to Clasmata to take care of my guard dogs on my frequent trips."

"How does he control the dogs if he doesn't speak?" I said.

"Hand signals, whistles, clucking noises, claps. He's ingenious at making noises. Somebody cut out his tongue in a fight he himself started and now he's a man of peace."

"The tongue causes many fights," said Moor.

"When do we leave for Forma?" I asked anxiously.

"Soon enough. Someone has offered me money to bring back artifacts. This sort of work is tedious for me. I'm not a natural adventurer. Who wants danger? But jewelry, that's something else again." He held up his hands and admired them. "Who would not want their wrists to glow with jewels? But I have almost as many jewels as I need now, enough to change completely every day for the rest of my life. I'm thinking of settling down and breeding soon, after I return from Forma. Do you two plan to breed?"

"We have no plans now," said Moor. "The future keeps finding us before we can make a plan."

"Then let the future come again! We'll leave to-morrow. I can use some good servants. I don't mean that! I consider us equals!" said Zem. His voice squeaked as he spoke. Later I was to learn that it squeaked whenever he lied. Sometimes it was hard to tell because he possessed an unusually high voice for a man, particularly a big man. "I swear to you, you will not be my servant. Moor saved my life once. And I'm the one taking the chance. It'll be two against one if there are any disagreements. I'll lose every debate."

"We haven't eaten in days," said Moor.

"What? Didn't my driver feed you? I told him to," his voice squeaked. "I swear to you I did. Let me feed you."

"You act like all the other immigrants to Artroro," I said. "It's hard to know when you tell the truth."

He laughed. "What? You mean you don't assume I'm always lying? How flattering."

"As a Soom Kali I would hope we could depend on you," said Moor.

"Unfortunately, you probably can. If I could just be more unreliable to people who can't help me, maybe I would get further ahead." He smiled warmly at Moor. "There are so few of our people here it's difficult for me. I feel lonely sometimes. Perhaps we can compete later, throw some knives." He turned to me. "No one can throw a knife like Moor."

"I've seen that."

We followed Zem into the kitchen. He walked slightly bow-legged, and his feet fell heavily with each step. Moor in contrast moved sleekly, the way Shami did. Zem tripped over some packages in the hallway, and his feet pounded to the floor. Moor and I smiled at each other. "You'd be surprised how graceful he is in an emergency," Moor said.

In the kitchen we ate a wonderful meal—since I'd left my village my meals often alternated between the minimum needed to keep myself from hunger and the maximum I could eat without feeling ill effects. Sometimes I went beyond those two extremes into feeling starved by the emptiness of my stomach and feeling stupefied by the fullness. Tonight I felt the latter, eating five different types of bread, a type of meat I'd never tasted that Zem said came from the sea, and all the fruit I wanted. I ate more than I'd ever eaten at once in my life, but Moor ate twice as much as I, and Zem three times.

During dinner, Zem told us he wanted us up early the next day to help him clean his ship. He also told us at dinner that the artifacts in his house came from many lands and that he sold them to customers or obtained them on commission. Evidently some wealthy Artroran customers had decided that the decoration of their homes would be enhanced if they obtained artifacts from Forma. The work was secretive. Obtaining these artifacts was not exactly illegal, however, in that the Forman government itself often sold them against its own laws.

"I'm happy to fill up my years with adventure," said Moor.

"I don't mind an occasional minor adventure," said Zem.

"Even that is not the Bakshami way," I said. "For instance, my grandfather filled up his years with wisdom. By accompanying you, I may be giving up my way for a life of escapade."

"You have already given up your way," Moor pointed out.

"I once gave up my way of life," said Zem. "But I didn't give it up voluntarily. It was forced upon me." He looked at Moor. "Do you have secrets from her?"

"I haven't thought about it, as I have few secrets. I've told her about your father."

He nodded. "I've never felt sadness, regret, or shame over my father. All my life, I did as he asked. The last thing he told me was how much he loved me, and then I killed him." This time Zem spoke forthrightly, without guile. Even when he used guile, he used it like an amateur. I already felt affection for his clumsiness and transparent lies. "I considered going to see your elders myself once, to ask questions about my father before I, that is, before he passed away."

The dogs ran playfully through the kitchen, Artie with a precious-looking box in his mouth. Zem smiled at them, uncaring about whatever it was Artie held. As always when the dogs played, Artie behaved straightforwardly, simply taking an item in his mouth and trying to hold on to it as Shami chased him and attempted to get the item. And when she took an item in her mouth, he simply tried to pull it away from her. But as the smaller one she played more deviously, biting his legs and ears to make him drop whatever he held in his mouth and then grabbing her prize. Artie, twice her size, happily played with her while she bit him until he squealed. Only rarely did he attack her so hard in retaliation that she rolled on her back in surrender. Often he was the one to surrender.

"In general he treats her with the tolerance of a man in love," said Zem. "I've yet to treat a woman that way."

"So has Moor," I said.

"You underestimate my tolerance of you," he said.

"And you overestimate my bad qualities."

"Ha!" said Zem. "Overestimate, underestimate. It's all estimation, that's the important thing. Tell me both sides of your story, and I'll tell you exactly what I think. Forget all this estimation, it'll get you nowhere."

"She trusts everyone," said Moor. "Her trust will destroy me, and you, too, if you don't watch out."

"It isn't my fault. It's the fault of all the scoundrels you involve us with. Where do you find these thieves?"

"Score one merit for Moor," said Zem. "It's folly to trust thieves. They're only doing what they must."

"As I am," I said. "I come from a sector where one trusts neighbor and stranger alike."

"One merit for the strong-legged woman! She must trust whom she trusts."

"She cares more for her dogs than she does for me," said Moor.

"Merit! Merit!" shouted Zem in his high voice.

"That might change if you cared as much for me as my dogs did," I said.

"She matches you every time," said Zem. "I suggest you both have equal merit. Therefore you needn't estimate anymore but consider yourselves equal in both folly and wisdom." He yawned extravagantly. "It's time for me to go to bed. You two should get to sleep."

"Will there be only the three of us on your ship?" I said. "And can the dogs come?"

Zem laughed and looked at Moor. "You're right. Those dogs again! Yes, they can come. But are you sure your dogs can stand the rigors of flying?"

"They flew in a plane in Mallarr without reaction. I, on the other hand, got sick."

"A plane is different."

"My dogs can do anything yours can," I said.

He looked angry for the first time since I'd seen him, but it was a child's anger, the type that's quick to appear and quick to dissolve. "I take great pride in my dogs," he said. "But they don't like to travel."

"I'm sorry," I said. "I only meant that I, too, take pride in my dogs. Since you feel the same way about yours we understand each other."

That appeased him. "My unspeaking friend will watch my house and belongings while I'm gone. I might tell you that you may trust him for anything."

"But you said you told him to feed us, and he didn't."

"Oh, did I say that?" said Zem, his voice rising into a squeak. Then his voice lowered as he continued. "All right then, I advised him not to feed you.

After all, I can't afford to feed every beggar who comes along. I owe Moor my life, but now he is two, with two dogs."

"He's generous in all matters but those involving food," Moor said.

"We're hardly beggars," I said.

"But you do beg," said Zem.

"Merit!" I said, and we all laughed.

Moor and I slept in a tiny room almost filled by the bed. In bed he told me that while Zem had changed since the last time he saw him, Zem still followed his feelings as he always had. The bed, like our meal earlier, was very fine indeed, and on this fine bed Moor and I once more practiced breeding in anticipation of the twenty days in a row when I came into season each year. Later when we slept, I dreamed again of riding on the fog. The next morning Moor told me he'd had the same dream, and in this way I knew our spirits had joined.

·~

part (six)

I couldn't eat much breakfast the next day because my stomach was still adjusting to my big dinner. Moor didn't eat much either, but Zem ate almost as much as he had the previous night. He seemed hurt by our refusal to eat a lot, but his natural good spirits returned in a moment.

The ship we would take to Forma sat inside an immense warehouse in back. The round ship was twice the size of Zem's house, and clunky, not as sleek as the Forman and Soom Kali ships I'd seen. There was a hard quality to the metal, as if nothing could break this ship. But I knew this wasn't true; I saw dents and nicks in the surface. Zem said it had taken him a lot of mistakes to learn how to maneuver his ship. He'd unexpectedly won the ship gambling and had taken only a few lessons on working it.

We loaded up packages of herbs, oils, and ointments—considered planetwide to be staples of good health. The aromas excited me. They were like the aromas of life itself to an Artekkan. The thought surprised me because before my travels I'd never regarded myself as an Artekkan, only as a Bakshami.

Like Moor, Zem owned a variety of knives, and he decided to bring several so that he and Moor could compete.

"The only time you should stop competing is when you've lost your self-respect and your good health," Zem said. "Then, you know you're defeated."

"Have you ever reached that point?"

"I've lost my self-respect, and almost lost my good health. But then I regained everything," he said casually. He looked expectantly at me.

"And then what?"

"That's when I won this ship."

"Why do you continue to compete? Perhaps you could lose your ship just as the previous owner did."

He looked pained when I said that, but it was a pain he enjoyed feeling—the idea of losing his ship thrilled as well as pained him.

All day we loaded and arranged. Later Zem tinkered with the ship as Moor and I watched and learned. We would take the ship briefly into space where the Formans were less likely to notice us, and then descend to Forma.

When darkness fell Moor and I spent a short time exploring the sights of Clasmata. Everywhere, I saw people engaged in acts of enormous strength, lifting motorsleds that had broken down, pulling diseased trees out of the ground, hauling great blocks of stone. Even Moor, hailing as he did from a culture where people revered strength, grudgingly admired the Artrorans.

The color of sand dominated Bakshami, and the colors of dirt, stone, and metal overwhelmed a visitor to Soom Kali. But here in Artroro the buildings, trees, and flowers all burst forth with an array of colors that gave me a jolt of excitement every time I walked out into the city.

The city was much safer than the countryside and villages, and apparently the Artrorans believed this was because the immigrants were naturally more violent. The lights on the paths didn't give off the eerie luster of the night lamps in the outskirts. These lights glowed with a quality that was both opaque and vibrant, not like the moon or metal but like someone's eyes, perhaps. I didn't feel I could see through the lights, but at the same time their vibrancy gave them a somewhat transparent effect.

We saw groups of people laughing as they leisurely walked the paths. The lights enveloped them in a milky luminescence that made them fantastic and beautiful, and I imagined Moor and me enveloped in the same fantastic light. Late at night Moor and I ate by a lake in one of the vast parks. One or two people wandered, but no one paid us any mind. Food stands floated on the lake for any boaters who might want a snack. Opaque, vibrant lights in the shapes and colors of fruits decorated the stands.

"Someday we'll return under different circumstances," Moor promised me. The wind refreshed us with its coolness in the warm night. A man sat on the grass nearby, staring wistfully out at the lake. An aura of great fatigue surrounded him that even the night's peacefulness couldn't penetrate. Seeing him made me realize that such an aura was beginning to surround Moor and me.

"And when we return we'll stop at one of the fruit stands on the lake?" I said.

"I promise," Moor said, in one of his responsive moods. It was an idle promise, but I felt as full of bliss at that moment as I ever had.

As they often did, the dogs nuzzled noses as if

kissing, and then they wrestled briefly before tearing into the darkness of some trees and back into the light of a lamp.

But we needed to move forward.

Back at Zem's, he was ready to leave. While he explained to his unspeaking friend what needed doing in our absence, Moor and I sat in the console room of the ship. He explained to me that there was some sort of magnet in the center of the ship. The Soom Kali found fuel-based ships more reliable, but the Soom Kali ships did not go into space, even for a short time. Like Bakshami's, their culture faced inward. Most of Artekka faced inward. Restophlin was the only planet of the Thirteen Sisters that could be said to possess advanced technology. In fact, when told what Restophlin had achieved, most Artekkans would say the achievements were impossible and broke the known laws of science. These laws had been proved, said the engineers of Artekka.

Out a porthole I could see the warehouse, gray stone walls, piles of boxes, and occasional vermin scampering among the boxes and against the walls. My grandfather used to tell me that a scientific law was like a box inside another box, inside another, and so on endlessly. Every piece of scientific knowledge a person possessed lay inside another, more important piece of knowledge. He said the laws of mystery were just as powerful as those of science, but that other cultures had lost their respect for mystery.

I'd said I didn't see why I couldn't do both, and he'd replied that very few have time.

Outside, Zem's friend had attached a tow line to the ship and had started to drag us out of the warehouse just as Zem entered the room where Moor and I sat. "Why is he doing that?" I said. "I thought this thing could fly."

"Of course it can fly. But it can't drive."

When we got outside, the warehouse behind us seemed suddenly inviting and predictable. Zem tethered all the dogs in special cages, and then tethered Moor and me. The vehicle that had dragged us outside drove back into the warehouse, and Zem's friend closed the immense warehouse doors. Next came an acceleration that made my whole body tingle unpleasantly, the way my legs did when they lost circulation. When that stopped I saw Artroro through the clouds. In the city the lights of different colors bloomed like flowers all around, while far away I could see the eerie luster of the apparently cheaper lights used in immigrant areas. Another ship descended in the distance, and as we climbed higher I could see the whole blue sphere of Artekka. Looking down, it was as if I were slowly adjusting a viewer so that everything below grew smaller and smaller.

Moor had grown excited and was struggling to untether himself. When he finished he hurried to the window and stared down below. I freed myself as well and joined him. A part of me felt exhilarated at the impossibility of the distances involved. That I could be so far above the ground I'd walked on not long ago! My adventures were like those boxes of which Grandfather had spoken, each adventure a small box within a larger.

Moor stood at the controls helping Zem. "This one?" he was saying, and Zem nodded. I set free my dogs. We'd tethered them in padded cages. Shami lay inside hers sideways with drool falling out of her mouth.

"Shami's sick," I said.

"It's temporary," Zem called out. "It happens to a lot of dogs. People, too."

And as if on cue, I gagged and needed to sit down. I leaned against Shami's cage while her eyes rolled up to meet mine.

"Don't worry, beautiful dog, I feel the same way. It's temporary."

Artie came over and nudged me and then Shami. I hoped Zem was right. I couldn't imagine enduring this for long.

Moor knelt beside me. "Zem says that as soon as he's done he'll give you medication." He brushed the hair from my face. "You're sweating."

"It's hot in here."

"It's cool."

"There you go again, tormenting me," I said.

"I don't torment you, only tell you the truth."

"That's what I mean. If the truth is not sometimes a torment, what is?"

Zem giggled at us from the console. "Maybe you shouldn't talk."

"Why? It's not my words that make me gag but this ship."

Zem came up and pressed something sticky on my arm. In a second I started to feel better. My head still swam, but more mildly. Zem had brought an ar-

the glass mountains

ray of medicines that represented a hundred different colors, tastes, textures, and properties. After a while I couldn't tell whether Shami was sick because of the ship or because she'd taken too much medicine. She licked Zem's hand as if to tell him she appreciated all the medicines he'd brought for her. She was truly a sweet child.

"Better?" said Zem.

"Yes, but I still have to concentrate to keep from succumbing to the sickness."

"Good, concentration on a worthy cause is an excellent way to pass your time."

I spoke quietly to Moor. "What was Zem like when you knew him before?"

"He was the most decent person I ever met."

"For me, that would be my father and mother."

Moor administered still more medicine to Shami. Like me, she made a partial recovery. She sat up, her tongue hanging out and her eyes appearing a bit loose in their sockets.

"Will she and I be able to withstand this?"

"You have no choice. Choices are not always a part of battle."

"I don't believe in battles then. In Bakshami it is said that there are no choices unless there are many."

"You are not in Bakshami."

I felt suddenly sorry for myself. "Ohhh, Ohhh," I said. "You torment me again. My head hurts." As soon as I'd spoken I felt sorry, for I saw how worried my words made Moor. "I'll be fine. If I could only lie down."

"I'll show you where to lie momentarily," called out Zem. He howled joyously, as Cray the storyteller

We fell silent again when we heard hooting sounds, almost like a larabird's mating call, from above. I strained to hear a sign in the hooting. Some light filtered through the trees, but I didn't see any stars. What sky I could see exhibited a sheen from clouds. I could almost smell the humidity from all around, from the moss and the damp ground and the droplets on the leaves. Long, reflective things crawled across the ground, so many I had to push them out of my way or else slip on them. I toed a white plant growing from the ground, and it cracked easily in half, the wispy white top falling off the stiff stem. When I picked up the top portion, although it almost filled my palm, it was as light as something the tiniest portion of its size. I brought it to my nose; it smelled faintly of dirt.

Deciding to wait until daylight to find our way out of the forest, we returned back to the ship for a last night. I was glad. I felt sick from the flight, and Zem and Moor got sick, too. So while Shami was making a recovery, we humans spent our first night in Forma lying down feeling nauseated. Zem got well first even though he made the most noise, groaning like a woman in labor.

Moor suggested that after we parted ways, we should meet back at the ship in twenty sunrises.

"Sometimes no idea is better than an idea if the idea is a bad one," said Zem.

"What!"

"If the idea is worse than no idea, it's better to act on no idea than on the idea. That way everything stays the same. If everything is the same, at least you know what will happen next. Don't leave me!"

Moor dismissed Zem's squeaky drama, lightly touching his friend's face with his palm. "Twenty sunrises."

"Don't leave the ship! Don't leave me alone!" We managed to appease him by promising we would keep alert for any unusually delicious foods to bring back for him. And then we left. Zem had given us Forman clothes to blend in, but none of us looked as pale as I'd heard the Formans were. But Zem said many foreigners lived in Forma as working-class partial citizens.

Outside, the sky sprinkled. Everything around us was so green the air itself seemed green. Artie, whose spirit had deteriorated while Shami lay sick, ran happily through the trees, crashing among the bushes and fallen branches, jumping over fallen trees, and stopping occasionally to smell the slimy crawling things on the ground. There were fewer than last night, but those that remained were as big as my hands. Artie pushed at them with his paw and jumped forward and backward. They crawled so slowly I didn't see how they survived. I picked one up. It tickled my palm as it slowly moved over my hand and up my wrist and forearm. When it slipped off, a trail of glowing orange secretions lay on my skin, and the trails began to sting me. So even a slow animal such as this could protect itself.

After an hour we reached a path. The going was nothing compared to some of the walking I'd done in the past. The remnants of sickness had worn off and I felt exhilarated by the humidity and surfeit of green around us.

We heard voices in the distance. Moor had had his hand on his knife, which he always hid in his clothes. Now his arms hung at his side, but I saw the readiness in his limbs.

We came upon a man and a woman who looked at us guiltily and hurried off.

"They didn't even seem curious about us," I said.

"They're probably taking time off from work. Forma is a working society like no other, but they think they're free."

"How can they think they're free?"

"Because they're free to quit their jobs if they wish, but food, water, clothes, and so on, can only be bought. And energy and seeds can be supplied only by the state. The fruit from these seeds they buy bears seeds that themselves cannot bear fruit."

"I'm glad they didn't ask any questions. I was raised to tell the truth."

"And why do you who by tradition lie to your lovers tell the truth to strangers? Those strangers might harm you."

"Let them try. I'll tie them up and bury them in the dirt."

"Your words are violent, Bakshami girl. You've learned to speak thus during our travels."

"And cut them into pieces the size of my fingers!" said Zem's voice, from behind us.

We turned around. Zem stood panting a few feet away.

"I didn't hear you," said Moor. "I'm disappointed

with myself."

"We made enough noise. But you were distracted by sparring with Mariska. If I fall in love someday, must I contest every point with my mate as you do?"

"If so, you'll have my sympathies," said Moor.

"And mine as well," I said. "But I encourage you, anyway. Find a tall Soom Kali woman when you get back and have the tallest children on the planet."

"I was feeling better and came to see you off."

We climbed down a slope and sat along the rocky banks of a river.

"It must be nice to have a home," I said wistfully. "It's odd to think of people having a home, here where we don't belong. It's very pretty."

"What, do you grow timid?" said Zem. "Who comes to a strange land for a home and not adventure? That doesn't mean I like adventure, but unlike you I don't wish for what cannot be."

"What I really would wish is only to stay with Moor forever, even when he only walks from one end of a room to the other," I said, following the Bakshami ritual once more. "He's my universe now. Nothing in the world matters to me except Moor. My love for him dwarfs my love for my dogs and for my family."

"How long must I tolerate these ritualistic lies?" said Moor. But he spoke with the satisfaction I used to see in my parents as they bantered.

"Until they become the truth," I said.

"Ah, you mean to say I must engage in the ritual with you in order to end the ritual."

I turned to Zem. "Who has merit here?"

Zem sighed and watched the water. "Being with you two has made me realize I don't understand merit when it comes to love." Zem threw several pebbles into the water, and we watched the ripples. "I've become more Artroran than Soom Kali," he mused.

"In Soom Kali we don't disturb a stone unless we plan to use it," Moor explained.

"Look here," said Zem. "Let's make it twenty-four sunrises. If there is danger I must leave, but not before then. And you must not hesitate to abandon me as well if I'm not at the ship within that time. The Formans' weapons are as good as anyone's."

He tripped over a rock and good-naturedly laughed it off. "Ah, the rocks get their revenge," he said. He was disarming when he wasn't lying. Because his engaging qualities and his lying lived side by side, each seemed more potent.

Zem and Moor hugged passionately, and we watched Zem walk off with his bags. He made surprisingly little noise as he traversed through the greenery.

"He loves you more than I do!" I said.

Moor and I sat and watched the lively river, reluctant to start our journey. Instead we sat and ate dried meat and hard bread. Such a meal would have seemed satisfying enough while I trekked through the desert; in this new land it seemed barely palatable.

3.

We followed the first road we came upon and reached a town at nightfall. On many roads someone stood in plain dress, just watching, and we learned that these people were there to watch for law-breakers. At five inns we offered to work for a room, but two innkeepers told us they were full because of some sort of town celebration, and three told us they didn't take "partials." They told us this politely enough, but suspicion clouded their eyes. So we spent our second night in Forma sleeping outside behind an inn. We'd inquired about a driver but had been told there were few people who would work for partials, especially partials who owned only a few provisions with which to pay for a driver. Apparently a minuscule minority of partials had sufficient funds to purchase other partials, but one look at us told all onlookers that we were not among the privileged—if it was a privilege to buy another human being. The person who told us all this chastised us for speaking only Artroran and not bothering to learn Forman. She said the "best" partials were the ones who learned the language. In this crowded land where lived the greatest enemies my people had ever known, perhaps I would find the guidance of which my grandfather once spoke. I could smell something sweet and grainy, and felt sure a dead Bakshami lay nearby; but it turned out to be baking nearby. The food the Formans cooked smelled like death!

For several days we walked through town after town, our strong legs never tiring. There were few motorsleds—only people authorized by the state could own them. Apparently, the government made people buy licenses for motorsleds, pay taxes for owning property, and even buy licenses for owning dogs!

There were amazing places in this sector where there were nothing but roads, curling and tying into each other in complicated and beautifully symmetrical patterns, up and down and past fields and forests lit only by the moons at night. In the towns, we saw inns and fueling stations with lots lit in purplish lighting that seemed to wash away color. But for some reason I found those colorless lots rising out of the darkness poignant. Like the plain lights in the immigrant sections of Artroro, these purplish lights of Forma seemed to symbolize a struggle to me, against what I didn't know. But such a struggle might mean both dejection and hope, and that's what moved me. I couldn't understand why these people we saw, most of whom possessed only a perfunctory hostility toward us, would want to destroy my sector. What I saw didn't fit with what I had hated all this time.

These were simple, albeit rigid, people, who worked incessantly and didn't have time to worry much about world affairs. There were a surprising number of Bakshami refugees living here. We asked all the Bakshami we met for news of my parents, but many were scared to talk to us, and the rest knew nothing. Of course all of them were only partials, none full citizens, though there were rumors of interbreeding. Through odd jobs and overheard conversation we learned that the planet Artekka was becoming more dangerous all the time. Artroro and Forma had officially joined forces, turning the formerly unimportant sector of Forma into one of the most powerful sectors on the planet. There were four important alliances now forming. The strongest, led by Artroro, also had the greatest expansionist tendencies. The weakest, led by a kingdom called Cassan, consisted mostly of a group of monarchies with delusions of superiority. The third was a small and mysterious alliance headed by Ou-Nal, or Land of the Fish. The inhabitants of this dominion were rumored to be the only people on our planet not descended from the inhabitants of the Hooded Galaxy. The people of Ou-Nal supposedly descended from an amphibious tribe a hundred galaxies away.

The fourth alliance of Artekka, led by the formidable armies of Soom Kali, was the second strongest, thanks to the size and courage of Soom Kali's warrior tribes. Artroro and Soom Kali were moving closer to one of their always-fearsome wars, and Soom Kali was seeking to strengthen its alliances.

Several Bakshami had told us that there was a farm in a certain section of Forma that hired Bakshami servants. At one time or another, many Bakshami passed through there. We headed immediately to the farm.

After walking for a few hours one night through hilly darkness, Moor and I came to a shop. The purplish lights, after all that darkness and foliage outside, seemed to signal the entrance into a small store, a half-life world of what turned out to be containers of every size, shape, and texture: hard containers, round ones, malleable, rigid, shiny, bright and plain ones. One whole aisle of the store was devoted to medicines for every disease and its opposite—oily skin and dry skin, fatigue and an overabundance of energy, constipation and diarrhea, too much fat and too little fat. While many of the people we'd encountered certainly had the pasty look of ill health about them, I didn't see how the populace could have one disease while it also had the opposite. The store taught me much about this culture, and how lost it was. And yet this culture possessed the strength to destroy mine.

With funds from odd jobs, mostly involving personal servant work for me and lifting work for Moor, I bought meat and dried fruit, which I felt quite addicted to. But we tried not to spend much money, even though there were consumer laws stating that you must spend at least half of the money you earned, with a large portion of the rest of your money going to taxes and licenses.

Though Forma was one of the more crowded sectors, most of the people lived in cities where employment could be found. Sometimes we didn't see another person for long periods of time, yet even when we went through the smallest towns all the shops were open, with a few lonely motorsleds huddled around. Often Moor and I walked silently. As we walked I spent all my time thinking about my parents, going over everything they'd ever said and their expressions and gestures as they said it, and every so often I'd remember something new.

I thought a lot about how my mother used to come in and comb our hair and check on us every night; every night, no matter if someone she'd loved had just died, if we'd displeased her that day or if she'd argued with my father. One night after she checked on us, I had heard her in an argument with my father. Later I found her standing on the verandah. I'd heard a noise

the glass mountains

and had gone to check. I'd never seen her look so sad and asked her what was wrong. "Every day you're mated, you learn anew how hard it is," she said, with some bitterness. I didn't know what my father had done, but I knew it had hurt her terribly. My father was a wonderful man, but somehow he had hurt her. And after that night, though my mother still loved my father, and though her soul was still joined to his in a way that transcended the rational world, she never again adored him in exactly the same way she once had. Thinking of that now broke my heart for them. I wished their lives had been flawless, unblemished. I wished they had never suffered for even a moment.

It was drizzling as we walked through a ragged community of houses fronted with huge trees, both fake and real rocks, and plain arrangements of flowers. Most of the lights inside the houses were off, but as we walked some sort of sensor lights snapped on at almost every house and bathed us in a warning glow.

A busy, dirty road stretched behind many of the houses. In these drab houses, we knew, lived the wealthiest partials.

I'd just come into season, and that night we lay in the drizzle and for the first time since Moor and I met we no longer just practiced breeding. We copulated with abandon, not knowing the consequences of giving birth on a planet we hardly understood; just as we'd come to Forma not knowing the consequences; and just as, despite all the predictions ruling the lives of the Bakshami, I hadn't been able even to guess at the consequences of any of my actions since the day my family left our village. Mine was the opposite of most people's lives on Bakshami, where the past was indistinguishable from the present and the future.

We were close to the Forman border with a sector called Hathatu-me, a sector as inconsequential as Bakshami had always been considered. Forma had supposedly annexed it long ago, and supposedly a few Formans wandered through the countryside every day looking for trouble, but aside from the freedom fees paid by Hathatu-me to Forma, the two sectors had little connection. The people of Hathatu-me were so unemotional and irresolute that when Forma approached them about taking over, they agreed readily and without fanfare.

Every day I saw partials throng the streets heading toward the rooms in the towns in which they worked, and all night they crowded the main streets, trekking quietly back to their homes. Theirs was a trek without purpose. They went home to rest so that the next day they could do more work.

According to the Formans, all this work was part of what made them the most civilized people on the planet. I thought my people had worked hard, but next to the Formans we were laggards. Oh, we'd worked a sixth, a seventh, in busy times a fifth of a day, but this work was secondary to our rituals and our storytelling. Only our rituals and storytelling were exalted, and both of them involved our families, friends, and neighbors. But here the hardest working were exalted, so that people declared with admiration, "He certainly is hard-working," and likewise declared with derision, "How lazy he is."

We were half a day from the farm of which we'd heard when the farm, in a sense, reached us. A man approached us on the road. He was short, with a small head and beady bright green eyes. With him walked several small children. "Where are you two going?" he said.

"We're searching for work, perhaps from a generous man like yourself," said Moor. "We heard there's a farm near here that employs many partials, especially Bakshami." We spoke in this obsequious manner to any Forman who stopped us, for we'd quickly learned that this was the way partials were supposed to talk. So far the worst reaction we'd encountered had been a few loud insults.

"Do you speak the language?"

"Not well, but we will learn. We're new here but eager to serve."

"I am Karrid. As one of the owners of the farm you mentioned, I am eager to teach such wretches as you. Come with me if you want to work."

We glanced at each other before following silently. I could see other partials watching us out of the corners of their eyes. That is, they didn't look at us, but their awareness was aimed our way. I had not yet learned this trick of seeing what I wasn't looking at. When I looked at something it was because that was what I wanted to see.

"What are you looking at?" shouted the green-eyed man.

I started. It was as if he had read my mind. "Why, nothing sir, I would look only at what you would want me to look at."

"I thought you were looking at my legs. Where did you say you are from?"

"I'm a refugee from Bakshami, sir, and I beg your forgiveness for giving you the impression I was looking at your legs. I can assure you that if you didn't want me to be looking at your legs then I was not."

"Go ahead and look," he said grudgingly, and turned and walked with his children while we followed. I did look at Karrid's legs now, and saw that one was shorter than the other, but he'd learned with great skill to walk in such a way that you could not tell without looking closely at the difference in length. In Bakshami there lived many famous wise men and women who limped. They were a sort of cult of elders, perhaps not more brilliant than the others but with different ideas about their powers. According to rumor, as the power of these limpers had grown, they'd willed themselves to develop physical deformities so that they never forgot their place as servants of the Glass Mountains and the traditions. And their limps reminded all that though their powers seemed unlimited they were but people like the rest of us. Of course, acquiring a limp was a somewhat wily trick, because the deformities of these elders made them seem all the more amazing to someone like me, who stared at them with the belief that the more deformed they were, the more brilliant.

So as I stared at this man's limp I thought he might secretly be a brilliant man instead of the simple one he appeared to be. He turned suddenly.

"Ah, now you were looking at my legs."

"Sir, as I said before I was looking at your legs only if you wanted me to be looking at your legs. Otherwise I was simply walking, seeing the fields around us."

"You were either looking at my legs or you were not."

"I am a peasant in your shadow, and what I am doing, was doing, or will be doing, is influenced not by myself but by your preferences and desires and even by the shadows of your preferences and desires that chance to fall upon me."

He continued to walk. Moor said quietly to me, "You must stop looking at his legs. He doesn't like it."

"I did not even notice till he himself brought it up."

"Well, please stop. My fortunes are now linked to yours, and if you give offense I shall be punished, too."

"The man is insane. He asks whether I'm looking at something I haven't even noticed, and then he tells me to go ahead and look. But when I do, he turns upon me and demands to know what I am looking at."

"Whether he is insane or not has no bearing on whether or not he is our master."

"Master! Look at his size. I could beat him myself simply by spitting hard upon him and watching while my spit knocked him off his feet."

"And if you did as you say, what of the Forman security who would descend upon you and show you who is master of whom?"

"Of that I know nothing," I conceded. "I can

speak only of this man."

As the sun fell I began to wonder whether Karrid expected to walk all night. His children made no noise the whole way, not once laughing in the way of children, not even asking simple questions of each other. Once I saw one look questioningly at another, and the second nod his head. And there were other glances and gestures, but all behind their father's back. As time passed, the man grew more tired, his limp became more pronounced and I realized how much energy he expended each day hiding his impairment. We walked until his limp grew painful to watch, and in the darkness we finally reached a small stone structure, a modest version of the smallest Soom Kali homes.

The man chased a few dogs out of a bed, motioning us to sleep there. We lay silently, uncovered and huddled together in the cool night. At first our dogs slept with the others, but finally we called Artie and Shami over to sleep on us and keep us warm.

In the morning a child, one we hadn't seen last night, came to wake us with vigorous shakes. I could see whose child it was in the expressionless green eyes, eyes of a boy destined to a life of drudgery.

"What kind of work will we be doing?" Moor gently asked the boy.

The boy lowered his head somewhat, and then looked over his shoulder once before answering. "We make bowls here," he said without inflection. He added with the slightest emphasis, "Beautiful bowls."

Apparently the farm workers stayed in another part of the farm. And so Moor and I crafted bowls in that silent family. We got paid a pittance for one day, plus a meal. Every so often as we worked, Karrid would look at me suspiciously, but after a while I knew he grew to trust us because he no longer hid his limp from us but limped freely just as if we were a part of his family. I grew fond of Karrid, even as I knew his beliefs—he supported the invasion of Bakshami on the grounds that his leaders said it should be so.

Each day was the same. It was the way of my old life except that this life was not mine. I was not meant to be here just as these people who had invaded a desert were not meant to live in a desert. Each day I used the brief time I had before I went to bed to ask around the farm for word of my parents. But no one could help me. In the mornings I got up and ate what someone had left us in the night, and then I went into the work room where I made clay bowls all day. In the evening, there would be morsels of food. I would hurry to eat before once again making the rounds, seeking news. I'd never known such immobility. My interest in breeding diminished quickly, as did all other interests. At the end of several days Moor and I had about enough to purchase a day's worth of food, so that we could take a day off.

We walked a long while to the far end of the huge farm and looked out upon the workers. The fields and workers stretched as far as I could see. I called to the one nearest me.

"Are you Bakshami?"

He gazed upon me suspiciously.

"I only ask because I am Bakshami, too, and have come here in search of my parents."

cynthia kadohata

The man returned to his work without reply, but another worker nearby answered instead. "What clan?"

"Ba Mirada. My father once served as a mayor. My mother sat on the interclan council."

The man who hadn't spoken before looked up with disgust. "I was a mayor, too, girl, can't you see we're busy."

But the friendlier man came nearer. "I know them. They work in the house."

"Both of them? Are both alive?"

He nodded. "Good workers, I hear. They may own a house one day." He pointed toward the largest house in sight. "They work in there, but don't bother them now, you may get them in trouble. Go when the work day ends."

I tried not to get too excited lest the couple turned out to be someone else, but all day I imagined touching my parents, kissing them, lying in their arms, smelling them, hearing their voices. That evening after dark Moor and I walked over to the house and asked to see my parents. The partial who answered the door directed us to a series of disheveled dwellings in the distance.

The dwellings were made of glass, and I knew Bakshami had constructed them. They had no doors, so when we approached the one where I was told my parents lived Moor and I walked right into the darkness inside. I heard nothing but the buzzing of insects.

"Mother? Father?" I called, and heard more buzzing. "Father! Mother! It's me, Mariska!"

Slowly someone began to move, and a candle was lit. I ran toward my parents but stopped when I saw their faces full of horror. Instinctively I turned around to see whether danger existed, but no one stood there but Moor.

"This is Moor-ah Mal. He's my friend."

My father rushed to me and shook my shoulders. "What are you doing? How long have you been here?"

"Father, we've come to take you home."

Though his hut was empty, he looked around himself with great panic and signaled me to stop talking. My mother hadn't moved, just sat up from the floor staring in horror.

"Father!" He slapped my face to silence me, then whispered, "We *have* no home. The Formans have taken over even the hotlands. We are lucky to have even this."

"But you are free to leave," I said.

"Who told you that?"

"Forma is a free country, I have heard it said. We have a ship."

"We owe money, we can't leave."

"Father, if you leave these borders you will owe nobody money."

"I am an honest man. I am also a man of tradition. My father once predicted that only through obedience could I keep my family safe."

"Father, what are you talking about?"

My mother came over now and led my father back to the mats. Then she turned to me.

"You will get us all imprisoned," she said. "We must follow the law."

"But we're breaking no laws."

"It is against the law to discuss not paying your debts."

"Then we won't discuss it, we'll just leave." She turned her back on me and blew out the candle and I heard her lie down on her mat.

"Get out before I call someone."

"Mother? What is it? Have I done something?"

She would not answer. Moor pulled me away, and we returned to our own room. The next day I worked all day and then afterward returned alone to my parents' hut. But someone had constructed a stone door on their dwelling. I shouted for them, but the door remained closed. A few partials watched as I shouted at the closed door, but no one spoke to me. I frightened them, and they frightened me, though we were all Bakshami.

That night as we lay in bed Moor warned me that we must return to Zem's ship. The wind fell softly upon our faces, as if to tell us that it was time to leave.

"I grow weary of this work," said Moor. "We must either take your parents by force or leave without them."

"I as well am always tired," I said. "I would rather walk to my death than work at this all my life. And yet I find myself pleased and proud when I receive my salary each day. And with every bowl I make I find myself calculating what fraction of my daily funds I have earned. I find these thoughts satisfying."

"We must resist that feeling."

"Why?"

"When you give your dogs freedom, they become your slaves. When you give them rewards, they become slaves to the rewards. You have become slave to scant rewards, just like your parents. The Bakshami make easy slaves."

"I am no dog and no slave."

"Mariska, here where we work my muscles are atrophying, my speed is of little use, and my head suffers from tedium."

"I must wait. My parents will come to their senses." I tried to remember where I'd heard that phrase, "come to their senses," but I couldn't remember. "I prefer a predictable life. Such a life has not been mine for too long now."

"We must leave this place," he persisted. "We will be out of time soon. I crave sleep for the excitement of dreaming to compensate for my waking ennui. Your parents must make their own fate."

"I will not leave them."

"Then we will take them by force."

"I cannot force my own parents!"

"We may have to knock them out."

"That is impossible for a Bakshami."

"Then it is impossible for them to escape because I see no other way."

"This discussion serves no purpose."

He didn't answer, and in the morning we made bowls again. I noticed it had become hard for me to get started in the mornings because my hands had grown stiff, unused to this sort of work. I noticed, too, that Karrid's mate was unable to work because her hands were always stiff. One of the other workers told me she'd once been the fastest bowlmaker in the household.

So all day I worked at my bowls, noticing the increasing perfection of my bowls, and feeling increasing pride in them. I lost interest in the outside world and thought only of my bowls. After work I always realized how bored I'd been all day, but during work all I thought of was my bowls, and even in my dreams I would see bowls and dream of making bowls that were more perfect than perfect. I put all the energy from my trek into making bowls. I thought about the bowls more often than about my parents. Slavery quickly becomes hypnotic.

The others were obedient and quiet, almost without personality except for Karrid's obsessions over his limp.

One day Karrid came upon me so quietly I was shocked when I suddenly noticed him beside me, staring. "I heard you have been making trouble," he said with surprising firmness.

"My parents work here, but I wished only to speak with them, not make trouble."

"It's too late to undo what has been done."

"But nothing has been done," I said.

"You have made trouble," he said.

He said nothing more, and this time when he walked away he held himself high and hid his limp, as if we were strangers again. Even I saw in his walk that we must leave, and though our exhaustion was severe that night, Moor and I prepared to depart.

When everyone else had fallen asleep, we hurried through the night, moving toward the place where my parents lived, unsure what laws we might have broken or what penalties might await us if we were caught. We were only halfway across the farm when we saw that behind us Karrid's home was now bathed in light. But no one seemed to be chasing us. Still, we hurried warily to my parents' hut.

The far end of the farm lay silent. In the black night the hut seemed dead, almost like a tomb. No matter how hard I pounded my parents would not answer. I began to believe they had moved. A few partial workers came out to see what the commotion was, but they immediately hurried back into their hovels. We now saw a motorsled in the distance.

"If we don't leave now, there may be no chance," said Moor.

"Father, they are coming. If you don't let me in, there's no chance for me. I don't know what will happen. But I will not leave without you." I was shouting now, and though everyone must have heard us from their hovels no one dared come out. "Mother! Father!" The motorsled headed our way.

"We must leave," said Moor.

"You must leave. Take the dogs. I'll meet you at the ship."

"You have no time."

"I will stand by my parents."

"Then you will perish alone. I will not wait for my demise. I am Soom Kali."

"I cannot leave." I pounded once more, until it seemed I had cracked the bones in my hands. "I cannot leave, Father, you must help me."

Now the motorsled had almost reached us. I had come this far only to be arrested. "Father, they're here. They've caught up with me."

cynthia kadohata

The door swung open and my father looked upon me with no expression. I grabbed my passive father and he ran listlessly beside me. Moor lifted my mother and carried her. She made no struggle.

As someone shouted in Forman behind us, we hurried into the tall fields and cut across to a busy road. It was almost morning, and the road was already thronged with partials going to work. We fell into place and moved at a moderate pace in order not to attract attention from those we passed. The brilliant sun rose on the horizon. But the sun rose on the wrong side of the horizon. It was the light from a fire, coming from the direction of Karrid's house. What it meant I didn't know, but I feared for Karrid and his silent green-eyed family. I did not understand the ways of Forma, nor did I entirely comprehend the purpose of authority. I comprehended leaders, those people whose surpassing wisdom and talent so outshone the judgment of others that one had no choice except to defer to them. But of authority I understood nothing.

Right before sunlight there were ships all throughout the sky, shining lights upon the ground.

"Could it be that they're searching for us?" I said. "A few partials?"

Moor said only, "Hide in the bushes."

I lay under some bushes with my parents and the dogs. The searchers never ceased all day, but they concentrated their efforts around where the fire had been. Smoke hung above them as if there were no wind at all. Moor, the dogs, and I lay unmoving the whole time, even soiling ourselves to avoid rustling the bushes. My parents didn't move either, and every time I glanced their way their eyes were open and unfeeling.

At night, with the ships gone, we headed back to the house to see what had become of Karrid. When we arrived we found the burnt bodies: children, and also the body of Karrid, his legs that he had hated so much scorched and blistered under him. He was alive. The scene reminded me of a smaller version of the massacre of my people in the desert. And yet these dead people had lived here. They could not be enemies of the Forman government; they themselves were Forman. I did not see how a Forman, even one who broke the laws, could be considered an enemy of Forma.

"Let us help you," said Moor. "Who shall we get to help?"

"No, no, I broke the law."

"But what law have you broken?" I cried.

"I knew you were colluding with your parents to get them to run from their debts. In truth, I felt for you. I also envied you, the way I first saw you walking with such brightness down the road. So I deserve all of this." He was weeping. "My children, my children." His children lay burned around him. My parents stood silently by.

"We'll bring you with us," I said. "We're going to our ship. We'll put you on my dog's back."

"I never wanted these legs," he said softly.

Moor was spreading ointments over Karrid's legs and then wrapping them in cloth.

"Then it's settled," Moor said.

Karrid was shaking his head. "I never should have

hired you for so long," he said tearfully. "In truth I broke a second law. I hired you for more than ten sunrises without asking you for your warrants. That's why I had to report you."

"You hired us and yet you reported us as well?"

"My conscience got the best of me. But I didn't realize it would come to this. They started the fire by accident when they stormed the place. It is only what I deserve. I broke the law!"

"But the law is wrong," I said. "And those who started the fire are wrong."

"Nobody has the right to criticize those who uphold the law. Let me die."

Moor spoke firmly now. "You must show us a way out of here," he said. "I have just decided. We came back for you and now your obligation is clear. Where I come from honor is not to be trifled with."

"Honor is following the law, young man. You have no honor."

"We must let him die if he wishes," I said. "Where I come from it is not honorable to force one to act against his will."

"We are not in Bakshami," Moor said sharply. Moor was by far the strongest of all of us, stronger most probably even than Artie. He stood up to his full height and his arms seemed to lie ready for anything at his side. "I insist," he said.

In this way we gained yet another companion.

4.

That night our reluctant guide rode on Moor's back

and mumbled directions. My parents plodded along in a daze. If it were not for the fact that they looked like my parents I would not have recognized them. The air was as still and untroubled as the towns through which we passed. Again I thought how it seemed impossible this could be the land of my enemies.

Aiding us tortured Karrid, that was plain. He wanted to turn us in, the way all his instincts implored him to do; yet some higher instinct told him that life was more valuable even than the law he adored. He suspected, and we knew, that if he turned us in we might be killed accidentally, the way partials sometimes were. So his instincts battled each other and his legs ached and oozed as he led us through this peaceful world that waged war. Several times people passed, and we nodded solemnly as they gazed at us suspiciously.

The stillness and the delightful air held no influence over the dogs. They seemed to feel tension everywhere and fought with each other so harshly that Karrid feared one would get hurt. Artie was much bigger, but Shami's fierceness possessed a demonlike quality. She darted in and out among us like some legendary beast. The dogs drew blood from each other. I was neither surprised nor greatly disturbed by this behavior. I'd often seen dogs act this way, sometimes in response to tension, sometimes for their own amusement. Artie and Shami continued to brutalize each other. I admired their agility and ferociousness and knew both of these qualities were at my disposal and would never be turned against me. But they were making too much noise.

"Quiet," I hissed, and they immediately ceased and became the sweet dogs I knew.

"How is your back, Moor?" I said.

"It will hold up because it must."

Someone passed a few measures away and paused to stare at us with alert distrust.

"Why is everyone here so suspicious?" I said when the stranger had passed.

"Who can say with certainty who is breaking the law and who not?" Karrid said. "Look at me, law-abiding all my life, and now I aid the likes of you. We must constantly be on the lookout for law-breakers."

"And what if you find them?"

"We must contact the authorities. Perhaps someone has already contacted them regarding us."

"We are breaking no law," I said. "Walking cannot be against the law."

"It depends where you walk."

"We walk through a town."

"It depends on the circumstances."

"The circumstances are we would like to save our lives. A world that has a law against saving one's own life is an irrational world indeed."

"It depends who you are. The law is not here to protect you. You are only partials."

"I would spit on that law if I could see it," I said angrily. I regretted my disrespect but not my anger.

"Fortunate for you then that you can't see it."

"And if I could and I did spit on it?"

He didn't answer, but Moor spoke for him. "The law here breathes with life just as a thunderstorm breathes with life. But unlike a thunderstorm a law possesses intelligence and intention. Don't spit on that which exceeds your power."

A new stranger passed, and I felt a vague fear growing in me. I began to wonder why these strangers happened to be passing on the same obscure road on which we walked. I couldn't tell whether my fear was groundless or justified. My stomach said it was justified. I would look into each suspicious face that passed, and even if we had not seen anyone for a long time I would wonder why so many people passed on this road. Why should anyone at all besides us travel on this road at this hour? Surely these people had homes. If they weren't passing just to stare with suspicion at us, then where were they going? It got so that I could scarcely contain my fear. Once I saw a hulking form far away and feared for our lives. But when the form grew closer it turned out to be a woman carrying a child in her arms and a pile of cloth on her head. And then I thought, If not to spy on us, why is this woman walking down this road with a child and a pile of cloth? The peaceful air held a virus of fear, and I had caught it.

Karrid was leading us to some underground tunnels that he'd discovered as a child. He said we might regroup there, hiding until the authorities moved on to fresh game. Then we might continue to Zem's ship. Karrid never told his law-abiding parents about the tunnels because they would have been obligated to tell the authorities, and he wanted the tunnels to remain a secret. As he spoke about the tunnels he seemed almost to forget his torment.

"I used to go down there first by myself, and then with my brothers and sisters. The tunnels stretched on forever. You could live there if you wanted! You could hide there! Across the sector there are other tunnels where certain mathematical cults live and speak in mathematical languages that only they understand. I've heard they spend all day discussing whether the number two is the number one split in half or two separate number ones. That the government tolerates them is proof that we're a free world. But the tunnels I'm taking you to are unknown. My brothers and I planted trees in front to hide them when we moved from there."

He fell asleep then, and Moor wondered aloud whether Karrid could be hallucinating, remembering a childhood that had never existed. So then I had a new fear to add to all the other fears overwhelming me. But on the outside I managed to appear calm. This thought gave me still another fear, that perhaps underneath his outer calm Moor was as scared as I was. I didn't like to think of Moor scared.

"Are you—" I started.

"No," he interrupted sharply.

"I was going to ask whether you're scared," I said.

"I know. I'm not."

"Not even somewhat?"

"I am always scared since I met you."

We came to a fork and tried to rouse Karrid, but he merely groaned. The tunnels were in the opposite direction from Zem's ship. We needed to decide whether to try to reach Zem's ship or to find the tunnels. Moor wanted to find the tunnels. He thought that we would not be able to make it to the ship in time. My parents did not voice an opinion. I searched the predictions and traditions for an answer, but none came. Therefore I voted with my logic, and with Moor.

Once, we saw a group of boisterous people walking toward us, and we immediately hid in some bushes. They stopped in the distance and huddled around something. Half the night seemed to pass before the group reached us and walked on. They moved in silence now, men and women but no children, and I could tell nothing from their expressions.

We continued after they'd left our sight. When we got to where they'd huddled, Moor pointed out something: a body sitting upright by the side of the road. It was a Bakshami—a partial—who looked eerily like my brother Maruk and whose bloodied face held insolence even in death. The body was still warm.

My mother fell to her knees before the Bakshami man and cried out, "Maruk! My son."

My father took her by the shoulders and said simply, "No."

"We must continue," said Moor urgently.

I formed a circle of leaves and rocks around the dead man, and we continued. "That will help to send him back to the hotlands, to become a part of the sand that bore him."

"We need to hurry," Moor said.

I stared at the dead Bakshami, whose life no doubt had been ruled by prediction as mine had been. Before the war few Bakshami who survived childhood died before their time. Seeing that dead man—whose life had been ruled by the same forces as mine and who so strongly resembled my brother—made me fear that all was chance now, for if he could die so might I. I could not know whether stopping would aid or hinder us, or whether hurrying would destroy us or save us. I saw this man watching the beautiful, peaceful road where flowers bloomed under the stars and promised all things to all passers. I remembered how many compulsive people stayed in the hotlands forever asking the elders questions about the future. They reasoned that each day circumstances changed; thus did their futures change in minute ways. What an elder might predict for me this day I had no idea. All was random now.

And in any case I was no longer in Bakshami. I was a partial now, in Forma, and I must act accordingly or else end up by the side of the road staring insolently at the flowers in the fields.

"He's dead," said Moor.

"I know," I said. "I was thinking he looked like my oldest brother."

"I mean Karrid."

He set down Karrid by the road as well, just a measure away from the Bakshami. I smelled an odor that was a mixture of Karrid's festering legs and the death of two friends.

"His legs won't bother him now," said Moor. Moor folded his legs so that you couldn't tell one was longer than the other. He hesitated. "Do you need to form a circle around him?"

"Perhaps I will." So again I placed rocks and leaves

around a dead man. Only then did we move on.

What we were looking for now was trees that looked as if they might be hiding an entrance to some tunnels. But I had no idea how a tree hiding an entrance might look different from any other tree. Karrid had told us which town he'd lived in as a child, and told us also what kind of trees he and his brothers had planted. In other words, he'd told very little of use to us. That night was the twenty-second from the time we'd arrived in Forma.

We slept all day and walked at night, and when we reached Karrid's old town we were aghast to see a huge sign in fifty different languages, apparently saying fifty times: "Visit the Legendary Tunnel—Purchase Passes Here." There was a map showing the location of the tunnel, and a pamphlet in Forman, Artroran, and a language I didn't recognize about how the tunnels attracted people from all over the planet and how this town had flourished after the tunnels were discovered a few years earlier by an amorous couple. Moor read to me from the Artroran.

Several branches of the tunnels were off limits, including one branch where, legend said, there existed a crevice where gravity was warped and people fell so slowly to their deaths that they would, according to the top scientists, probably starve before they burned to death at the center of the planet. Down another branch lived people who could see in the dark and hated all but themselves. One off-limit branch remained unexplored simply because for some reason people grew so frightened when they neared the branch that none dared venture forth. And so on, for eleven off-limit branches. If you even leaned over the crevice you would be caught in its pull and fall to your death, and if you even neared those who saw in the dark they would try to destroy you. A few people had accidentally learned these things, but whatever else was known about these branches had been learned through experiments with dogs. So said the signs and pamphlets Moor read to me.

"What kind of insane people would throw dogs down a crevice?" I asked.

When we went to the caves we found wooden booths apparently open during the day and selling all manner of tunnel paraphernalia.

"We should go in," Moor said.

My father spoke up for the first time since we'd left the farm. "But the sign says it's open only during the day."

Moor politely did not reply, but I replied for him. "Shall we let a sign stop us when we've come so far?"

"To what purpose do we enter against the law?"

"We will go in," I said firmly.

"Karrid insisted the tunnels were elaborate," said Moor. "He seemed to believe we could hide out in them."

"Again I ask, to what purpose?"

"We can hide in there, I tell you," I said. "Fate has brought us here for a reason." Or, for no reason, I thought. And even though I'd sworn not to abide by the predictions, I added, "It's dark in tunnels, the opposite of our world full of blinding sunlight. Maybe that's what my grandfather meant when he said I would find a guide somewhere the opposite of

Bakshami. And Karrid says the tunnels are a way of getting to Hathatu-me. No one will pay attention to us there."

Father did not answer, so we entered the tunnels, which were artificially lit for as far as we could see. We walked until the dogs grew restive, and still we could not see the end of the light in the main tunnel in which we walked. We began randomly to take offshoots, all of them marked with signs and lit by lights that emphasized their jagged shapes.

Apparently the Formans drove through here with vehicles during tours. We knew that, outside the tunnels, daylight might come at any moment, and a vehicle might then travel through these caves. So we didn't stop. I grew as exhausted as I ever had during all my walking. At least during the trek to the hotlands, I could sleep each night. Here there was no night or day. My legs felt stiff and arthritic, and the artificial lights made my head throb. Beyond the point when I first felt I could go no further, we were relieved and overjoyed to see that an offshoot of the tunnel through which we walked was not lit at the end. Moor's superior eyes spotted this sheltering darkness. As we hurried toward it we could hear noises far away, and as the noises neared we heard laughing. We hid in a lighted offshoot. A motorsled whizzed by full of people laughing. After that scare we rushed into the darkness, running desperately so that we could be engulfed by the safety of darkness. Unlike those who fear first what they don't know and then what they do, we feared only what we knew, which was the sounds of laughter behind us. When we reached the darkness we collapsed briefly, and then rose and kept going until we collapsed again. This time I fell asleep.

When I awoke I felt Moor at my right, Shami upon my chest at the left, and Artie at my feet. I heard my parents' breath. I felt a warm happy comfort and wished to stay in this cool cave forever. One by one my companions awoke, and when I could sit up without disturbing the sleep of another I sat up and gazed in the direction from which I thought we'd come. But in that and every direction only darkness met my eyes.

"We ran so far I can no longer see any light," I said.

"Speak softly."

"Do you suppose it is daylight outside the caves?"

"I don't know." He touched my arm to silence me, and we sat listening. There was no noise anywhere except my own breathing. There was not the slightest breeze against my face. I could see nothing and hear nothing. But Moor's senses were keener than mine, and he didn't lift his silencing touch from my arm. So we sat and sat until I could hear it, too, a soft sound, almost like the sound of water trickling. But, just as skin is unmistakable even when it is hiding among items of like color, the faraway sound of human voices was unmistakable to me. And I knew the voices were getting closer—that's why I could hear them now.

Moor pulled me and the dogs up and led us away, whispering that he would lead us in the direction opposite the voices he heard. We dared not turn on the lights Karrid had given us. Instead we moved away from the sounds of life in the same way that, earlier, we had fled the lights in the tunnels. Again we moved until I felt I could move no more. My parents never complained, but I knew they were exhausted. The dogs, also tired, whined occasionally. Though stronger, faster, and more agile than me, they needed more sleep.

Because I could not hear the voices unless I concentrated and stood still, I trusted Moor completely and found the same sense of relief in this trust that I'd once found in my trust of my parents. Finally he removed his hand from my arm and spoke. "I haven't heard them for a long time," he said softly.

My mother, who hardly spoke anymore, said, "If it's been a long time, why do you tell us only now when we've been so exhausted? Whether it's night or day outside, we have been walking a night and a day's time."

"Whoever's following us is probably resting, and we must as well," said Moor. "We must hope that when we leave this cave we will be somewhere safe."

My mother persisted. "Who are they? Why don't they take a motorsled?"

"They have one," said Moor. He spoke in my ear, though, so my mother couldn't hear, and I knew he'd grown angry with her. "Perhaps they don't know exactly where we are, just that someone is in here. They may have lights, but my hearing so exceeds the power of my sight that I can't know with certainty."

Moor didn't speak again, just sat down. We ate some of the provisions we'd brought and then lay on the rock ground. I could feel in the darkness that Moor's mood had softened, and though much still troubled him, he also seemed strangely relaxed and content, almost complacent. This was something new, something I'd never known in him. As he sank into sleep, I soothed him with affectionate ritualistic lies, about how my only desire in the world was to knead his feet when they tired of walking, and to kiss his temple when his head hurt, and to rub against his skin like a dog in the mud. But then I found I really did desire these things, and I kneaded his feet, kissed his temple, and rubbed against him like a dog in the mud.

I awoke later—how much later I don't know—to hear my father talking softly to no one in particular. He was in mid-sentence, as if he'd been speaking for a long time. "...never been without sight for so long," he was saying. "Did you know I was a mayor once? And now what good is it?"

Moor touched my arm. "We may have to leave soon. I think I heard something."

"Already?"

"I don't know how much time has passed."

"Maybe we should leave now even if you don't hear anything more. We can get farther ahead of whoever follows."

"I can't know where they are unless I hear them."

I looked around, saw nothing, but I imagined I could see Moor's shape, not see it exactly but know its presence with my eyes. "Perhaps we're followed by friends," said my father. "And we can't be sure which of the forbidden branches we've followed."

"If they're friends let them shout it to us," I said. "Until then, I will believe otherwise. Therefore, we find that we can be saved only by the voices of those who would destroy us." Moor leaned his head against my shoulder. I reached for his face and closed his eyes.

"I wonder how my father fares," he said. His lashes tickled my hands as his eyes reopened. This time I let them be. "My father used to have a room he kept just for himself. We never saw the inside of that room. He kept it locked and went in and out only when no one was watching. One day I found the keys and sneaked in, and discovered nothing but refuse in there, dirty platters and torn garments and the remains of all sorts of food. Nothing more. He did nothing in there but eat alone and brood. He caught me in that room and beat me so hard my mother feared I would die. When I got better she took me to Mallarr. On that trip she was killed. He changed after that. He never beat me again. But I have no desire to return to him even now."

"He was kind enough to let you go."

"The only kind act he ever performed. I appreciate it because I know kindness is difficult for him. In Soom Kali duty is easier than kindness. Sometimes in the act of following our duties we find ourselves performing acts of kindness. Perhaps my father felt he was only performing a duty."

"But we will return to see him one day," I said firmly.

"We'll go back," he said. "I promise you."

"I know I've asked you before and that you're honest. But let me ask you again. Have you regretted helping me?" We whispered to each other in the dark. "You might have been a great warrior."

cynthia kadohata

"A warrior's life at best is thrilling and lonely."

"I hate war and yet I fell in love with a warmonger."

"Sometimes I think two contradictions are more likely true than two harmonious facts."

"Even now at this moment, you have no regrets?"

"No."

"I could have spent my life in peace on that farm," said my father.

I said, "I can't tell whether the people are half free or half slaves."

"And where can you tell that? In Bakshami, where the people are slaves to the heat? Or in Soom Kali, where they're slaves to their own rigid rules?"

"Bakshami has always been free," I said. "So has Soom Kali. Only in Forma does the government make war on its own people."

There was a long silence. Then: "It's time," Moor said. We roused my parents and the dogs and started off again, walking as fast as we could without Moor losing the voices he heard far behind.

I wondered, and knew he did, too, which of the eleven forbidden caves we'd wandered down. Ultimately it didn't matter: whatever dangers we would face, we would face them.

I couldn't even hear my footsteps upon the ground, nor could I see a thing. Then Moor said urgently, "Run!" while at the same time momentarily preventing me from running by grabbing at my hand and pulling me close. I felt his swift hands yank the pack off my back and fling it aside to help me go faster. I felt his desperation. His lips brushed my cheek as he pulled

the glass mountains

off my pack. In a moment his pack dropped as well, and with it the last of our provisions. Voices echoed throughout the caves. I thought I saw the softest of lights far behind us, upon our path.

There is a joy to running for your life in nearly complete darkness. The six of us were alone with our speed. My panic was filled with the force of life and with the desire to keep not only my beating heart, but everything I'd ever known and seen and touched. All of that was there with me as I ran. I'd never run thus, in such darkness. I didn't even harbor the hope that nothing blocked my way, because I knew that if something blocked me I would not see it and nothing could be done, and therefore I shouldn't worry about that now, I should worry only about speed. So I had no hope and yet I was not hopeless but rather reckless. Moor and I laughed insanely at the recklessness we felt. Even my parents and the dogs half howled and half laughed with recklessness. And we were all laughing in this way as my father and the lovely Shami fell toward their deaths. Shami had been running to the left of us, and I heard her nimble footsteps end suddenly. Moor's laughing cut short as she plunged howling down the famous crevice. A second later my father groaned as he realized he, too, had plunged into the emptiness.

I stopped and saw that behind me a light shone and was moving quickly forward. "Father? Shami?" I said, unbelievingly.

"They're caught," Moor said. My mother still ran with mechanical steps ahead of us.

"Let me give them my hand."

cynthia kadohata

"Don't go near," he hissed. "It pulls you in."

"That's only legend."

"I felt it as I neared, like a hand beckoning me to die."

Shami whined, a whine that was weak from her terror. The light drew closer, and for the first time I saw the shapes of people, in a motorsled. I leaned not more than the width of a finger toward the edge of the crevice and felt dizziness fill my head and make my thoughts thick and heavy.

"Father? Answer me."

"Save yourself," he called out.

At the sound of his voice my hand for the first time found the place on my knife that made it feel like an extension of myself. I leaned over, fighting the dizziness, and threw the knife in the direction of my father's voice. He groaned, and I heard nothing else but Shami's whining. My father would never suffer again. Shami whined once more.

"I have only one knife, sweet puppy," I said. I fell to the ground and felt what Moor had, something like a hand beckoning me to die, pulling at me, making my brain dull and heavy. And then I felt something else as well, a pain piercing one leg so that I thought my leg was being cut in two. Something was pulling my other leg out of its socket.

Through the pain in my legs and thickness in my head I could hear Moor calling, "Mariska! What are you doing?" I didn't know where I was, or what I was doing. "We must run," he implored. "They're very near."

I heard growling and realized my pain came from

Artie's teeth pulling at my leg, fighting with the crevice for my life. Moor pulled my other leg. I doubted my body was strong enough to withstand the strength of Moor and Artie on the one hand, the crevice on the other. The beckoning hand tightened its grip. In proportion, the pain in my legs increased horribly and then I was sitting by the side of the crevice with the man I loved and the dog I'd raised. My head felt clear and my legs throbbed.

"I can't move," I said. "My legs."

Moor shouted, "If you love me you must run." There was bedlam, lights and voices and shouting. Moor fought off a Forman, and I staggered away. Artie and I ran, knowing that if we took a wrong step we, too, might fall to our deaths. Artie pulled at my clothes to make me hurry. My feet betrayed me as I stumbled, and my hurt legs bumped the hard ground. The absurd joy was gone. We bolted toward a fork. I staggered into the fork and all noise ceased. My legs made me want to cry out in pain with each step. I repeatedly darted into huge boulders and finally collapsed in terror and crawled toward the last boulder I'd hit, thinking that at least I might hide behind it. I felt blood flowing down my face from where I'd fallen against the rock. There was a sort of tiny cave, and I pulled myself into this cave and scrunched up, drawing in my legs and squeezing them to me.

There was no noise anywhere in these tunnels where noise carried so easily. I did not want to be first to make a sound, but neither did anyone else, if anyone else was even there.

.⌣

cynthia kadohata

part (seven)

I lay fearfully in my hole.

I heard a dull whine but felt so scared I couldn't even tell whether it was myself who whined. And then I realized that the whine came from far away, that it was my darling Shami as she realized she couldn't escape. After a while her whine was joined by a wailing from Artie that was so loud and full of the force of life it seemed more appropriate to birth than to death. Then silence.

I was barely able to move. I refused to show myself. And so the time passed, though how much time passed I don't know. I feared I would die like this— no one would be able to reach me, and I would no longer be able to maneuver myself enough to get out. It was hard to breathe in my hole; I felt I was barely getting enough air to live.

I didn't know whether I was dead or alive. I fantasized about how delightful it would be to let out a scream that would echo throughout the caves, and to run forth and be destroyed by the weapons of...I didn't know if anyone waited out there.

At moments I feared that the Formans were only torturing me, waiting until I had suffered so unbearably I preferred death to this existence. Then they would come in and save me from this insufferable cavity. Other times I felt certain no one was left but me. I had no idea what had become of Moor or my mother.

In my hole I learned about all the different types of misery, misery of loneliness, misery of loss, misery of immobility. I had known in the past the sort of acute pains that come from falling and cutting myself, from accidentally burning myself working on glass, or from getting hit by a powerful gust of sandy wind. But this kind of pain, the pain caused by stillness, was something new. It had seemed like nothing at first but built up moment by moment until finally it began building with increasing speed, so that it turned into something else altogether and produced a loathing of life and of myself such as I had never felt, and had never heard of anyone feeling in all my years in Bakshami. The more I couldn't move, the more I hated myself.

When I wasn't noticing the pain in my back, or my legs, or the horrible pain in my neck, or the hunger that wracked my stomach, I thought of Moor and my family, and of Shami falling to her death. I didn't know whether she would burn to death at the center of the planet, or whether she would starve to death from her slow fall. I hoped she would starve. Either death would be harrowing, a slow building up of pain similar to what I myself was experiencing, but starvation would be less painful. In starvation Shami might even experience a type of vertigo that she would take for enlightenment.

Shami's loud yelps and howls had ceased long ago, and except for an occasional vague cry in the distance, I didn't hear any noise. Once, from my troubled sleep, I thought I heard the last call of Shami, the dog I'd once saved, growling and cursing in a manner so savage it seemed to emanate a physical force that scratched my face and pulled at my hair, begging me to reply. And I woke up and returned the call, realizing this might be the last time she would ever hear me. I screamed and cursed as savagely as she had, until it was no longer me but something that possessed me that called out to her. Artie joined me. She answered, and then we were all cursing together. When we finished, my ears hurt from my own voice reverberating in my hole.

There was no sound. But I could not know why. Perhaps I'd stunned the Formans into silence. The fear I'd been living with welled up in me, and now I felt scared not that the Formans were still there but that they weren't, and I was alone in these awful dark caverns.

Something reached into my hole to touch me, and I froze. There was a whimpering then.

"Artie?" I called out softly, and he whimpered again.

I tried to move but couldn't without causing even more pain than I already felt. If I was stuck here for the rest of my life, I would rot in a place where my bones would never be discovered, would never migrate to the great mountains of my homeland.

"Artie!" I said again, this time joyfully. "Artie! Artie!"

He whimpered more, and I knew his heart had broken. Instead of trying to get out, I lay weeping and fearful in my cave. Without guidance I was nothing. My life had always been laid out for me by those who loved me, and now, as far as I knew, no one who loved me still lived or knew that I lived. Who would guide me?

I played a rhythm with my fingers against the rocks, but I didn't leave my hole. In this way I passed time until my fingers grew tired. Then, full of stale air, without hope and without feeling in my extremities, I decided to leave my hole. I'd almost forgotten how to will my hands and feet to move and cried out in pain as I stretched a foot tentatively out. When I finally emerged I found myself as frightened as ever and needed to fight the urge to creep back in. Still, as frightening as it seemed outside the hole, at least the air was fresher out there. So I continued crawling in the dark, feeling for other tiny caves in which Moor or my mother might have hidden. But I felt that, for the first time in my life, I was completely without human companionship.

Artie and I stumbled forward in the cave, and I realized that he whimpered from weakness. He normally ate a great deal and had not eaten for some time.

I would not have thought myself capable of greater despair than I'd already felt. But for some reason the despair I now felt over Artie's hunger overwhelmed my fear and even my pain. I forgot where I was, or why or how, and felt only a pure despondency that engulfed me in a sort of shimmering hot light which was not of the rational world but of another world I had never visited. I curled up as tightly as when I'd inhabited my hole and watched this light all around me. I felt somehow that everything I'd ever done had led to this moment, a moment when there was nothing left for me: Moor and my mother missing, Father dead, and Shami even still falling to her death when my intention from the start had been to save everyone I loved. So how was it that somehow all of this was connected to what had come before, to playing games with my sisters and brothers, to watching my parents create ever more spectacular shapes and visions in glass, to lying against my parents at night and listening to Cray the storyteller as he regaled us with tales of what had once been and what had led us to be who we were and who we would become. Nothing he had ever told me seemed to lead here, to this dark cave. And all of this left me with nothing in the present, except a future as dark as my past had been filled with sunlight. So I wondered whether this was to be the direction of my life, this movement from light to darkness, and whether this was the logical end.

Artie's paw groped at my face and roused me. Over and over again he started sticking his weak paw on my face and in my mouth. At first I thought he was trying to tell me of his great hunger, but then I realized what he really wanted: He wanted the meat on his bones to feed me. And with that frightening thought the hot shimmering light disappeared, and I was back in the dark cave, enveloped in cool close air and huddling against the warm body of my dog, our stomachs crying out for food. I listened to the cries until I grew faint. Then I got up and desperately dragged Artie through the cave.

When I grew tired I lay on him and felt his com-

the glass mountains
287

forting breath lift my head up and down. But as my mind wandered I suddenly realized that he had stopped breathing.

"No!" I cried out. I crazily stuck my own hand in his mouth and then jumped up and dragged him some more and kept dragging until I collapsed. He had lost his life. For the first time in my life I sobbed, wasting the water in my body for tears and then desperately licking my tears to retrieve the water. I decided to die here with Artie. First I would give him a proper ritual. I groped around for stones and pebbles that I formed into a circle around him.

I passed the "night" in the soundless dark, frightened by the tiny sounds I imagined I heard, and felt so scared of being in the open that I again craved to return to my hole. When I couldn't fall asleep I took two stones and with them played the first simple rhythms I'd learned as a child. The rhythms lulled me as much as I could be lulled, and finally I fell asleep.

When I woke, I considered dragging Artie's body back to the crevice, where at least he might have company. But it was so dark I could not be sure that I might not fall in myself. And I couldn't part with my dog. Nor, I found, could I stop when I possessed the energy to go forward. So I dragged him with me, feeling along the wall and going along the narrow tunnel. I walked until Artie's body began to stiffen, and I dragged him still. All this insanity seemed not dreamlike but intensely real.

I had got used to a sickly fear that pervaded this tunnel and realized a person could get used to anything. But once, when I woke after a nap, I saw above me a tiny prick of light. I hadn't seen it earlier—it must have been nighttime out. Suddenly I realized that the air was a bit fresher here, and the fear I felt less acute.

No matter how hard I tried, however, I couldn't find a way to climb up toward that hole. Even if I could have, I don't know what I would have done next. It was just that the prick of light drew me to it with its beauty and promise. Reluctant though I was to leave it, I knew I mustn't stop. I had no idea where I might escape, and I didn't want to risk falling to fatigue or starvation if I chanced to be only a day or two from escape. Every time I lay down I stared all around me, searching for another prick of light. When I didn't see any others I wondered whether I'd imagined the light, just as even now I sometimes imagined for a moment that here or there I saw light.

Slowly, I became aware of something, a thin, fine smell that wove itself through the stuffiness. The smell, which I couldn't place, seemed ravishing in its beauty. I felt intoxicated. There was almost no time left for me now. After every interlude of sleep it had become harder and harder to rise and to move. But this new smell energized me. I followed it until I grew dizzy with its beauty. I could place it now. It was the scent of fresh air, with bits of trees, with dirt, with animals and rocks and clouds all mixed into its lovely brew. Finally it grew so strong I stumbled forward as fast as I could, dragging Artie's corpse. I closed my eyes to concentrate on the smell, so that no other sense but that of smell guided me. When I suddenly reached my destination all my other senses were stunned by what they found. I was outside.

I suppose it was all nothing special, just a dry canyon with a few trees, a sputtering string of a river, and an overcast early evening sky. But I lay down and rubbed my face in the dirt and slurped at the string of a river. I put handfuls of dirt in my mouth and chewed and smelled and felt the texture of life on my tongue. I happily spit out the dirt and started to wash out my mouth in the trickle of muddy water.

So my face was dirty and my mouth full of muck when I met a man I thought at first might be the guide my grandfather had spoken of. But he was the opposite of a guide.

He was a plain smooth-faced man hovering over the bodies of my mother and Moor, both of them unconscious, maybe dead, Moor bleeding from a bandage on his back.

"Are they alive?" I ran over and found them both bleeding.

"Are they your friends?"

"Yes, we were together in the caves."

"I happened upon them," he said calmly. "The caves are dangerous. You shouldn't go in them."

"We were chased."

"Ah." He half smiled.

"How long have they been here?"

"How can I know? I myself have been here only a short while. I bandaged the boy, poor thing, he's lost so much blood." His mild gaze fell upon Artie. "I believe your dog is dead."

cynthia kadohata

"I know," I said angrily. "Don't you have any ointments or something for them?"

"I'm a fisherman. But I have already given them some juices that will help. You must feed them some meat." He nodded so subtly toward Artie that I was not sure he had nodded at all.

Both Moor and my mother had become skeletal, and both mumbled in their sleep. I started a fire and cooked some roots and could not stop myself from looking Artie's way. He had been the most magnificent dog that ever lived. He had not died from starvation but from a mix of despondency, hunger, and, perhaps, a desire to provide me with food. I asked forgiveness and impaled him with a branch that I suspended over my fire to cook. The smell of this food roused Moor somewhat. When my dog was cooked I chewed his meat and put part of what I had chewed into Moor's mouth, part into my mother's.

And in this way I saved my mother and my beloved from starvation.

They didn't quite wake up that evening, but I could see they were improving. My new companion sat up agreeably on a rock all night, not sleeping at all so far as I could see. Whenever I attempted conversation, he answered agreeably that I was quite right.

I passed a night as quiet as the day and in the morning woke before sunrise. My companion had already started a fire and begun cooking some roots. As he ate he stuffed his cheeks so full they both stuck out in humps that he chewed down in quick little bites. Every so often he would rapidly spit out bits of food that apparently were hard to chew.

the glass mountains
291

The sun rose at the horizon. I was staring at the sun, just finishing up my roots, when I heard a snore and saw the man sitting upright with his eyes closed.

I cleaned up the breakfast remains and waited for further improvement from Moor and my mother.

2.

"Did you clean up?" was the first thing the Hathatu-me man said upon waking. "I'm very tidy myself. Of course if you didn't want to clean up, that would be fine, too."

"I cleaned up."

He stood up and threw dried bugs into his mouth, a whole handful, and he spit out the shells with dazzling rapidity. I watched with amazement as the shells flew out one after the other.

"That's quite a trick," I said.

"Yes, it is."

"How come the Formans haven't overrun your country? At least there's a little water here, and greenery."

"Oh, we pay them their money and that satisfies them."

"The Bakshami should have paid them as well."

"Bakshami is no longer."

"Then it's true the hotlands have been over-taken?"

"So it is said."

"And the people?"

He shrugged. I felt no more sadness, just anger, at the Formans, at these passive Hathatu-me, and

cynthia kadohata

at my own people. The world had changed, and they had not possessed the will even to try to protect themselves.

"Do you think Forma will attack Hathatu-me despite the payments?"

"They likely will."

"And you take it so calmly?"

"No more calmly than your people did, I believe."

"But look what happened to us!"

"Like you, we are not a fighting people."

"But you must learn to become so if you will survive."

"Perhaps we won't survive."

"But how can you accept that so easily?"

"No more easily than your people did."

We didn't speak for a while. Then my companion glanced up at the sun. "I must go soon." He looked at me with the mildest curiosity. "What happened to the three of you in there?"

"Chased by Formans," I said.

He smiled serenely, an ordinary man with a simple, almost substanceless, manner except for an ever-present serenity. "That happened to a friend of mine once. The Formans are a strange lot."

"You were born in Hathatu-me?"

He smiled and bowed his head somewhat.

"The Formans say they own you."

"No human has an owner."

"You're too optimistic. Many of them own and are owned."

He smiled agreeably. "Perhaps you're right after all."

"If you were a slave you would know it's so."

"I shall dwell on that."

"Do you not hate the Formans?"

"My hatred wouldn't make much difference, that much is certain."

"I've never met such an opinionless man," I said.

"Perhaps you're right in what you say. Of course there is always the chance that you are wrong."

His mere presence began to make me want to take a nap. I fell asleep and awoke to see him gazing mildly at me as he stood ready to leave. "Your friends are recovering," he said. He pulled me up with a gentle but firm force, and took my hands. Up above I heard a familiar whirring, and when I gazed up saw several Forman ships flying overhead.

"It's beginning," he said. To my surprise, he began weeping silently. Strings of liquid poured out of his nose. "You must get back now. I wish you luck. Take good care of your friend. He is Soom Kali. The Soom Kali have my fate in their hands. If they should lose the upcoming war..."

"But where are you going?"

"I must get home to see my family." He rushed off, crashing through the brush until he disappeared.

As I ministered to my mother and Moor, I could not understand that Hathatu-me man and his mild ways. The Formans might be about to take over his land, and he had no intention of fighting, no intention of trying to save his sector as the Soom Kali would soon need to fight to save theirs, and, indirectly, his as well. A great war lay before the planet. Moor and I must return to Soom Kali to persuade a jury not to kill him for the death of his soldier friend; then we could live there and fight there, for ourselves and for the child that I now felt growing inside me. I did not know who among my family had lived and who had died. I did not know whether the Glass Mountains still rose majestically above the sand or whether they now lay in ruins under the sun.

Two days later Moor opened his eyes. We didn't speak, just smiled and touched. I lay next to him, and we slept together. A few hours later I awoke to see him cooking at a fire.

"You should rest," I said.

"There is no rest for a Soom Kali man in war."

"There is no war."

He peered above, and we saw a fleet of Forman ships speed past. We hugged and watched the ships pass. Then Moor returned to his cooking.

"We must revive your mother and move on."

I crouched beside my mother, whose eyes remained closed. But color had come into her cheeks.

"I don't know what her life will be like without my father. She may not want to live."

"She will have to make that decision herself."

Two days later, as I lay beside her staring into her face, her eyelids fluttered and opened.

"Moor!" I said. Moor and I leaned over my mother.

She glared at us with eyes that held something I had never seen in them before. So strange was her expression that it took me a while to realize what her look meant.

"You hate me!" I said. But then the expression faded and she closed her eyes and slept fitfully.

Moor told me they had taken a different tunnel to the outside. In their tunnel, they'd been attacked repeatedly. In the end, Moor said, it was my mother who had saved him, by killing their last attacker with Moor's own knife.

"Why does she hate me?" I said.

He was silent.

When my mother was strong enough, we traveled into a nearby town, where we easily found a Hathatu-me ship that would take us back to Soom Kali. In fact, the Hathatu-me were so mild and agreeable, I think we would have been able to find a ship to take us to one of the moons and back if only we had asked.

The driver of our ship was as agreeable as the man I'd met outside the caves. Nowhere did I find the guidance my grandfather had promised me. The time for predictions had passed, just as seasons passed in other sectors. And now the season of war had arrived.

At my request, we flew over my barren homeland. My heart soared as I saw the Glass Mountains shining, way in the distance. I was raised for peace, but found myself surprisingly impatient to defend those mountains and whatever was left of Bakshami.

When we reached Soom Kali, we found the entire populace preparing for war. Even Moor's sickly father had been recruited to help manufacture weapons. All trials had been suspended—no Soom Kali would be put to death when every body was needed for the war.

The strip of barren land through which I'd once passed was now peopled with Bakshami refugees learning to fight. Among the students were Jobei and Leisha, who had left the Glass Mountains not long after I had. They had decided that the only way to save the great mountains was to leave them and learn to fight. Among their teachers was Moor's friend Panyor, with whom Tarkahna had mated. And another couple I knew lived there: Ansmeea the Young and my former betrothed, Sennim. They were married now.

Every day I took classes on the art of soldiering. What I learned in my hand-to-hand battle classes was that falling was a type of magical enterprise for me. As I hurled through the air about to land it was almost as if I could calculate the movements of each of my muscles and project which combination of movements would cause which kind of landing. Strangely, those moments in the air, a time of fearful anticipation for most students, were a time of great joy for me. Sometimes I suspected that the teachers picked on me often—hurling me up and across and down, forward and backward and around—just so they could watch me fall. I felt my babies—twins— inside of me as I twirled through the air. And always I landed with grace. After watching my brilliant falls, the Soom Kali teachers would compliment me lavishly, the way they did with only their most prized students. Moor would flush with pride.

My brother Jobei could not keep up in class. He had aged astonishingly. His small rotted face shocked me, and he had begun to hunch his shoulders as if they burdened him. His legs were as thin as the sticks we'd once played together. And yet, in his stick-like legs, sloping back, and decimated face I saw an even greater nobility than I'd seen in him before. If I tried to judge him as someone still alive, he appeared ugly and small, but if I saw him as one half-dead, he appeared noble and great, a man who had given his life force to kindness and generosity. And I knew that, in honor of him, it was proper that I should look upon my own brother as half dead.

Panyor contacted Maruk and Sian, now fully integrated, but they refused to move to our strip of land. Maruk and Sian had children, and both my brother and his wife had joined the army and received new promotions recently. They didn't want to give up their thriving military careers to move to a forsaken strip of land to be with me. Apparently the generals made great favorites of them.

· I spoke with Maruk only once, and he seemed as proud, daring, and kind as he had when we were children and I'd admired him so much. He looked like an adventurer, smaller than many Soom Kali but nevertheless large enough, and as handsome as any soldier in the sector. But pretending to be who he was not had made him a Soom Kali. His Bakshami childhood was forgotten. It was like with the romance ritual. He'd pretended to be Soom Kali, and to protect himself and his children, strove to make the pretense real. Being a man of great resources and determination, he'd succeeded. I couldn't help respecting the way he'd invented himself. Very few could have accomplished what he had. But in the process he'd become more like a Soom Kali soldier than many of the real Soom Kali soldiers I met.

"I would hope that your family could join mine in this strip of land," I said.

He looked at me with the old love in his eyes. "I would still die for you," he said. "But if you could know how great was our struggle at first, to live here and worry constantly of not integrating successfully. If you could know that, you would also know with what relief I wake up every day now, when I realize that in truth I am Soom Kali. I have become Soom Kali. It would not be possible for me even to remember the rhythms I once knew by heart because I am no longer what I was."

As he spoke these last words I was ever to hear him speak, I saw a flash of the old, kind Maruk, the Maruk who'd protected me all through my childhood and who I would have died for. I still would have died for him. But he would not have wanted it so. And so the brother I'd once venerated left my life forever. That night I played rhythms for him as if he had died. I had no brothers left.

In class the next day and every day thereafter I felt obsessed with my studies and oblivious to pain. Every evening when I got home from warrior classes, my body was covered in cuts, gashes, and bruises. Everyone thought I was insane to study thus when I was pregnant. But I was addicted to the joy of falling, just as a bird might be addicted to flying. In classes, I would think of my father, my brothers, my family— past, present and future—and my dogs, and I'd fight with a fury I hadn't known I possessed. But one day in class the fury didn't rise in me as it used to, and I realized that my worst memories had become scars rather than wounds. I remembered what my mother had told me long ago, and I knew that my soft heart had mended, rather than breaking like a hard one. My father was a part of the same dream that my past had become. He had formed me as much as anyone or anything in my childhood had, but now my childhood, like Maruk's, was gone. I came to think of my father and Maruk as magical, like the wisest elders, or like the magical childhood I now saw I'd had.

As the days passed, Panyor helped many Bakshami build their houses. He told us about battles in which he'd fought, and about ships he'd flown. He gave classes and lectured to the Bakshami who'd moved into our new village. The Bakshami were surprisingly good at learning of war—after all, according to legend, the Bakshami had descended from a Soom Kali man and a beast. We grew confident in our ability to defend ourselves. We were such impressive students of war that a couple of the finest warriors in Soom Kali honored us by moving to our colony. Even Zem returned from Artroro and became one of the most flamboyant and lazy members of my new village.

On the day that Artroro officially declared war on Soom Kali, Moor and I decided to hold our mating ritual. The night before, I sat up by myself, thinking about the time long ago when I'd seen a wave of sand pounce upon a man. That stranger had appeared in our village like the first flea of summer, a harbinger of the scavengers and bloodsuckers who soon descended upon our quiet lives, scavenging for the remains of war.

I sat on the ground by a couple of lonely trees. Most of the landscape in our colony had a lonely quality. I felt eyes on my back. I turned smiling, certain it was my future husband. But it was my mother, staring at me with haunted eyes. She rarely talked to me since my father had died. I thought she blamed me for my father's fate. His remains were trapped in Artekka's hot center, never to become a part of the hallowed Glass Mountains. The hate flashed for a moment, then burned itself out, to be supplanted by an expression I had not seen in so long I could not quite place it.

"What are you thinking?" I said.

"I was thinking how proud I am of you," she said simply.

We held each other and cried. When the sun rose, our relationship had changed in that way all parent-child relationships change eventually. Now I was the grown-up, taking care of someone more helpless than myself.

And in this state of mind I faced the great wars of my future.

•◞

the end

cynthia (kadohata)

I've been writing since 1982. When I was 25 and completely directionless, I took a Greyhound bus trip up the West Coast, and then down through the South and Southwest. I met people I never would have met otherwise. It was during that bus trip, which lasted a month, that I rediscovered in the landscape the magic I'd known as a child. Though I'd never considered writing fiction before, the next year I decided to begin. I sent one story out every month, and about forty-eight stories later, *The New Yorker* took a story.

Cynthia Kadohata lives in California.